AN AMERICAN BULLET

JOHN STONEHOUSE

Copyright © by John Stonehouse 2018
All rights reserved.

John Stonehouse has asserted his right under the Copyright, Designs and Patents Act 1988 to be identified as the author of this work.

All rights reserved. No part of this publication may be reproduced or transmitted in any form or by any means without permission of the author.

This book is a work of fiction. Names, characters, places and incidents are either a product of the author's imagination or are used fictitiously. Any resemblance to actual people, living or dead, events or locales, is entirely coincidental.

Cover Design by Books Covered
Interior Layout by Polgarus Studio

ISBN 13: 9781723779626

Chapter 1

Raton Pass, Colorado.
December 2002

The air in the rocky-sided pass is heavy, deadened—the sky above the tree line the color of lead.

Jimmy Scardino takes a final hit on his Camel cigarette, he tosses it into the snow, eyes the rail line running south into the pass—it's white-over.

He checks his watch, knocks snow from his hair. Turns back to the stolen Buick Roadmaster at the side of the gravel road.

Easing in behind the wheel, he drives the station wagon thirty yards to a grade crossing —feels the raised steel tracks beneath his tires.

He stops the car, cuts the motor.

Stepping out, he swings the door shut.

Half a mile back along the rail line is a collection of buildings—Fisherville, a track-side settlement. Businesses and houses are barely visible in the late December afternoon. It's near dusk, nothing moving. Nobody's seen him. Nobody's seen the car.

Colorado spruce and limber pine line the gravel road where it disappears into the mountain wood. He moves between low branches, stooping into the trees to a clearing in the fading winter light.

He pulls out a second set of keys, spots the double-cab Tacoma pickup. Closing down the last cold yards, he fights an urge to run.

He reaches the pickup, opens up, climbs in, fires the motor.

He checks the clock on the dash, nods to himself.

Almost time.

⊥

On the long climb through the Raton Pass, the Amtrak passenger train fights for traction.

Clarke Tanner in the engineer's seat, peers through the windshield—the forward light beams filled with swirling flecks of white.

He glances at the main panel on the operator console—the train is picking up speed, finally descending; running downhill after more than an hour.

The rail heads will be iced. He sees a letter *'W'* picked out at the side of the track—the whistle post for Fisherville, ten miles north of the Raton tunnel.

A quarter-mile on, he can just make out track-side yards and buildings.

Two grade crossings at Fisherville—the main road, then a second, gravel road at the northern end.

He checks the speed, the train's accelerating, nearing the limit for the track.

Conductor Ross in the seat beside him reaches for the heater control. He cranks up the dial, rubs at the arm of his sweater; "Getting worse out there."

Tanner starts the sequence of air horn blasts—two long, a short, then another long. "You catch a weather update at Raton?"

The conductor nods, stares out of the side window at the snow. "Trainmaster's office say there's a storm headed in. Possible Cat-4."

Tanner sounds the air horn again—repeating the sequence of long and short blasts.

Tracts of white powder are settled on the hills lining both sides of the pass. Ahead, snitch-lights glow on the sides of the flashers at the main crossing.

"How is it up to Chicago?" Tanner says.

"Not looking real good."

The engineer watches the signals at the highway. Beyond the main crossing, a shape draws his eye where the forest line comes down to meet the track.

He eases up out of his seat, stares along the cone of the forward light beam.

Windshield wipers mark the time in beats.

Tanner's breath catches in his throat.

⼈

His hand floats toward the automatic brake-valve handle.

Something is out there. Something on the track.

Five, six hundred feet ahead, not more.

He sounds the horn in a long-drawn blast.

Conductor Ross snaps around in his seat.

"Son of a bitch…" Tanner pulls on the handle, putting the brakes into full emergency.

"Jesus," the conductor says, "get off the line." His voice is hoarse in his throat.

The engineer stares at the car across the track—the closing speed too great now, no way he can get the train stopped. They're in full emergency—nothing more he can do.

"*Move back…*" the conductor shouts.

Tanner stares at the station wagon in the lights.

He feels his heart in his chest.

Starts to brace.

Chapter 2

Forty miles north, Deputy US Marshal John Whicher steers his Chevy Silverado down I-25 in the worsening snow. Freight trucks are slowing on the long approach into Raton Pass. Cars and pickups switching lanes, throwing up a dirty white spray of slush.

Whicher checks his rear-view mirror, throws a look back at the empty rear seat. He thinks of Charles 'Cutter' Maitland, his passenger, scant hours ago.

The marshal flexes his fingers on the wheel, stretches out his shoulders. *You did your job*, he tells himself, nothing more.

Maitland would likely be staring at three feet of empty sky through a slit-window in a cell, now. A twelve-by-seven unit. Solitary confinement. A concrete bed.

They'd made the run north out of Texas, Maitland chained to a 'D' ring in the Chevy floor. Whicher signed him over to the prison guards, he was lost to the world from that moment. The marshal shudders at the thought of it, despite himself.

Florence Supermax. The Alcatraz of the Rockies.

He flicks through channels on the radio, settles on a station playing Johnny Cash. The last rays of sun sink behind the mountains in the west, blood red against an iron sky.

Raw sound fills up the space inside the cab.

Whicher frowns. Everybody says the man in black is dying.

He stares out through the windshield, thinks of Florence—a sprawling high-security complex. Something in the air there, malevolent, brooding. An absence. An inexplicable kind of void.

But Maitland had it coming, he was into organized crime from the time the school board kicked him out at fifteen. A murderer at eighteen, he spent ten years carving up rival crews for the mob. The feds caught him with burnt human remains in a tarp in the trunk of his car.

Maitland tried to plead-down, testify for the government. But then he'd run out from everybody, the feds, the mob. He was rearrested in Dallas, his life forfeit.

Whicher thinks of home, of the long ride back to Texas. Five hours. Maybe more, if the weather got worse.

He eyes the heaps of snow lining either side of the roadway. Dark outline of a mountain beyond the cold glass windows of the truck.

His cell phone starts up.

He checks it, sees the USMS number—the Abilene office on the screen.

He knocks off the music, answers; "Whicher."

"John, this is Evans…"

Whicher recognizes the senior marshal, the Abilene department boss on the line.

"Where are you now? Are you still in Colorado?"

"Yessir."

"Did you get Maitland delivered?"

"Yes sir, I did."

"I need you to do something," Evans says, "urgent. I need you to get to a place called Fisherville. Fast as you can."

Whicher looks at the interstate stretching out. "Sir, I'm running south on twenty-five. Around fifteen miles from the state line."

"It's the north side of Raton Pass," Evans says. "There's been a collision. A train and a vehicle."

Whicher searches ahead for exit signs.

"I need you to get to Fisherville," Evans says, "and meet with a Marshal Corrigan. I can't discuss this over the phone, but it's priority-one, urgent."

Whicher hits the blinker, switches over to the right-hand lane.

"In three states, you're the closest marshal with security clearance."

"Marshal Corrigan?" Whicher says.

"Offer any and all assistance."

"How do I find him?"

"Find the train. Corrigan was riding onboard."

The road in is silent beneath the wheels of the Silverado—the steep-sided valley blanketed in snow.

Whicher clears the edge of the mountain forest, sees the pulsing red and blue lights of emergency vehicles.

A single frontage road runs parallel with a rail track—work yards and houses spread out, a group of sheriff's department vehicles at the front end of a double-height passenger train.

He eyes the locomotive unit, sees ambulances, a fire truck.

He slows the Silverado to a stop.

From the seat beside him he takes his heavy, wool ranch coat. He shuts off the motor. Steps out into biting cold.

Putting on his Resistol hat, he slips the dark gray coat over the jacket of his suit.

Groups of people are by the side of the train. Whicher sees two men in railroad caps in the center of one group. He slips out his US Marshals badge. Makes his way toward them.

A sheriff's deputy steps in his path.

"Who's in charge here?"

The deputy indicates a woman in a duck down ski-jacket and hiking boots.

Whicher steps around the deputy, strides toward the woman—six-one, a busted nose, at thirty-eight, he's in good shape.

The sheriff turns at his approach.

The marshal lifts his hat an inch. "John Whicher, US Marshals Service."

"Kim Dubois." Her face is angular, the features sharp. "I'm the county sheriff."

Whicher looks around the circle of people in the strobe and flash of lights. "Is there a Marshal Corrigan here?"

The sheriff's eyes narrow. She gestures for him to step away from the group.

He follows her ten yards to the head-end of the train—glances at it, in the dark he can't see much.

"You're the second person to ask for Corrigan since I got here," the sheriff says.

"Ma'am? Is he here?"

"No. And according to the train conductor, his name's not on the list of people traveling." Sheriff Dubois puts her gloved hands into her jacket pockets. "One of the passengers approached me, claiming Corrigan was on the train with her. Accompanying her. A young woman."

The marshal cuts her a look.

"They opened up some of the buildings back there to get people out of the cold." The sheriff takes a hand from her pocket, points down the frontage road. "Back there. I think they took her to that old bar."

Dim light is showing from a stone-built, two-story saloon.

"What happened here?" Whicher says.

"The train hit a car."

"Did anybody get hurt?"

"As a matter of fact," the sheriff says, "it doesn't look like it. The car had no occupants. The train hit it, but not too fast."

"Where's the car at?"

The sheriff angles her head toward the dark line of the forest. "Up there. They backed the train here after they hit."

Whicher sees lights a few hundred yards farther up the track.

"A Buick Roadmaster," the sheriff says. "On a Denver plate. Stolen, it looks like."

"And it was just on the line?"

"Parked." The sheriff nods. "Deliberate. The crew about got the train slowed, but it mangled the car pretty good. I've got people checking on it now."

"Can I see this young woman?" Whicher says.

"You can see her."

"You tell me anything about her?"

Sheriff Dubois makes a face.

The marshal squints at her beneath the brim of his hat.

"She seemed a little strange."

"How's that?"

"Disturbed," the sheriff says. "Or something." She shrugs. "I don't know, that's how it seemed to me."

⋏

Set back from the track, the saloon shows a single light bulb in its grimy window. A sheriff's deputy stands beneath the porch roof, looking out at the stationary train.

Whicher shows his badge. "Sheriff Dubois says y'all have a young woman here—asking after a US Marshal?"

"Are you Corrigan?"

"No." Whicher shakes his head. "But I need to see her."

The deputy moves aside, gives him a look. "She's blonde, wearing a long coat. You'll notice her…"

Whicher steps into the building, into dim light in the old bar room. Handfuls of people sit at tables, the place is disused, practically derelict—the ceiling coming down, the counter covered in dust.

The air inside is chilled, cold as outdoors, at least there's no wind.

A young woman sits at a table in the corner; she's in her thirties, her face sculpted, mid-length hair. Blonde, dark blonde, expensively cut. Her full-mouth is pressed shut. Whicher thinks of an Italian movie actress. She draws her coat around her, a fur-lined coat with an oversize hood. Her eyes flick to the uniformed deputy at the door, animal tension in her face.

The marshal approaches her table. He shows his badge.

She stares at him a moment, eyes intense blue.

"We talk someplace?" He gestures toward the door.

She pushes back her chair.

He leads her out of the building, outside into the falling snow.

At the edge of the frontage road, white-laden branches of spruce and pine move in the bitter wind. He stops in the lee of the trees. Nobody is near them, nobody close enough to hear.

"Sheriff Dubois says you were riding the train with a Marshal Corrigan?"

She puts up her hood.

"Ma'am? Is that right?"

She turns in the faint light from the saloon, eyes the scattered groups huddled at the side of the track.

"Where is he now?"

She takes a breath.

Whicher puts his head on one side.

"I don't know."

"Ma'am?" he says. He looks at her.

Thoughts are passing behind her eyes, one following

after another. Finally, she looks at him directly. "My name is Lauren DeLuca."

He waits for her to say something more.

Her gaze is disconcerting.

"Why were you traveling with Marshal Corrigan?"

She doesn't answer.

"How come he's not here?"

She steps toward him, suddenly. "You have to take me into custody."

"Ma'am?"

"You have to," she says.

"You're asking me to arrest you?"

Chapter 3

In the darkness of the woods, Jimmy Scardino lights another Camel cigarette. He cups the glowing end in a leather-gloved hand. But nobody's seen him.

Two sheriff's vehicles have driven part-way up the gravel road—neither one of them clocking the Tacoma set back in the forest clearing.

All around the train it's a regular light show, everybody focused on that.

Belaski had found the spot—for a Polack, the man had a knack, Jimmy had to admit.

Fresh snow is falling all the time, covering every track they've made. Safe as houses. Only thing bothering Jimmy is the goddamn cold.

He shivers. Stamps down in his boots. Wind howls along the narrow pass, penetrating even beneath the trees.

Where the hell was Belaski, though?

Son of a bitch.

How come he hadn't made it back?

Whicher studies the young woman named Lauren DeLuca.

"You were traveling with a US Marshal? You were on the train with him. And now you don't know where he's at?"

She stiffens. "Let me see your badge again."

Whicher thinks about it—doesn't respond.

Her eyes widen. "Who told you to come here?"

He hutches his shoulders against the cold.

She looks to the saloon, to where the sheriff's deputy is still standing beneath the porch roof.

"Y'all were riding the train?" Whicher says.

She doesn't answer.

"Where were you traveling? Was Marshal Corrigan with you when the train collided with the car?"

She nods, brushes a strand of hair from her mouth.

"Right with you? Sitting with you?"

"The brakes went on suddenly," she says. "It was obvious something was wrong—very wrong. There was noise, lots of noise, screeching, the train was shaking. Then a bang, a horrible bang. We stopped. He told me to stay where I was. He said he was going to check on what had happened. That's the last I saw him."

The marshal looks into her face.

"We started to reverse," she says. Her eyes are hooded, deep in thought. "They told us we had to get off, I haven't seen him since he left his seat."

Whicher glances down the slope to the track. "And this all is how long?"

She lifts her arm, pushes back the cuff of her heavy coat. "Almost an hour."

Whicher thinks of his department boss, Evans, calling on the interstate. Corrigan must have called it in—there was no other way USMS could have known so fast.

He stares at the double-height passenger train. "I have to go speak with somebody." He points at the saloon building. "Go on back, wait with the deputy."

For a moment she looks about to argue. Something in her face changes, she turns, walks away to the saloon.

Whicher pulls out his cell, keys a number, clamps the cell against his ear.

Nothing.

He checks the screen, the network's down at barely one bar.

Lauren DeLuca enters the saloon building.

The deputy turns, grins as she passes.

At the train, Sheriff Dubois is walking with two men dressed in Amtrak blue. Whicher steps down the slope, hustling toward them. He raises a hand.

The sheriff spots him. "Did you find her?"

"I found her."

"See what I mean?"

The marshal doesn't answer.

He takes out his badge, shows it to the two crewmen, the metal cold against his exposed skin. "Like to speak with y'all."

Snow is thick on the shoulders of their coats. "We're having a bad night already," the elder man says.

"I ain't looking to aggravate it. But you want to run me through what happened?"

"My name's Ross," the man says. "The train's in my charge." He indicates the crewman beside him. "This here's Mister Tanner, the engineer."

Whicher feels the cold already seeping through his leather boots. "You were driving?"

Tanner nods.

"I have to get to my unit," Sheriff Dubois says. "I need the radio." She strides off down the side of a passenger car.

"Sheriff said somebody left a station wagon parked up on the rail line, that right?"

Tanner shoves his hands down into his pockets. "We came into Fisherville below the limit for the track. The horn was sounding, everything was done right…"

"I only want to know what happened."

The engineer gives a shake of his head. "It was damn near dark already, the snow was bad. We saw a car. I put the train into full emergency, that's the fastest way I can get it stopped."

"There's no chance we could've avoided hitting it," the conductor says. "We can't steer around."

"I hit the button, called dispatch," Tanner says. "We reported the collision immediately."

"Dispatch put out the call to roll an ambulance," the conductor says. "They had our position, the time…"

Whicher looks up the line toward the front of the train.

"I got out," the conductor says, "the station wagon was spun around on its front axle, the rear all smashed to hell. I had a flashlight, I could see nobody was inside. I checked, just in case it was something weird. There was no sign of a body thrown clear."

Whicher nods.

"We checked the train," Tanner says, "checked the engine for fuel leaks, for fire. The passenger cars were alright, there was no sign of derailment…"

"We backed up into Fisherville," Ross says. "Tried to keep spectators away."

The marshal lifts the Resistol hat off his head, knocks snow from the brim and crown.

"Five minutes later the sheriff's department was here," Tanner says.

Whicher runs a hand through his head of fine brown hair. "One last question. Do y'all have a Marshal Corrigan on board?"

"Sheriff Dubois asked us that already," the conductor says. "We weren't notified of any law enforcement personnel traveling. I checked the passenger list, a hundred-twenty-plus people. No Corrigan."

"Y'all sure?" Whicher blows the air from his cheeks. "Have y'all done a head count?"

The conductor stares through the dark, eyes hunted. "There's an issue with that…"

Whicher replaces his hat, pulls the brim forward.

"Three people got off at Raton," the conductor says, "the last stop. Two tickets were bought for cash at the automated vending machine in Raton—according to our system. We can't be a hundred percent sure two people actually boarded there. The door attendant thinks it was only one."

"You're a man down?" Whicher says.

"We may or may not be. Anybody can buy a ticket," the conductor says, "it doesn't mean they have to get on board. It's not like an aircraft, people get on and off all the time. But based on tickets sold against a straight head-count—we could be one person light."

♶

Whicher pushes up the slope toward the old saloon, boots slipping in the fresh fall of snow. Moving fast, he tries to work some heat into his body. At the door, the deputy exchanges glances with him.

Inside, in the bar room, the marshal scans the folks seated. He turns on his heel, walks back outside. "That blonde lady in the long coat? She walk out of here?"

"No, marshal."

"She didn't leave the building?"

The deputy looks at him. "She's not in there?"

The marshal re-enters the saloon, walks the length of the counter, all the way to the back of the room.

An older couple is seated at a table. He turns to them. "You folks see a lady come in here wearing a long coat? Long coat with a fur-lined hood?"

"She stepped out in back," the man replies.

"We thought she might be looking for a restroom…" the woman says.

The man raises an arm, points to a doorway right at the end.

Whicher strides to it, walks through, tries the light switch. It's not working.

He steps into a pitch-dark corridor. "Anybody back here?"

He works his way along the black space, arm out, feeling his way. A void opens into another room, he enters, sees light from a single, dirt-smeared window. He can just make out piles of boxes—shapes, broken furniture, general garbage. At one side of the room is another door. He steps to it, grabs the handle. It opens.

Outside, in the snow on the ground he sees footprints.

Wide-spaced.

Somebody's run.

⸎

The tracks in the white-over ground lead along the back of an adjacent house. A wood-panel fence marks the edge of the property, the marshal follows down a gap between the fence and the forest's edge.

Back out on the frontage road, one set of footprints blurs into another, half the train passengers have walked the area. The marshal scans left to right—searching for anything that sticks out.

At the rear-end of the train, the rail line disappears into the Raton Pass. He stands, stares into the black sky, snow flurries swirling.

No way she was headed up there—up in the high mountains, on foot. She was supposed to wait in the saloon with the deputy. But she'd run. She'd run out the back.

He sets off at a jog, runs the full length of the stationary train. In the pulsing lights from ER vehicles, he can see about a quarter of a mile.

Nobody notices.

A thought hits him—*if she's run, nobody will notice her either.*

Trees and a rocky-sided pass hide the road out of Fisherville—beyond it, the interstate is miles away. But where else could she go?

His eye comes to rest on his Silverado.

He runs down to his truck, drags snow off the windshield with the arm of his coat. He gets in, fires the motor. Switches on the headlights, stares at the radio transmitter on the dash.

A woman asks to be arrested. Next minute, she runs.

He moves the shifter from park into drive, swings around onto the road.

Passing the city-limit sign, he throws his hat on the empty passenger seat.

The wipers fight snow, headlights drilling out into the night.

He keeps his speed low, feels the steering light, the tires losing traction.

No other vehicle is headed out of Fisherville—the road's white over, no wheel tracks—nothing's recently left.

In the edge of the headlight beam, a shape moves—he takes his foot off the gas.

Something is at the side of the road.

Then gone again.

Whicher stares out into the dark.

A hooded figure.

The truck lights pick out a face—turning to look back toward him.

He's sees a flash of blonde hair.

Pressing down on the gas, he accelerates in the truck.

He draws level.

The figure turns to look at him—it's her, she looks in through the window—shocked, now, at the sight of him.

He stops. Pushes open the passenger door. "Ma'am? What the hell are you doing?"

She spins away, lunging through the deep snow, headed for the woods.

The marshal stares after her. He grabs a flashlight, snaps it on, pulls the keys from the ignition.

Running around back of the Silverado, he's already struggling to see.

Pushing into the tree line, the ground is harder, the air scented. "*Ma'am,*" he calls out. "*I'm a law officer. Ma'am you need to stop…*"

Sweeping back and forth with the flashlight, he sees nothing, just the narrow beam glaring from the trunks of pines, then vanishing into black.

Something moves to his right, he turns the light in its direction, sees the back of her coat.

She's running, twisting, turning.

He sprints after her, light beam bouncing, the air cold, dead-feeling against his skin.

Running flat out, he feels his lungs begin to burn. "*Stay where you are…*"

She glances back for just a moment—leaps sideways.

Whicher tears by a deadfall of branches, sees her scramble for an incline through the dense-packed trees.

Reaching into his coat, he pulls a Ruger revolver from his shoulder-holster.

His foot hits a root, he trips, rolls, comes up again, onto his knees.

She's blocked now, blocked in—trapped by a bank of sheer rock.

She turns.

"Please…" her voice catches in her throat.

Whicher kneels in the cold earth, lungs heaving, gun arm outstretched.

She fights for breath; "Don't kill me. Please don't kill me…"

Chapter 4

The lumber yard office is cramped and cluttered—Whicher leans against a paint-chipped radiator at the window.

The woman in the fur-lined coat stares at a spot on the floor.

Outside, in the warehouse, a sheriff's deputy stands guard.

"My name is Lauren DeLuca," the woman says. "I was traveling on the train with a Marshal Dale Corrigan." She sits forward in the office chair. "I'm in the witness protection program. I'm traveling to attend a trial."

"Marshal Corrigan is your escort?"

She shifts her weight. Nods. "He's supposed to get me there, to Chicago."

"Why'd you run out?"

She doesn't reply.

The marshal lets out a breath. Two hours back he was on the interstate, thinking only of the long drive home to Texas. Warm in the cab of the Silverado. "You have no idea where Marshal Corrigan is at now?"

She shakes her head.

"Why did you run?"

She wraps her arms about her sides.

The marshal eyes her.

She looks up. "I'm afraid for my life. The train hit that car," she says. "Corrigan got off. I don't know what's happened, since then."

"I need to make a call," Whicher says.

No reaction.

"I need you to step outside."

Her face blanches.

"There's a deputy out there," Whicher says, "assigned by Sheriff Dubois. I want you to step outside and stand right with him, while I make a call. You need protecting any, he'll protect you."

Her eyes drill him.

He looks toward the phone on the desk. "I make the call, you can step right back in here."

She rises from her seat.

Whicher opens the office door, stares out into the warehouse—it's dark, piled with cut planks and beams.

A diesel space-heater drones by the back wall. Beside it, a bearded deputy warms his hands.

The marshal fixes the man with a look. "The woman in here with me is stepping on out," he says. "I got to make a call. But she stays right by your side."

The deputy nods, taps at a pair of cuffs clipped to his duty belt.

"You don't need to cuff her." Whicher steps aside, unblocking the door.

Lauren DeLuca walks out of the office, takes the few paces to the deputy.

Whicher shuts the door, picks the phone off the desk.

He punches in a number for US Marshals Service, Abilene. Stares out of the window at the falling snow.

The call picks up.

"Evans."

"Sir, this is Whicher. I'm in Fisherville."

"With Corrigan?"

"No sir, we've got some kind of a problem out here. I got to Fisherville forty, fifty minutes back, I found the train. There's a sheriff in charge of the first response—Sheriff Dubois. I asked her did she have a Marshal Corrigan present, she told me no. But she said a woman was asking after him."

"Have you seen the woman?"

"She's right outside the door. With a sheriff's deputy."

"Corrigan called," Evans says, "straight after the train collision."

"There's a hundred-odd passengers here," Whicher says, "plus the sheriff's department, plus fire and ambulance crews. But no sign of him. Sir, if he's here, I can't find him. Which office is he out of?"

"Albuquerque."

Whicher thinks it over. "This train hit a car abandoned on the track. The woman, Miss DeLuca, says he left his seat to check out what happened when it hit. She hasn't seen him since."

"Lauren DeLuca is in the witness security program," Evans says, his voice tight. "She tell you that?"

"Yes, sir. She did."

"She's a federal witness in a major trial."

Whicher nods at his own reflection in the window glass.

"She's traveling to Chicago," Evans says, "she's a key witness, the trial's due to start."

"What kind of a case?"

"Organized crime."

"Mob crime?"

"Corrigan is her close security officer. She's considered at high risk of attack. You need to find Corrigan and keep the witness safe."

"The train conductor says there's no record of him being on the train…"

"That's standard security, there won't be."

Whicher reaches for the door, pulls it open, covering the phone with one hand. "Miss DeLuca—step back in here, please…"

"Look for Corrigan again," Evans says, "I'll call back in five minutes…"

"Use this number, sir," Whicher says, "there's no cell reception here."

"Five minutes," Evans says. "You be by that phone."

Out at the grade crossing, a fire truck shines working lights at the point of collision with the car. A tow-truck winches the wrecked Buick clear. In the spill of light at the side of the track, Whicher sees the handful of people watching.

He recognizes Tanner and Ross, the engineer and

conductor stepping forward to look at the rails.

Sheriff Dubois is at the edge of the group. Whicher peers into the pine woods lining the track beyond the road.

The sheriff strides a few yards from the track side into the snow. She nestles her chin into the collar of the duck down ski-jacket. "Don't tell me your date ran out again?"

The marshal looks back down to Fisherville, to the yellow square of light in the dark—the office window of the lumber business. "Your deputy has her down at the wood yard."

"You figure out what's going on?"

"I can't find hide nor hair of Corrigan," Whicher says. "But the woman's in the witness security program."

The sheriff makes an 'o' shape with her mouth.

"Corrigan's supposed to be security, the woman's in transit."

"I put the word out," the sheriff says, "but none of my people here have seen him. If he presents himself to anybody, they'll whistle."

Whicher looks off into the snow-laden trees. "Anybody searched them woods?"

Sheriff Dubois glances over her shoulder.

"Somebody dumped that Buick," Whicher says. "They had to go someplace."

"Those woods go on for miles. I've had a couple units take a look up the road," the sheriff says. "Just to make sure it's not some kid—some meth-head getting his rocks off derailing a train."

"No sign?"

The sheriff shakes her head. "Whoever it was, they most likely dumped the car then went back down to Fisherville. Nobody would've seen them, it was dark already, everybody's keeping inside."

"How about if they're out there?"

"To search those woods, I need to keep everybody here for hours, freezing. You think your Marshal Corrigan is out there?" the sheriff says. "I'll lend you my flashlight."

Whicher blows the air from his cheeks.

The sheriff looks at the sky. "What do you intend doing?"

"I have a witness to protect," the marshal says.

"By the Grace of God, we have no serious injuries here," Sheriff Dubois says. "The train's still in working order. If the rails are good, they're going to move."

"They going back to Raton?"

"Nope. They're going on. They're going up the line—to La Junta."

⅄

Back in the lumber yard office Whicher snatches up the ringing phone.

"You find Dale Corrigan, marshal?"

"No sir. There's still no sign."

"You have the woman with you?"

"Yes, sir I do."

"The situation has been escalated," Evans says. "I'm going to need you to put down the phone right now and take a call from the officer in charge of her case. The man's name is McBride. Inspector McBride. He's a senior marshal with the WITSEC program. I've spoken with him, given him your number there. He's going to call you, he'll take it from here. Whatever he asks you to do, I want you to go ahead and do it, understand? You're assigned this now, emergency status."

The marshal sits at the desk.

"You take your orders from McBride till further notice. Put down the phone," Evans says. "Pick it up it, when it rings."

Whicher replaces the receiver on its cradle. He gazes around the empty room.

Outside, the rumble of the train's engine dips and rises. Snow is starting to stick to the cold glass panes at the window.

He stands, opens the office door—checks, sees Lauren DeLuca with the sheriff's deputy in the warehouse.

The telephone sounds again.

The marshal lifts the receiver, places it against his ear.

"My name is Inspector McBride."

"Yessir."

"You have a young woman with you."

"Right outside my door. With an armed guard."

"Marshal Evans assures me your security clearance is good for this," McBride says. "I double-checked with the Division Marshal. The young woman you're with is one of the highest-class assets we've ever had on the secure program."

Whicher thinks about it, says nothing.

"She's being moved in secret," McBride says. "Her escort is unavailable on his cell."

"Sir, there's hardly a signal in the pass here…"

"He had enough to call me," McBride says, "at least once. He called, told me the train had collided with something. And now there's no sign of him. That correct?"

"Yes sir, it is."

"In which case, I'm assigning you as close protection," McBride says. "It's your job to keep her alive."

Whicher stares at the door.

"You hear me?"

"Yessir."

"I'm not going to tell you any more than I have to," McBride says. "But the Illinois Attorney General's office need her—they need her testimony. Chicago FBI think a bullet's waiting for her. I don't doubt it. After this, I don't doubt it at all."

Whicher steps from the window, stands with his back to the wall.

"Get her to Chicago," McBride says.

"How y'all want me to do that?"

"You ever work witness security?"

"No, sir."

"Rule one—the less people that know a thing the better. Apart from myself and Marshal Evans, you're the only person knows where the witness is right now."

"Sir, the sheriff here knows, Sheriff Dubois."

"How's that?"

"The sheriff handling the incident with the train."

"Alright," McBride says. "I'll deal with that. You served in the army, before the Marshals Service, that right?"

"Yes sir, I did."

"Then you'll understand a need-to-know basis. On the phone, we won't use names. You get the witness to Chicago any way you can. Whatever it takes, we'll handle the expense. Tell nobody. Nobody knows where you're going, what you're doing or who you're with. You have family?"

"Excuse me?"

"We'll call them for you, let 'em know you won't be home."

"I live alone."

"Alright," McBride says. "Alright, good. You don't make any calls. Whatever happens, you talk to me only. I'm going to give you a number. When you get to Chicago, call it."

"How about updates?" Whicher says. "I let anybody know where I'm at?"

"No-one," McBride says. "Not even me."

Whicher holds the warehouse door open on its rusted steel runners. A cross-wind whips snow along the pass, he watches it drifting as the night temperature falls.

At the edge of the frontage road, a thick white layer is on the roof of the Silverado.

He slides the door closed, turns back into the warehouse, takes the Marshals Service Glock 19 from the holster at his waist.

He checks the gun over; releases the magazine, it's full. One spare magazine at his belt, spare ammunition in the Silverado. He taps the Ruger in the shoulder-holster, his back-up weapon of choice. "We need to move before the roads get any worse."

Lauren DeLuca stands in the shadows. "Where?" she says.

Whicher looks at the bearded deputy—then back at her, expression pointed. "Never mind where."

He buttons the wool ranch coat to his throat, slips the Glock into an outsize pocket. Studies her a moment in the darkened warehouse—trying to see the marked woman beneath the cover-girl face.

She takes a pace forward.

Close enough for him to feel her physical presence.

"Wait here," he says. He wraps a hand around the butt of the Glock.

⁂

"You're not going anyplace in this," Sheriff Dubois says.

"How about up on the interstate?"

"The roads are getting worse by the minute."

Whicher checks the hills to both sides of the pass—covered, white-over now, pine and fir and juniper heavy with snow, wind blowing streams of powder from their tops.

"The weather service is predicting full-out storm conditions." The sheriff gives a lop-sided grin. "You want to bunk in my jailhouse?"

"Ma'am, I need to get away from here, disappear."

The sheriff lowers her voice. "You think somebody tried to put a hit on her?"

"Her close security's missing," Whicher says. "No accounting for why…"

Sheriff Dubois brings a gloved hand over her chin. "You think that's what we have here?"

The locomotive's engines grow louder, turning over, revving, dropping, the night air shaking to the sound.

"The roads are going to be cut till morning," the sheriff says. "Till they can get all the highway crews out."

Whicher sees the conductor, Ross, approaching.

"*Sheriff,*" the man calls out. "*I want to board the passengers…*"

"You go right ahead."

"The train's leaving?" Whicher says.

"We got nothing for 'em here. If the operator says it's okay to roll, I'm lettin' 'em roll. We've got everybody's names," Sheriff Dubois says, "in case we need to follow up on something. We'll keep looking. That wrecked Buick ought to tell us something, it must have come from somewhere."

Whicher nods.

"We're gaining nothing keeping the train here, there's hotels for folk up at La Junta, or maybe they'll keep on going." She looks at Whicher. "You need any help from me?"

"Ma'am?"

"You want a ride out?"

Whicher thinks of Chicago—a thousand miles distant.

"I can get you away in one of the all-wheel-drive units," the sheriff says. "As far as Trinidad, or maybe Raton."

Scattered groups are making their way down toward the

train, attendants and crew, travelers trying to shelter from the cold.

The marshal watches the nearest passengers already headed back onboard. "Y'all have any female officers here tonight?"

Sheriff Dubois looks at him.

"Do you?"

"Maybe," she says. "What's on your mind?"

⊥

Inside the lumber yard warehouse, a blonde deputy shrugs off her winter coat.

She lays it on a stack of fresh cut two-by-four joists—takes the heavy woolen coat Lauren DeLuca's holding out in exchange.

"Go ahead, Cheryl," Sheriff Dubois tells her. "I'll see you get the uniform coat back."

The deputy pulls Lauren's coat over her shoulders. She takes the clip from her hair, lets the blonde strands fall about her face.

"Put up the hood," the sheriff says.

The deputy shrugs, raises the hood, lets her fingers rest a moment in the soft, fur lining.

"I'll go out first," Whicher says.

Holding the Glock by his side, he draws the door of the warehouse open.

"You're just going to ride on back to the department, Cheryl," Sheriff Dubois says. "Don't worry about it, hon."

The marshal steps out, sees the Las Animas county

sheriff's truck, motor running.

All around the train, passengers are streaming back to get on board.

"Alright," he calls over his shoulder. "Let's move out, let's go."

He strides to the side of the truck, the female deputy in step behind him. He scans the view along the road, left to right.

"I get in?" the deputy says.

The marshal opens up. "You can get in."

The young woman jumps inside. She angles her head toward the warehouse. "Who is that in there?"

"Nobody."

"She sure has a nice coat," the deputy says. "For a nobody."

Whicher shuts the door, bangs on the roof.

The truck pulls out of the yard, moves along the frontage road—past the city-limit sign.

Whicher steps back into the warehouse—watches till the truck's gone from sight.

He pulls the door closed.

Lauren DeLuca's wearing the deputy's discarded overcoat.

The sheriff pulls out a bobble hat from the pocket of her ski-jacket. She tosses it over. "You can wear this, too."

Lauren catches the hat, stares at Whicher.

He nods to her. "Just get this done."

⚔

In the churned up snow around the train, Whicher stands at the back of a group of passengers and rail car attendants, one hand around the Glock in his pocket.

He shields Lauren with his body, checks for the sheriff's deputy following behind.

The passengers start to climb onboard.

"You have a cabin?" Whicher says.

Lauren points toward the front-end, up the track.

The marshal nods, looks along the side of the coach car—lights reflecting in its stainless-steel skin. He scans the few houses, the workshops, the old saloon.

"Sir?"

Whicher turns as a train attendant gestures at the empty doorway.

The marshal climbs up, into a narrow space, dirty meltwater of ice slick in the center stairwell.

Lauren climbs in behind him.

The sheriff's deputy boards last.

Whicher moves along a corridor, through the press of passengers checking left-behind belongings, shrugging off coats, trying to locate seats.

He checks for the deputy—still behind them.

They pass through two coach cars, a lounge car, a diner.

Three sleeper cars are at the head-end of the train, set back from the baggage car and the double locomotive. A narrow corridor is flanked with roomettes to either side. They reach a center stairwell, the corridor dog-legs into a blind turn.

"Up there," Lauren says.

Whicher follows the corridor along the side of the train, a row of sleeper cabins is directly ahead.

"The second door."

"There a key?" the marshal says.

"They only lock from inside."

Whicher steps forward, slides open the glass-panelled door to the room.

All the drapes are drawn, the lights dimmed.

He takes out the Glock, enters—checks the cabin space, the small bathroom.

"Alright," he says. "Come on in."

She shakes her head. Steps in behind him.

Whicher registers the look on her face. "There's no other way out of here tonight."

"This can't be safe."

The marshal eyes a small tote in the overhead rack.

"That's his," she says.

"Corrigan's?"

"He had it with him."

Whicher steps out of the room, sees the deputy waiting at the end of the corridor. "Hang tight."

"Sheriff says to get off, before the train moves."

The marshal nods, slides the glass-paneled door closed.

The locking mechanism is a flip-over metal bracket. "We'll get off at the next station," he says, "or at the one after that."

Lauren only stares at him.

"All the roads out are blocked. This here's fixing to be a major snow storm."

"If somebody followed me," she says, "if somebody tried to stop the train, you think they followed that sheriff's truck?"

He looks at her. "We don't know what all happened."

"You think they followed that woman wearing my coat?"

He tips back his hat a fraction. "Let me ask you something?"

She glares at him.

"You think they'd expect you to get right back on here?"

⽊

Whicher sits by the window, the rocking motion of the train steady, now. Holding back the dark blue drape, he looks out at the white-over land.

Snow is tumbling from the sky, falling heavier than ever. Forty-five minutes, the train's been moving, running dead slow—just enough speed to keep headway, keep momentum, clear the rails.

Descending from the pass, from the high mountains, the track's running north-east, now, out into flat land—the Colorado plains.

Whicher closes the drape, sits back, eyes Corrigan's tote in the overhead rack. Nothing in it of any use, no documents, just a change of clothes, a wash bag, two boxes of .40 caliber Smith & Wesson ammunition.

He glances at Lauren—sitting opposite in the jump seat.

She's out of line with the door, by the heater vent. Feline, coiled.

The borrowed deputy's coat is gone now—Whicher

handing it back to the sheriff's man before he stepped from the train.

A black sweater clings to the curves of Lauren's body.

"You don't have another coat?" he says.

She shakes her head.

The marshal takes his heavy wool ranch coat off the pull-out table by the window.

She eyes the exposed space where the coat was—Whicher's semi-automatic Glock laid out on the checkerboard top.

"You want this?" The marshal holds out the coat.

Her eyes rest on his.

Whicher extends his arm.

Her face softens.

She sits a fraction forward. Reaches over, takes it.

Opening it out, she puts it on, pulls the loose folds around her.

The clack of train wheels fills the cabin again. She's barely spoken since they pulled out from Fisherville.

Get her to Chicago, Whicher tells himself. Nothing more. *The less you know of her the better.*

Lauren sits back, turns her face to the side, breathes in lightly though her nose—a cat taking his scent.

He pushes down a lingering sense of unease. Thinks of the storm. Snow was drifting in the pass by the time they'd been headed out. Covering everything, all tracks.

Lauren studies him.

"You want to sleep?" he says. "If you want to, go ahead."

She doesn't reply.

"I can pull down a bunk." He glances at the overhead sleeping platform.

She shakes her head. "I don't think I could."

The marshal crosses his arms, feels the solid form of the Ruger in the shoulder-holster beneath the jacket of his suit. "In the army, that's what we'd do."

"That's what you did?" she says. "Before this?"

"Never know when you'll get another chance."

She sits low in the seat, his big coat engulfing her.

Whicher eyes the locking metal bracket on the door—it won't keep a man out.

Above it, a privacy-curtain covers the inset glass panel, he pulls it tighter, makes sure it's secure.

"Don't you think that deputy could have stayed on the train?" Lauren says.

"When we get off, I don't want anybody to know about it."

She thinks it over. Dips her head. "What do you think happened?" She looks at him.

He doesn't answer.

"Did you talk to Marshal Corrigan's boss?"

"I talked to him."

She shifts her weight in the jump seat, wraps her arms about her, holding on to her sides.

The marshal watches her a moment. Listens to the sound of the wheels against the rails.

"They told me they could protect me…" she says.

"Tell me about Corrigan?"

Her eyes search his face—the broken nose, broad mouth, wide-set eyes, hazel to green. "Aren't you afraid?"

Whicher runs a hand down his tie. Puts one boot on top of the other.

"He seemed experienced," she says. "He seemed to know what he was doing. I only met him when they told me they had to move me. Can you think of any reason he would have left the train?"

The marshal leans back into the seat.

With no answer.

Chapter 5

Jerzy Belaski rises from his place in the second coach car. Pulling down his watch cap, he steps into the aisle, starts to make his way along toward the front of the train.

He passes through a connecting corridor, steps into a lounge car.

Passengers are spread out, talking—drinking coffees and sodas. He eyes the packed snow clinging to the curving glass roof of the carriage.

Beyond the observation windows, nothing shows but the blackness of the night, striated white.

An attendant is in the aisle ahead, checking tickets.

Belaski makes a show of twisting sideways, looking to get past to where a handful of passengers are watching a movie.

"Sir, one moment," the attendant says. "We're double-checking numbers, making sure we've got everybody onboard."

Belaski gives a hawkish grin, no warmth—his gaze flat, deadened.

"Can I see your ticket?"

He reaches into the parka he's wearing, pulls out a square of printed card.

The attendant reads it. "You got on at Raton?"

Belaski nods.

The attendant studies the ticket, makes a note, gives it back. Unsettled by the man's demeanor, he steps on down the aisle, avoids looking at him again.

Belaski takes a seat near the group gathered watching the movie. He sits a minute, his face turned toward the screen. Thinks of the sleeper cars, just beyond the diner.

Glancing back down through the lounge he sees the attendant step out, move on to the rear.

He stands, passes through into the empty diner car.

Kitchen staff are somewhere downstairs on the lower level, he can hear them.

Moving straight through without stopping, he reaches the first of the sleeper cars—roomettes lining either side of a narrow strip, then a center stairwell, a small lobby.

Beyond it, the corridor dog-legs right then left.

At the head of the stairs is a washroom—unused. He enters, locks the door behind him.

Unzipping the parka, he pulls off the watch cap, runs a hand through his dark brown hair. The figure looking back in the mirror is unsmiling; shy of six-feet, though most people think him tall. His eyes have a strange cast, an inner light. Almond-shaped, slavic, gray. His body is hard, his mouth clamped—at odds with the world.

Taking out his cell phone, he sees a network showing. He searches the list of stored numbers, presses to call, holds the cell up to his ear.

Jimmy Scardino picks up. "Man, *what the fuck*? I'm following the goddamn train—the hell are you doing?"

Belaski bares his teeth in the mirror. Wipes a finger under his long, hooked nose. "The road follows the line of the track…"

"You going to get this shit done?"

"It follows right till La Junta…"

"Get fuckin' moving—or get off."

"She's with the man," Belaski says. "The guy in the hat." He reaches behind his hip to a cut-down holster inside the waistband of his cargo pants. Takes out a threaded-barrel SIG Sauer P226. "You got any other cars out there?"

"Are you kidding? In this?"

"Only you?" Belaski places the gun on the basin of the washroom. "There's only you on the road?"

"I haven't seen another vehicle in ten miles."

"Watch for me, then."

"You're going now?"

"Just stay close to the train."

Belaski shuts off the call. He slips a six-inch black, metal cylinder from his pocket—a suppressor. Taking up the SIG, he winds the cylinder onto the exposed threads.

He shoves the pistol into the front of his waistband, half-raises the zipper on the parka, checks the gun doesn't show.

Tapping down his coat, he feels for the ski-mask in a pocket, pulls it out. It's made of black fleece, with twin-eye holes. He rolls it part-way onto the top of his head, stopping just above his brow.

He puts the watch cap on over it.

Motionless in the mirror, he pictures the sleeper cabin half-way down the car. He can't risk forcing the door, he'll give them too much time to react. He'll have to get the guy out.

He unlocks the washroom, steps out.

The lobby and the stairs are still empty.

Moving down the corridor, he takes the blind turn, listening to the sound of the train.

The sleeper cabins are in a line in front of him. He stops halfway along the corridor, studies the blue drape across a glass-panelled door.

He raps a knuckle against the glass, hard.

"Message for Miss DeLuca."

He knocks again, harder still.

"Message for you, ma'am. Open up, please."

He cuts away, jogs to the end of the corridor, steps around the dog-leg corner.

Ducking into the vacant washroom, he slips out the suppressed SIG.

He rips off the watch cap, pulls the ski-mask down over his face.

He holds the door an inch ajar.

Lines up with the SIG.

🟊

Whicher holds the barrel of the Glock on the center of the cabin door.

Lauren slips out of the jump seat.

"Get back as far as you can…" Whicher breathes.

She flattens into a recessed space behind the bathroom wall.

The marshal stares at the door.

Any shot will pass straight through.

He grabs at the edge of the privacy curtain, yanks it—the glass panel shows an empty corridor—a few yards visible to the side.

Nobody can be asking for Lauren; nobody on the train knows her name.

He steadies the gun, unfastens the fold-over metal lock, slides open the door.

Nothing.

Just the sound of wheels against the rails.

He counts a beat. Leads with the Glock, swings sideways, out into the corridor.

Empty.

No-one—nothing either way.

He moves toward the dog-leg, trying to widen the line at the blind turn.

He stops. Checks back over his shoulder—Lauren's at the threshold of the room.

"Step back in, lock it."

Pistol raised between both hands, he eyes the thin-skinned cabin walls; no protection.

He takes a breath.

There's just the clacking of the wheels on the rails.

Above the drumming of his heart.

ᛏ

He called to her—he called out.

Belaski heard it—the man out of the cabin now, he was out, he was telling her to get back in.

He raises the SIG.

Curls his finger at the trigger.

Pushes open the washroom door.

⋏

Whicher sees the black, ski-masked figure—holding up a semi-auto.

He fires in the same split-second as the gunman.

Reeling, he scrambles to get back around the turn in the corridor.

There's a muffled scream, voices—someone shouting in a cabin.

Staring along the iron-sight of the Glock, he hears a thump, feet moving—feels a strange sensation—sharp, cold air.

The sound of wheels on the rails is louder, now, above the ringing in his ears.

Something is open.

A door open.

Wind is rushing up the corridor, harsh, cold wind.

Leading with the gun, he forces himself to step around the corner.

Nobody is in the lobby—the door of the washroom's open, no-one inside.

Whicher jumps down the stairwell, to the lower deck. Into an entry lobby, a tight, square space.

Black sky shows at one side of the carriage—snow swirling, frozen earth rushing by.

The door's wide open to the outside

The marshal's stomach comes up in his chest.

He spins around, lowers the Glock.

A carriage attendant appears at the top of the stairs.

"US Marshal," Whicher calls out. "Stop the train."

Chapter 6

The ground rushes at him as Belaski hits the bank of snow—rolling, twisting into the stinging swirl of white.

A sickening pain pulses through the back of his head. He comes to a stop, pushes up from the ground.

He sits on his haunches, hands at his knees. The train pulling away into darkness.

Doubling over, he starts to retch.

His mouth is full of spit, he pulls the ski-mask from his head, puts a hand into the hair at the back of his head. Blood is beneath his fingers, oily, warm.

He steadies himself, still clutching the SIG. Presses his fingers into white powder beneath him, feels the burn from the cold.

Rising, he takes in the bleak, flat land, the driving snow.

Looking back down the rail line, he strains to see into the dark.

No point of light shows from any house—no farm, no settlement. A black outline of trees is just visible. Between the flat fields he can make out a road, raised banks at either side, covered in snow.

He spots it, now—sees it out there.

The single set of moving lights.

⊥

The train conductor, Ross, is at the head of the stairwell. "What in the name of God is going on?"

The noise of seized brakes fills the entry lobby.

"Somebody just took a shot at me," Whicher says.

The conductor clambers down the stairs as the locked wheels start to grip against the ice-bound rails.

"They took a shot, then jumped."

Ross gapes at the open doorway. "You want to stop? You want to get off?"

The marshal stares out into the snow—finding anybody will be next to impossible. "Can you call ahead?"

"Engineer's already calling dispatch," Ross says. "We have to stop, now, recharge air, get pressure back in the brake-line."

"Tell dispatch to send out the nearest police unit."

The conductor swallows, stares out of the open door, at the blur of snow.

"You know where the next grade crossing is at?"

"We could find it…"

"Y'all keep the doors locked," the marshal says. "Get law enforcement out, have them search the train at the next station."

"You want a car out here? In this?"

"Get 'em to send out a unit. We're getting off."

⊥

Red light streaks the snow at the side of the grade crossing. The train is slowing to a walking pace.

Set back from the crossbuck is a white Ford Explorer, its light bar popping.

Whicher waits in the entry lobby of the sleeper car, Corrigan's tote and Lauren's case in his hand.

Lauren's at the foot of the stairwell, wrapped in his heavy woolen ranch coat.

Thirty minutes have passed. Thirty minutes to stop, reset the brakes and move up to the nearest crossing point with a road.

The train grinds to a dead stop.

Conductor Ross sticks his head out of the open door, cranes his neck, checking up and down the line.

Whicher scans the white-over prairie—nothing out there but the law enforcement Ford Explorer.

The driver steps out of the vehicle. He stands, huddled in the wind and snow.

The conductor waves the marshal out.

Whicher drops from the train, feels the cold wind nail the back of his suit.

In the doorway, Lauren turns, climbs down.

The conductor watches as they step back, clear of the line. "Otero County Sheriff's office say they'll have people at La Junta."

The marshal touches a hand to the brim of the Resistol.

Ross speaks into a two-way radio. The train's exhaust note rises.

Whicher turns side-on as compressed air hisses—the train begins to move away.

He walks toward the waiting vehicle.

The driver steps around to the rear door, motions for Lauren to get inside.

Whicher lifts the luggage in after her, slides it onto the rear seat, pushes the door shut.

"Officer Kyle Guillory," the driver says.

"Whicher, US Marshals Service."

"I'm supposed to meet with you here," Guillory says, "help out. That's about all I know."

The marshal studies the man—he's in his thirties, heavyset, a fleshy face reddened by wind. He's wearing a police cap, a padded tan jacket—a city badge, *Millersburg*, sewn above the right pocket.

"I can't tell you much," Whicher says, angling his head toward the rear of the Ford. "Be obliged if you don't ask."

The officer glances into the back of his vehicle.

The marshal eyes the snow chains strapped around the big Ford's tires. "Whatever help you can give us, we can use." He takes a last look at the train—moving off into the dark.

"You don't have any coat?" Guillory says, above the wind.

Whicher steps to the front passenger side. "We get in?"

"Hell, yeah."

The marshal climbs inside, feels heat blowing from the air vents. He thrusts out his hands.

Guillory swings in behind the wheel. "You're going to freeze your ass off out here," he says. "It's fixin' to be a real good one." He gazes out through the windshield. "Looks like we're headed south of minus-four Fahrenheit. Plus significant precip." He turns to Lauren in the back seat. "Evening, ma'am."

She nods, saying nothing.

"You make it out here okay?" Whicher says.

"Pretty much, with the chains."

"What's going on with the roads—there anyplace we can get to?"

"You're not from Colorado, are you?"

Whicher shakes his head. He takes his hands away from the heater vents, rubs at the sleeves of his suit.

"It'll get severe, this way," Guillory says. "I came five miles, is all."

"From?"

"From Millersburg."

"So, can you get us back to there?"

The officer nods. He moves the shifter into drive, turns the Ford around, away from the railroad line.

Beyond the road, there's just a smudge of black sky, a blur of horizontals.

"What kind of a police department y'all have?" Whicher says.

"We're not that big of a town—around a couple thousand," Guillory says. "The department runs to two men. Me. Plus my boss."

The marshal peers out at the glare of the SUV's lights.

"We have a station house, an office."

"Anybody else know about you picking us up?"

"No, sir."

"Who took the call?"

"You mean, from the rail folk?"

Whicher nods.

"I did. I took it right at my house."

"You tell anybody? Before you came on out?"

"No, sir." The officer steals a look at the big man in the hat.

"Alright." The marshal says. "If you can get us to your station house, I need to make a call." He turns back to Lauren, tries to catch her eye.

She sits with her head turned to the window, staring out. A cold reflection in the curved black glass.

Chapter 7

In the driver's seat of the Toyota Tacoma, Jimmy Scardino lights another Camel from the cherry-red end of the last. "I put my lights on now?" He blows smoke. "I mean, the main beams?"

Jerzy Belaski looks at him from the passenger seat. "Keep 'em off."

Maybe it was the eyes—always pissed-looking. Like a pissed-off teenager. Brown hair plastered to his forehead, the hook of a nose. A hawk, what he looked like. *A Polack hawk.*

The tail lights of the vehicle ahead glow dull red in the distance.

"I follow the train out of the pass," Jimmy says, "is one thing." He points a finger out of the windshield. "A white cop car ain't the same—in all this shit."

"You want to shut the hell up?"

Scardino clamps the cigarette in his mouth, steers the truck down the center of the road. Better not to provoke the son of a bitch. Better just to let him be. The guy was off the deep end, a mad-whack. Mean. Fast. But good at what he did—Jimmy'd seen his handiwork, didn't need to see it twice.

Anybody needed taking care of, Belaski'd do what needed to be done. But nobody liked him, back in Chicago, back in the neighborhood. Nobody among the men.

Belaski shifts his weight, takes a cell from out of his parka pocket.

He stares down into his lap—at the screen.

Not a single bar of network showing.

⁂

The city-limit sign looms out of the dark at the side of the road—*Millersburg*—Whicher casts an eye over the buildings at the edge of town.

Board-clad houses are set in big plots—open barns around them, rough timbered, the houses old, tall, their roofs steep-pitched.

Scant light shows in any window. Along the tree-lined route, branches hang low beneath the weight of snow.

No other car is moving.

There's not a living soul in sight.

Whicher eyes a row of grand houses faced with stone, sees a bright-lit area ahead—a broad intersection, flurries swarming the orange-glow of the street lamps.

A handful of businesses are spaced about the main road—a grocery store, an outdoor supply. An auto shop. A bar.

Guillory points at a double-wide brick building—at the

far side of a one-room church. "That's the station house."

The town is silent, the only sound the faint whump of the tire chains on the road.

In the lots between buildings, solitary cars and trucks are covered in snow, abandoned to the night.

Whicher looks from one end of the intersection to the other.

"Winter time," Guillory says, "the middle of the Comanche Grasslands, it'll get quiet." He steers off the main street, pulls into the empty lot of the police department.

The marshal stares through the windshield. "How 'bout you head on in, put on the lights?"

Guillory looks at him.

"You want to give us a minute?"

The patrolman shuts off the motor. "If that's what you want."

He pushes open the driver door, levers himself out against the wheel.

A blast of frozen air enters the cab before he swings the door shut.

Trudging through the thick snow, he finds a set of keys, opens up.

From the back seat, Lauren lets out a constricted breath.

Whicher turns around to her. "Nobody knows we're here. Sheriff Dubois said there was no way out by road."

Her head moves lightly from side to side.

"We need to go on inside the station." He holds up the collar of his suit jacket, pushes open the door. "The son of a bitch that took that shot at me jumped, right?"

She looks around out of the window, despite herself.

"You see him get off at that grade crossing?"

"You know for sure that he jumped?"

⋏

Officer Kyle Guillory pours coffee into three identical white mugs. The sound of a boiler rumbles from somewhere out of a back room, the radiators in the station house all ticking.

Guillory puts out the coffee, shifts hunting trophies aside on the top of a cluttered table. He flips cream and sugar sachets from a cardboard box.

Whicher takes up a mug. "I use your phone?"

"Go right ahead."

The marshal crosses to the door of an office marked, *Chief of Police*. "I step on in here a minute?"

The patrolman nods.

Whicher enters, puts a boot tip to the door, pushes it closed.

Alone, he takes in the room—wood-paneled, rows of photographs—Officer Guillory plus another man in uniform; the boss, the chief of police.

The marshal sits at a corner of the desk.

From his jacket he takes out his cell, finds the stored number. He keys it into the office land-line.

He checks his watch. Nine-thirty.

The call picks up.

"Who is this?"

Whicher recognizes Inspector McBride.

"Sir, it's Marshal Whicher."

McBride exhales into the phone. "Marshal—I told you not to call."

"Yes, sir, I know that. But something happened—about an hour ago. Somebody made an attempt…"

"An attempt?"

"On my traveling companion. I'm not calling y'all for help."

A beat passes.

"Then what do you want?"

Whicher stares around the office. "Sir, did any word come back yet on my companion's previous escort?"

"Not at this time."

The marshal stands, lifts the phone from the desk. "I've asked for a train arriving at La Junta to be boarded and searched. The Otero County Sheriff will be handling it. Maybe you ought to call. The attempt was made on the train, the attacker or associates may still be onboard. We got off. But now we're pretty much boxed-in, account of the weather conditions."

"Can you keep moving?"

"Not real likely," Whicher says. "At least, not any time soon."

"This is a land line you're calling on—not a cell?"

"Yes, sir, it is."

"Your companion is safe?"

"She's safe, and nobody's coming in here—where we're at is pretty remote."

"Who knows where you are now?"

"One other person," Whicher says, "an officer on a

small-town police force. I'm calling from their station house."

"In the circumstances, maybe I ought to take the number."

The marshal reads off the number written above the keypad. "Sir, I been thinking—maybe it's time I knew a little more about the person I'm traveling with?"

"Not a good idea."

Whicher rolls his tongue around the inside of his mouth.

"The less you know of her, the better," McBride says.

"You don't think it could help?"

"No, I don't. Did anybody see you arrive at that station house?"

"No, sir."

"If they had people on the train, they know where it stopped, where you got off, they could likely track you down. If you're in country, in a rural locale, there can't be many places you could go. I'm guessing that police station is right in the middle of town?"

Whicher thinks it over.

"It's the kind of place they might check, they might watch. You need to find somewhere till you can move again, a place no-one's going to notice you, nobody's going to see."

The marshal eases out the chair from the desk—he sits.

"Keep on with what I told you," McBride says.

"Just keep right on?"

"Unless you can't."

Whicher thinks it over, lets the phrase sink in.

Unless you can't.

AN AMERICAN BULLET

✶

Lauren DeLuca sits at the far side of the office in the marshal's coat. Her legs are crossed, her face a mask. Cheekbones a perfect curve in the light of the office lamp.

The marshal drains his second mug of coffee.

"Why do you keep checking your watch?" she says.

Too long.

Too long since Guillory set out.

He was headed over to the far side of town, to his house. To bring them something to eat, bring a winter coat for Whicher.

Lauren puts her head on one side, blonde hair falling in an arc. "Do you think he's alright?"

"Snow's pretty bad out there."

Her foot begins to bounce. "How long do you think he'll be?"

Whicher shifts in his seat. "Why don't you tell me something about you?"

She draws the big, wool coat around herself.

"Maybe it could make a difference," he says, "if I knew who was coming after you…"

"I agreed to testify in a trial. In exchange, I was promised protection."

He runs a hand over the day's growth of stubble at his chin.

"How much of this have you done?" she says. "Witness security?"

"I've done a lot of things, ma'am."

"I hope you know what you're doing."

He nods. "One thing I do know…"

"What's that?"

"Mostly—folk that end up in witness security, they're from a pretty damn serious background."

"A serious background?"

He looks at her. "That's to say—a criminal background."

⋏

On the long wall of the Millersburg outdoor supply, snow is inches thick on top of the payphone booth.

Jerzy Belaski feeds in quarters, checks both directions along the sidewalk. No footprints show, the ground is unmarked—only his own boots have disturbed the fresh fall.

No headlights show in any direction.

Behind the wheel of the stationary Toyota, Jimmy Scardino looks out, runs a hand through his thick head of wavy, black hair.

He's smiling. Smiling at nothing.

Belaski keys the numbers on the freezing phone.

It rings twice, three times, picks up.

He hears the sound of music playing—ambient noise, voices, people talking.

"Mister Coletti?"

He pictures the South Side of Chicago, a neighborhood bar.

"It's Jerzy Belaski."

"What?"

"Belaski…"

"What the hell do *you* want?"

There's a rustling noise at the earpiece, the speaker goes dull. The sound changes, the music quieter now, no voices—a backroom.

"We ran into a problem," Belaski says.

"What God damn problem?"

Genaro Coletti. Still the construction foreman he once was.

"Did you hit the train?"

"We hit it."

"Did you get it stopped?"

"We stopped it, but we couldn't get right to her." Belaski stares at scuff marks on the side of the payphone booth. "By the time we had her escort, the sheriff's department showed up…"

"Where are you?"

"Colorado. She got herself tight in with law enforcement."

"The fuck is wrong with you?" Coletti snaps. "What the hell is going on?"

"I bought a ticket at Raton," Belaski says, his voice even. "I got on the train."

"Jimmy park that station wagon on the line?"

"He parked it. We got the train stopped, but we couldn't get to her."

"Ah, Jesus Christ."

Belaski keeps his speech slow, deliberate. "The train didn't wreck, they got it started up again. She got back on, I got on. Jimmy followed in the truck…"

"What the fuck?"

"We picked the spot for that," Belaski says. "Just in case. The rail line follows the road from Trinidad to La Junta. It follows the track for miles."

"Yeah? Shit."

"I tried again on the train, but there was another cop—I took a shot, but there was no way to get the jump, I had to bail, had to get out. They stopped the train in the middle of nowhere. They got off."

"Where?"

Belaski eyes the snow. "Around forty miles from La Junta. Millersburg, it's called."

"You know where she is now, I mean right now?"

"They went into a police station."

The sound changes again—Belaski pictures Coletti covering the phone with his hand, cursing him out, only barely in control. Balls but no brains.

Jimmy Scardino stares out through the windshield, shifting, nervous in the Toyota.

"Millersburg?" Coletti finally says.

"I'm just letting you know…"

"That I sent a spray-hitting prick to do a man's job…"

"So you know what's going on…"

"Yeah? So far, so fucked up."

Belaski leans against the side of the booth.

"I'm sending help."

"There's a storm going here, it's snowing like crazy. No way anybody's getting in through this."

"Then you listen to me," Coletti says, "this gets taken

care of, tonight. Or you're out—I find somebody else."

"Nobody's coming in here." Belaski grinds his teeth. "Nobody's leaving."

"Anyway it needs to get done, you get it the hell done."

The call clicks out.

Chapter 8

Officer Kyle Guillory's Ford Explorer lights up the trunks of blue spruce and limber pine lining the trail through the woods. The tall trees have kept the forest track clearer than the metaled roads, sheltering the ground from the ceaseless fall of snow.

In the back of the vehicle, Whicher sits with Lauren DeLuca. In his lap, a borrowed coat from Guillory; a deer camp jacket made from tight-weave wool.

He glances out of the window at the frozen night, grateful for the coat, for the warmth of the blower in the Ford.

A half-mile into the woods, they're starting to slow.

Whicher sees a clearing in the trees—in its center, a cabin, built from rough cut logs.

He looks at Lauren, still she hasn't taken off his coat.

Guillory lifts a finger, points from the wheel. "There's no regular power. But plenty of lanterns, a bunch of firewood, it'll warm up pretty quick."

Lauren edges back into her seat. "There really aren't any hotels? Or motels even?"

"Nothing till you get to La Junta," Guillory says. "And no way we're getting up there, not in this."

"Couldn't we stay at the station?"

"We need to change locale," Whicher says.

Lauren looks to Officer Guillory. "Could we stay with you?"

"A place like Millersburg is too small," Whicher says, "too much of a risk of somebody noticing."

"But if we don't go out?"

Guillory brakes the Ford to a stop in the clearing, leaves the motor running. "If y'all don't want folk knowing you're around, this'll work about as good as anyplace you could get."

⊥

The wood stove is going strong—bright flame leaping, a stack of cordwood set on the plank floor.

Heat is seeping through the cabin space. Whicher adjusts the sliding flue on the stove.

Set about the place are propane lanterns, the log walls hung with antlers. It's solid—dry, well fitted out. A family hunting lodge—his father's before him, Guillory said.

In a corner of the room, Lauren DeLuca takes out the folded contents of a blanket box. Rugs. Thick wool blankets. She lifts them out, looks at each one briefly. Throws them onto the back of a chair.

The burning logs glow orange-white, air roaring in beneath the three-legged stove.

Whicher takes a few steps into the kitchenette in back.

He can make out a sink, a drainboard, storage racks, wire-front cupboards.

He tries the faucet. A thin stream of water starts to run. A cistern must be out there somewhere. Not frozen, it must be insulated. Whatever, he knows better than to drink.

He shuts off the faucet. Rows of bottled water line the floor against one wall—store-bought water, hauled in from town.

On the counter is a rucksack, left by Guillory—filled with crackers, coffee, cans of chili and beef tamales. Whicher looks at the gas stove. "You want somethin' to eat?"

She tosses the last of the blankets onto a folding, army cot.

The marshal holds up the rucksack to the light from a wall lantern.

Lauren steps to the kitchenette.

"You going to take off that coat?" he says.

She looks at him. "Do you want it back?"

Whicher studies her. Her face is in shadow.

"Are you going to take off that hat?"

He places a hand on the crown of the Resistol, flips off the hat, puts it down on top of the kitchen table.

She unfastens the coat.

In the dim light he can barely see her eyes.

"You look better without it," she says. "Without the hat."

She takes off his coat, walks to the stub of an antler on the wall. Reaches up, hangs it on the bone hook.

For a moment neither one of them speaks.

Whicher rifles the rucksack. "You look better out of my coat."

He swings the bag onto the table.

She takes it, starts to unpack everything from inside.

The marshal takes a lantern from the wall, stares at a slit window high up on the rear side of the cabin, snow filling the frame. All the other windows are shuttered—lacquered pine planks closed against the panes.

He moves to the back door. It's locked with two bolts, top and bottom. He slides them back, opens up.

"What're you doing?" she says.

Outside, wind is moving in the trees, the air dead, thick with snow.

"I need to check on something."

He grabs Guillory's coat. It's made of black and red plaid, lined with sheepskin, fastened with a heavy, brass zipper.

He puts it on, steps out, pulls the door closed behind him.

Light is showing at the slit window on the back wall. A thin shaft, bright against the snow beneath the trees.

He moves into the clearing, woodsmoke swirling. Looking into the trees along the track he can see twenty yards—then nothing but black.

No sign of anybody out there.

He feels the snow in his hair, melting against the heat of his neck.

Silence—silence but for the wind—a high keening in the tops of the trees.

He turns back to the cabin, to the slit window, searches

for a shutter—finds none. He steps to the back door, knocks snow from his boots. Re-enters the kitchenette, slips home the two bolts.

Lauren DeLuca looks at him. "Is everything alright?"

He pulls out a chair, sits at the kitchen table. Shrugs off the coat.

From the holster at his hip, he takes out the semi-automatic Glock. He places it on the worn, pine boards. "You know how to shoot?" He looks at her.

Her face is clouded. "Not really."

He nods. Draws the big-frame Ruger revolver from his shoulder-holster, holds it in the flat of his hand.

"You carry two guns?"

He places the revolver on the table. "This one belonged to a buddy of mine."

"It looks a little old-fashioned."

"It'll get the job done." The marshal tilts his head at the square-looking semi-auto. "That's the USMS standard issue."

She takes a breath. "You watch the door, then. I'll fix us something."

She picks a box of kitchen matches from the counter top. Lights a burner on the stove, turns the flame down low.

"Do you want coffee?" She lifts a can from the rucksack. "Do you want some of this chili?"

He clicks open the cylinder on the revolver, spins it. "I'll take whatever you got."

"I guess you weren't counting on this," she says, "any more than I was."

He looks up from the table.

"Spending a night in the woods," she says.

He presses the cylinder closed, shakes his head.

She takes a can opener from a rack of kitchen utensils, sets the steel jaws onto the top of the can.

"This morning, I took a man out to a prison facility. Florence ADX. Highest security prison in the country."

Her face is in profile as she empties the can of chili into a pan.

"Mob guy," the marshal says.

Her eyebrow arches.

"From Chicago. Originally. I was thinking; maybe you would have known him?"

⋏

The track between the trees is pitch black—Jimmy Scardino sits behind the wheel of the Toyota, lights out.

The motor in the pickup is shut off, the temperature falling. Scardino rounds his shoulders, tries not to shiver. "How long you want to wait on this, man?"

Belaski looks at him. "If nothing happens, they'll settle."

"I say go in. Get it done."

"They'll be less alert." Belaski shakes his head. "We wait."

He stares off out of the windshield, mouth compressed beneath the hook of a nose.

Scardino thinks of arguing, thinks again, curses beneath his breath.

He sits back in the driver's seat, watches Belaski from the corner of his eye.

The man was barely breathing—taken up with some thought; consumed. He'd just be that way—*possessed,* some called it. With his weird kind of energy. Up close you could see it, sense it—feel it coming off of him. His eyes dead, the way a shark's eyes were dead.

"What're you looking at?" Belaski speaks without turning.

Scardino doesn't answer. He looks off into the gnarled, black woods.

Along the side-trail, set back from the main track, there's just the creak and moan of unseen branches.

Following the SUV had been easy—out of Millersburg. The cop, the woman, and the man in the hat.

Hanging back, way back, they'd seen them go up into the woods. They'd waited in the pickup. On a side-trail, to see what occurred.

Fifteen minutes later, the Ford had come back out again. Just the driver in the cab.

They'd followed the wheel tracks it had made to a cabin.

"You're not worried?" Scardino says. "You're not worried about getting away? In this whole shit ton of snow?"

"Would you rather be up in that cabin?" Belaski says.

Scardino looks at him.

"With somebody outside, waiting. Somebody like me."

⚘

On the army cot along the log wall of the cabin, Lauren DeLuca lies sideways, her head on her hands.

The canned chili and tamales are finished. Whicher feeds

a split log into the wood stove, closes the iron and glass door, twists the handle against the latch.

He steps into the kitchenette, lifts a chair from the table. "Two kinds of people wind up in witness security," he says. "Family members of people that agreed to testify—and the witnesses themselves."

He sets the chair down by the iron stove.

She sits up on the cot. "I told you already that's what I am."

"Nobody gets in WITSEC over nickels and dimes."

She takes a breath through her nose.

He lets his eye rest on hers a moment. "For a federal prosecutor to take an interest, only key testimony is enough. I know you're going to a major trial, a mob trial."

She blinks, slowly.

"So you're high-level. An insider."

The wind blasts against the cabin walls, rattling the wooden shutters at the window frames.

The marshal stands. He listens a moment, eyes the slit window on the wall in back.

He takes the Ruger from the table top. Sits again, rests the big-frame revolver against his lap. "How long have you been in the program?"

She looks at him, the fire's shadow flickering across her face. "A little over nine months."

"How long with your previous protection officer?"

"Corrigan? I never saw him. I only saw people if they told me I had to move…" She stops—composes her face into a practiced mask.

He tugs at the collar of his shirt.

"They told me not to talk."

"They told you that?"

"To anybody."

He listens to the sounds of the cabin, hears only the wind outside.

⁂

In fourteen years on a two-man police department, Kyle Guillory can't think of a single occasion necessitating a night in a hunting lodge—with a woman like her.

He peers through the snow driving in across the Comanche Grasslands, steers the Ford Explorer to the end of the county road.

The junction with the track is marked only by white-over fence posts sweeping downhill from the line of trees.

He could apply to the sheriff's department, Las Animas County Sheriff. Get a job with them, he tells himself; find himself something new. Fourteen years ought to count for something. Marshals Service—maybe he could apply to that?

The man, McBride, had called the station house—the call diverting from there right to Guillory's place. The station phone was set up that way, he'd been about to go on up to bed, coming on midnight. Guillory shakes his head, moves the shifter into low.

The tire chains bite in the hard packed snow.

McBride had said he was an inspector with the US Marshals Service. Insisted on talking with the other marshal, even when Guillory explained he wasn't there. He'd said it was urgent; Guillory would've left it till morning, the storm the way it was, only getting worse.

There was no way to call the hunting lodge, not a hope in hell of getting any signal.

Ahead, the track dips through a hollow near the edge of the woods. Guillory sees the glinting snow reflected in the headlights. It could be deep there—the kind of dip that could hold a drift.

He keeps his speed steady, wary, ready for the feel of slipping wheels. Thinks of Comanche braves, hunters, men lost in the night, men like him. Lit by camp fires, the hides of their tepees weighted down with chunks of stone. The Ford chews its way through the dip—and out the other side.

He steers on into the woods, darkness enfolding, headlights glaring back from low slung limbs of trees.

Through the wheel, he feels the thump of chains on the winter tires.

He thinks of coming up, coming to the lodge again, kicking back, once the weather shakes out.

His foot comes suddenly off the gas.

He straightens, sits up in his seat.

A shape is out there—a shape in the truck's main beams.

Where the track kinks left into the woods, there's a vehicle. A parked vehicle, just sitting—lights out.

He lets the Ford slow, listening to the rhythm as the chains strike the ground.

He can see it's a pickup, now—a Toyota. No way anybody's going to be out—not in this, not in the middle of a winter storm.

Behind the glass of the driver window he sees movement—a face turning to look.

He feels his heart rate climb in his chest.

Tells himself it's okay.

Chapter 9

Jerzy Belaski stares back down the track, past Jimmy Scardino's head, at the lights in the woods.

"It could be hunters," Jimmy says.

Belaski reaches for the overhead dome light—moves the switch to stop it from coming on.

He leans his weight forward. Takes out the suppressed SIG.

The lights approaching are thirty yards away.

"Maybe they won't stop…"

Above the glare of headlamps, more lights begin to flash, colored lights—red and blue.

"We're not in Garfield Park," Belaski answers

The vehicle's stopped moving.

A door opens, the driver's door.

A man steps out.

A tight, white beam snaps on, a flashlight.

Scardino reaches to a door-pocket, he takes out a mid-size Springfield XD.

"Put that away." Belaski eases open the passenger door.

"Just get him talking." He drops, crouches to the ground.

Moving down the side of the pickup, hidden from the headlights, he reaches the tailgate.

He risks a look at the vehicle down the track.

He can't see a partner.

Rural cops, he tells himself—*they'd work alone*.

The flashlight shines directly into the cab of the Toyota.

The cop nears the side of the pickup—gun trained on the driver-side window.

"Police officer…"

Red and blue light fractures the dark.

"Open up. Step out of your vehicle." The sound of the man's voice is dull, flat in the noiseless woods.

Scardino opens the driver's door an inch.

"Keep your hands where I can see them," the officer shouts.

The door of the Toyota creaks on its hinges.

Belaski edges around the back of the pickup, still crouched—he studies the man now standing at right-angles to him—a police cap on his head, a padded jacket. Heavy face. Like an Iowa pig-farmer.

Scardino gets a boot on the ground, his hands out in front of him, no gun.

"Step out, turn around, put your hands on the roof of the truck."

Jimmy gets out, straightens.

The officer steps sideways to the front of the Toyota. Moves the flashlight onto the registration plate. "Chicago?"

"Uh?"

"You're from Chicago?"

"I was just driving, man. I needed to get out of the snow."

Belaski crouches at the tailgate. For a moment, he thinks of the control, the absolute power—the lives of both men in his sights. All he has to do is squeeze on the trigger. He feels the beating pulse in the muscle of his thumb.

"I want to see driver's license and registration," the officer says. He steps back directly behind Scardino.

Jimmy turns his head a little. "My license is in the truck there…"

Belaski hears the lack of any clue in the man's voice.

"Put your hands behind your back," the cop says.

"What? What for?"

"Just do what I tell you."

Raising the pistol, Belaski takes a shallow breath. He stares into the side of the cop's head.

Squeezes off two rounds.

The man's head snaps sideways—blown out.

He falls, deadweight, into a crumpled heap.

The blunt thump of the gun echoes in the mass of trees.

Jimmy stares at Belaski.

Belaski marches to the cop's body.

Scardino fumbles out a Camel from his jacket—lights the cigarette, draws the smoke down deep. "Are you fucking crazy?"

"Waiting game is over." Belaski glances at the lifeless form.

Turning on his heel, he walks down the track to the man's vehicle—the Ford Explorer from before. Pausing by the open door, he listens—nothing from the radio, no sound.

"Drag him into the woods and get in the truck," he calls back. "Follow on behind me."

"What're you talking about?"

"Just do it, Jimmy, for Chrissake. Get the guy's hat. Get in the truck, drive up behind me. You see me stop, you stop. That's all you have to do."

Chapter 10

Smoke is swirling in the clearing, wood smoke in the snow-filled air. Fifty yards back on the track with the Ford Explorer, Belaski watches Jimmy Scardino work his way around the forest's edge—around the back of the cabin, out the other side.

He shakes his head at the man's efforts; labored, stumbling—Scardino had just enough luck to be born into family, the family of a made man. He never would've made it from the streets.

Jogging slow along the side of the clearing, Scardino reaches the Ford. "Only thing I could see was a strip of light around the back. On the wall, up high."

Belaski nods. "There's no way of getting in."

"No way quiet…"

"So we drive up in the cop's SUV."

"Right up to the cabin?"

"They hear us, they'll have to check it out." Belaski takes a final look. "If they don't, I'll stick the cop's hat on, I'll go on up." He yanks open the door of the Ford, swings in behind the wheel.

Jimmy glances at the Toyota, another fifty yards back along the trail.

Belaski starts up the motor, puts on the lights.

Jimmy looks at him, grim faced, he gets in.

The tire chains bite on the soft ground. The vehicle starts to move forward.

Jimmy takes off a glove, pulls the Springfield from the pocket of his jacket.

The headlight beams reach ahead through the frozen air.

"How they going to know it's cops?" Jimmy says.

Belaski reaches up to the switch to turn on the light bar.

Jimmy nods, teeth glinting in the light from the dash.

"I park up, they see this, they ought to recognize it," Belaski says. "Tell you what, though—the guy in there with her has already seen me. Back on the train. He got a look at me."

"What difference does it make?"

"How about you do it, you put on the cop's hat? I'll pull around so you're facing the cabin. When he looks out, he's never seen you before."

"Man, I don't know…"

"I got you covered, Jimmy." Belaski hands the man the dead cop's cap.

⁂

Sitting by the wood stove he can see both doors, front and back. At first it's just a flicker that catches Whicher's eye.

Lauren's resting on the army cot, knees drawn up.

The marshal studies the propane lantern on the wall. Maybe the gas is running out?

From the edge of the shuttered window is a snatch of red light. A snatch of blue.

He stands, picks the Glock off the kitchen table.

Lauren shifts on the cot.

"Put out the light," he says.

She looks over at him.

Above the wind is another sound; a motor. The marshal moves toward the front of the cabin.

Lauren slips off the cot, reaches for the lamp, turns down the dial.

The gas putters, dies. Only the wood stove lights the room.

Whicher steps to the door, slides back the cover on a four-inch square of glass.

Outside, the clearing is filled with bursts of red and blue light. Popping, swiveling.

A white Ford Explorer is twenty yards from the cabin. "That's Guillory."

The SUV is side-on, he can barely see the windows, they're covered in snow and ice.

"It's gone midnight," Lauren says.

"He's got everything lit up."

"Is he coming in? He was coming in the morning…"

Whicher nods. "He's not getting out."

Something could've happened, the marshal tells himself—the sheriff's office were going to be boarding the train at La Junta, maybe they found something. They could've picked up the guy that jumped.

"He's lit up like a Christmas tree," Whicher says, "I guess

he wants us to know who it is." He reaches to the top of the door, unfastens a bolt.

"Are you going out?"

He opens the door, steps off the porch. Walks out into falling snow—wind scouring, whipping ice crystals into his face.

Nearest to him, a cop in the passenger seat grins.

Guillory, at the wheel, is in darkness.

Whicher checks step—the passenger's not the chief of police, not the man from the office photographs.

He senses movement.

The grinning man starts to raise something.

Whicher dives left as the window glass explodes.

He rolls to the back of the SUV, holds up the Glock, fires three rounds into the rear-hatch glass.

The Ford's wheels spin—it lurches, rips away out of the clearing.

Whicher stares as it races down the track, lights flashing through the trees.

He squeezes off two more rounds.

In the door of the cabin, Lauren DeLuca's staring.

He gets to his feet. "*Stay there, get back inside…*"

Sprinting across the clearing, he reaches the track to the woods.

Beneath the trees, the ground is firmer—he runs into the black, cold air knifing his lungs.

He stops.

A shape is out there, looming.

He stares down the sights of the gun.

Chapter 11

The dark form of a pickup truck sits to the side of the track beneath the trees. Whicher scans the blackened woods, chest heaving, sweat breaking on his skin.

Approaching, he can see it's a double-cab Toyota. Nobody inside.

He steps to it, grabs the door on the driver's side—it opens.

Keys are hanging from the steering column.

The cab smells of cigarettes.

He jumps in, starts the motor, turns on the lights. The fuel gauge shows the tank half-full.

Shifting into drive, he presses down on the gas, steers out onto the track, toward the clearing. The wheels of the pickup hit the churned-up ruts of snow from the Ford. He pulls up in front of the cabin, leaves the motor running.

He steps out. "*Lauren,*" he calls.

The cabin door is closed. He jumps up on the porch.

He puts a boot against the door.

Inside, in the light of the wood stove he sees her—she's

at the back of the cabin. The glint of a long blade at her side.

She holds up a butcher's knife.

"We have to go," he says.

He takes the boxes of ammunition from Corrigan's tote.

"Put on my coat. Where's your case?"

She points at the floor by the cot.

Whicher grabs the case, grabs the plaid hunting coat.

Lauren sets down the knife. She looks at him, face pale, her eyes rounded.

He steps from the cabin, jumps down off the porch, throws the case into the back of the crew cab.

Lauren follows him outside, shivering. She stares at the Toyota.

"Get in," he tells her. He climbs inside, behind the wheel.

She steps up into the cab, pulls the door closed.

"We need to get the hell out of here."

Lauren puts both hands to her face, spreads the skin taught across her cheeks.

The marshal shifts into drive, steers out into the track in the woods.

"Where are we going?" she says.

He strains his eyes to see beneath the overhang of trees—the world down to the width of twin headlight beams. "Somebody knows where we're at," he says, "that's all that matters."

"How can anybody know?"

ㅅ

Jimmy Scardino's blood is wet on the seats of the Ford—broken glass all over the cab.

Belaski hears the sound of a motor, sees lights moving, flickering in the trees.

A split second—all it'd taken. The big man went down, shots were coming through the back, glass everywhere, blood flying—blood and pieces of bone.

The last shot caught Jimmy in the back of the head.

They were fish in a barrel, he'd gotten them out.

He thinks of dragging Jimmy from the cab—he was passing out, blood gurgling from his mouth. Nothing he could do, he tells himself; *nobody's going to know.*

He pictures holding the muzzle of the SIG to Jimmy's temple. Squeezing. Making sure.

He feels the rush in his veins, now—the surge of anger. Everything going to shit; the whole damn thing. He sits in silence, in the darkness, motor shut down. Watching the lights moving ghost-like. Jimmy's Toyota coming down the forest track. A bright phantom.

It draws level with the off-shoot in the woods. Speeds by.

He starts the motor in the Ford, leaves his own lights extinguished.

To follow the tail lights—trailing red into the dark.

Chapter 12

Lauren DeLuca pins a finger on the open page of a road map—the land is a whiteout, smothered. "There's supposed to be a highway at the end of this."

Whicher steers through an alien landscape, amorphous shapes, indistinct, trying to pick out fences, power lines, signs of the road.

"We have to keep heading north," Lauren says.

The marshal squints into the glare of white, thinks of sandstorms overseas in the desert. "Hard telling which direction we're headed…"

She looks up.

"We're going north," he says, "near enough."

The look of panic subsides, she raises the map on her knee.

Whicher focuses on the feel of the truck—the grip, speed, momentum—thinking like the armor officer he once was.

"How about fuel?" Lauren says.

He nods. "We got fuel."

"What if we get stuck?"

Snow races sideways through the air, shot-blasted in the light of the pickup beams. "We ain't getting stuck, we're finding that highway."

"What if we can't?" She clicks on a reading light. "We should be getting close." She stares at the map.

"Tell me about yesterday," the marshal says, "you got on that train—where y'all start out?"

"Albuquerque."

"You got on the train with Marshal Corrigan, just you and him?"

She nods.

"When?"

"Midday."

The marshal thinks about it. "That's twelve, thirteen hours back. What time you think the train hit that car in Fisherville?"

"Around five," she says. "Five-thirty."

Whicher peers out into the night, the wipers on the Toyota freezing up—starting to smear. He turns up the heat, dials air onto the windshield. "You get a look at the license plate on this? It's from Chicago."

She reaches up, switches off the reading light.

"That's a thousand miles from here—seventeen hours, straight. They knew," he says. "Ahead of time, they knew. How'd they know to come out all the way from Chicago?"

She doesn't answer.

"Nobody on the WITSEC program ever got killed," the marshal says. "So long as they did what they were told."

He feels her eyes on the side of his face.

She says; "Don't let me be the first."

The gradient is changing, Whicher feels it, feels the pickup cresting a long slope.

Stretched out above the plains land is a smear of light—a broken band maybe half a mile ahead. "That's highway."

Lights are moving, lights just visible through the snow-filled air.

"Chicago's north and east—I say head west, head the opposite way."

Lauren eyes the dash, face lit up in the glow of the dials.

The marshal eases back on the gas, wary of the deep-looking white mounds at the sides of the road. "I was a scout," he says, "in the army. Used to breaking a trail."

She sits back, turns to stare out of the window.

"Lauren—that's not your real name, is it?"

He glances at her.

"Lauren is. They told me to keep that part, I'd be less likely to mess up."

"Tell me about Marshal Corrigan?"

She stiffens. "I didn't know him…"

"You had any other close protection, anybody else know who you were?"

She shakes her head.

"So far as you know, there's nobody else?"

"There has to be somebody."

"Why you say that?"

"If somebody came to try to kill me."

No cars, he can't see cars. The highway is close now, just a hundred yards—but something is blocking the way—a white bank lit up in the pickup beams.

"What the hell is that?"

Whicher gets off the gas, the Toyota slows.

A dirty bank of snow is piled at the end of the road, across the intersection—where the highway crews have passed with their plows.

The marshal drives on toward it—the bank is big, the plow trucks must've passed and re-passed, each time adding to its size. Pin pricks of light show above it; the sides of a moving freight truck.

He drives to the end of the road, lets the pickup slow to a stop.

He shuts off the motor, grabs Lauren's case. "Come on, get out."

Pushing open the driver's door, he steps out, leans into the wind.

He starts toward the piled-up bank, the snow already over his boots.

Glancing back, he sees Lauren out of the pickup, now.

At the foot of the mound he starts to climb—up six-feet of ice and snow.

Sinking to his knees, he throws the suitcase forward, scrambling, pushing with his hands, his elbows, the cold intense.

At the top he can see the highway stretched out—white-over. Cars are moving in the distance, a rig and trailer approaching.

He tosses Lauren's case down the bank. Pulls at the zipper on the plaid coat.

With freezing fingers, he eases out his badge-holder, the Marshals Star on the front.

Staring at the oncoming rig, he scrabbles down to the roadway. He steps out into tire tracks on the hard packed snow.

"*What the hell are you doing?*" Lauren calls out.

Headlights are in his eyes, the rig lets out an air-horn blast.

He holds out the badge, locks his legs.

The truck lights dive, spray bursts from the sides of the wheels.

The rig slows as the marshal steps back.

The driver's door opens.

A head appears. "*Are you crazy?*" the driver shouts. "*You son of a bitch…*"

"*Peace officer*," Whicher calls out.

"You step in front of my truck—a night like this?"

"United States Marshal. Requesting you assist."

⋏

Belaski sees the freight truck pull out.

He clambers up the bank, sees two big letters on the back of the trailer—an *H* and a *T*.

Nothing is on the highway where the truck was, no reason for it to stop—they'd flagged it down.

Memorizing the letters, he jumps back down to Jimmy's Toyota on the snow-bound road.

AN AMERICAN BULLET

Shaking from cold, he eyes the silvered chains on the law enforcement Ford.

Despite the shot-out passenger window and the holes in the rear-hatch, he gets back in.

He shifts to low, raises the revs. They couldn't get Jimmy's pickup over the bank—they'd ditched it, they didn't have chains.

Steering the Ford into the mound of white, he feels the steel-links on the tires start to cut and grip.

All-wheel-drive; he can clear the bank.

He can clear it.

He can make it.

He can catch them.

Chapter 13

High up in the cab of the Freightliner, the driver leans forward at the wheel. He's bearded, skinny, wearing a woolen Broncos hat.

"Where you headed?" Whicher says.

"Pueblo."

"How far is that?"

"Twenty. Twenty-five." He pushes at the sleeve of his sweater. "God knows if the truck can make it. I been stopped in Lamar, again in Swink."

"How is it further east?"

"The same. Like this."

The marshal looks at him.

"You can barely see a hundred yards. I come out of Dodge City this afternoon, from Kansas. It's been bad all the way—snow and broken down vehicles. Only gettin' worse."

Lauren sits silent between the two men, arms folded.

The driver jabs a thumb over his shoulder at the sleeper cab. "If it gets too bad, I guess I can bunk down."

The wipers beat back and forth on the windshield.

"Get us to Pueblo," Whicher says, "we'll get out."

♏

Belaski checks his driver mirror—a single set of lights behind him, nothing else out on the road.

Wind is streaming through the broken window, the muscles of his body starting to seize.

He eyes the freight truck in the distance, he can tail it, catch it. To stop it on the highway, to stop it and then to get to her— there'll be the escort to get past, the driver of the truck.

He lets his speed drop, listens for anything on the police-band radio—still nothing, no report of anything wrong.

The Ford is shot up, if he pulls alongside the rig, they'll recognize it.

The freight truck starts to pull away, he lets it disappear in the dark and snow.

Belaski eyes the transceiver on the dash-hook, reaches for it—pulls hard, ripping it from its moorings.

Switching on the red and blue flashers, he steers out into the middle of the twin-lanes, lets his speed fall away.

He checks—sees the vehicle behind start to slow.

Belaski rolls the Ford to a stop.

He puts the suppressed SIG in the pocket of his parka. Watches for the car to come to a halt.

Pulling the keys from the ignition, he steps out, walks fast to the stationary vehicle—an old Chrysler sedan.

Inside, the driver's a young guy in a hooded sweat. Nobody with him.

"What's going on?" the kid calls through the window.

Belaski draws the gun from his pocket. He points it at the young man's face.

The kid's eyes go wide.

"Get out of the car." Belaski steps to the driver's door.

The young man folds forward, stumbles out.

Belaski gets in, points the gun at the kid's midriff. But doesn't fire. Robbing, not killing—two separate wires in his mind; different lines.

The kid's jacket is on the passenger seat, his cell on a dash-mount.

Belaski tosses the jacket out onto the road. Puts the car into drive.

⁂

Three o'clock in the morning, downtown Pueblo is deserted. Ice at the banks of the Arkansas River, snow blowing thick in the air.

Ahead, along the sidewalk, a motel building is lit up. Whicher eyes the cars and trucks outside in the lot.

Beside him, Lauren buries her face in her upturned collar.

The marshal takes a hand from his pocket, points along the sidewalk at the motel lobby.

"Anywhere," she says, "just get us out of this wind."

Whicher scans a side-street, thick with snow, blurred halos at the street lamps.

Lauren slows her step. "Why do you keep on looking?"

He clamps his hat down on his head. "Army habit."

"You think somebody will be out there?"

Two hours, now.

Millersburg, two hours back.

The woods, the cabin.

Thirty long miles behind.

⁂

Parked at the curbside in the stolen Chrysler sedan, Belaski watches a city police car make its way along the street.

The Chrysler's covered in salt and snow—only its headlights showing—no way to see the make or model, no way for the cop see the plate.

Parts of the city are blacked out, the power down—law enforcement would be busy with a hundred things.

The patrol car reaches an intersection—makes a turn, continues on its way.

Belaski studies the building fifty yards off. A motel. One entrance. An eight-feet high wall in back.

They'd walked.

The two of them, after the truck set them down.

Half a mile into central downtown, they'd found a motel, they'd gone into reception. Five minutes later, a clerk opened them up a room. They'd gone in. They hadn't come back out.

Wind nudges at the car, rocking it. Belaski huddles in the cold.

They'd feel safe, now. Finally. They hadn't seen him. All he needed was to pick his moment.

He stares down at the SIG on the passenger seat, thinks

of putting the can-like suppressor to Jimmy Scardino's head.

Jimmy was dying, shot up, he was only going to slow it all down.

But still.

The son of a made man.

Belaski's stock would be in free-fall, everything he'd worked for, year on year.

How to justify, how to explain?

Deep shit.

Deep, deep shit.

He thinks of the big bastard coming out of the cabin.

Your life is mine now, Belaski breathes in the silent car.

The terms of the deal on Lauren DeLuca were irreversible—killing the man who shot Jimmy Scardino would be personal accounting.

He checks his watch, checks the cell phone in the well above the shifter—it's showing full.

Three o'clock in the morning in Colorado, four o'clock in Chicago.

He can't call him, can't call Coletti.

Cold rage roils in the pit of his belly, he clamps his mouth tight.

If he can get it done, only if he can get it all done, he tells himself.

He pushes back in the driver's seat.

Only then.

Chapter 14

Mounds of white bury the cars parked in the motel lot—through a gap in the drape at the window, Whicher studies a weak sun, hanging low.

From the bathroom, he hears the sound of running water. He rubs the stiffness from his shoulder, thinks of scant sleep in a motel chair, Lauren resting fitful on the bed.

He checks his watch. Seven thirty.

The sky is dense, gray—snow tumbling, spinning through the air.

He lets the drape fall, thinks of Guillory—only Guillory had known they were in the hunting cabin.

He pushes down the thought, crosses to the nightstand, lifts the phone from the cradle.

He listens to the sound of the shower starting up. Keys a number, hears it ring.

Lauren is moving around inside the bathroom.

The tone of the call changes—re-routing. It picks up.

A man's voice comes on the line; "McBride."

"Sir, this is Whicher. I need to talk with you."

The inspector clears his throat.

"I'm on a fixed line."

"Alright," McBride says. "But don't talk, just listen…"

The marshal catches the note in the senior man's voice.

"Sheriff Dubois called last night, from Fisherville," McBride says. "She had her people search the woods around the train collision site, had them search with dogs. They found Marshal Corrigan."

Whicher swallows, feels a dryness in his mouth.

"He'd been shot in the back of the head. Close range. The sheriff said he'd been dragged into the woods, they couldn't see much blood."

The marshal turns to face the door, sits heavy at the edge of the bed.

"It's snowing so damn hard, they can't exactly tell—they think he was shot someplace, dragged in after. Without the dogs, the sheriff said they never would have found him. I called the number you gave me last night," McBride says. "I spoke with an Officer Guillory—he said you weren't there…"

Whicher eyes the Glock laying flat beside the phone. "Sir…"

"I asked him to get word to you—Guillory's now missing. He's missing but they found his vehicle, shot up. With blood in the cab."

McBride exhales long into the phone.

Whicher hears guests moving around in the motel, dull noise, the sound of muffled voices. From the bathroom, water drums in the shower.

"Somebody attacked us last night," he says. "They were using Guillory's unit…"

"I don't want to know where you are," McBride says. "Guillory's vehicle was abandoned on a highway—some kid reported getting stopped, he thought it was a cop. The guy made him get out, he took his car."

"Did you talk to him? This kid give a description?"

"Reporting officer was from another county," McBride says. "He went off duty, they can't raise him, everything's messed up on account of the storm."

The sound from the bathroom changes, no water running in the drain.

"I don't know how somebody could've shown up last night," McBride says. "I don't know how that could've happened. Sheriff Dubois says she's sending the canine team…"

Whicher keeps his voice low. "Do I come in?"

"The trial starts in two days, weather's predicted to remain severe. Flights are canceled, travel by road's all to hell. I don't know where y'all are at, I don't know how you're going to get to Illinois."

The water starts up again, Whicher hears movement, the shower in full flow.

"Anytime you get near anybody," McBride says, "it seems like they find out. I don't want you coming in, I don't want her around people."

Whicher glances about the room. "I could get her to a US Marshals office?"

"We knew she was a risk," McBride says. "When they sent her down from Chicago, they called her the-dead-woman-walking."

The marshal stands, picks the Glock off the nightstand.

"Listen," McBride says. "You got two days, I don't know how you're going to get anywhere, we can't even get you on a flight. If you can't move, if you can't do it, y'all find the biggest police station or USMS office you can. Better yet, FBI."

Whicher stares at his reflection in the motel mirror. Fits the semi-automatic in the holster at his belt.

ᛎ

An hour later, the diner on West Third is warm, lit up bright—half-full with working men in coats and boots.

Whicher eases in to the red leatherette of a booth where he can see the door.

Lauren slips in along the opposite side of the table.

The glass front of the diner is fogged, shapes moving beyond it, out in the street.

Whicher studies on the menu card.

A waitress approaches. She fills two china mugs with hot coffee.

The marshal takes off his hat, sets it onto the seat beside him. Orders huevos a la Mexicana, with corn tortillas.

"Ma'am?" the waitress says.

"Just the cinnamon pancakes."

"Get something more," Whicher says.

Lauren looks across at him.

The waitress taps her notepad. "If you want, I can get you the same?"

Lauren shrugs.

"We'll take the pancakes too," Whicher says.

The waitress writes up the order.

Lauren sips her coffee.

"We need to eat," Whicher says. "I don't know when we will again." He watches her eyes roam the faces of customers in the diner. Nobody close enough to overhear.

"McBride called."

Her eyes come back on his.

Whicher lifts the chipped white mug, blows steam from it. "Guillory's gone. He's missing." He puts a hand to the window, wipes it down, checks along the sidewalk.

It's empty—a city bus rolling along at the end of the street.

"We keep going," he says.

Lauren lets out a breath.

"Law says I have to get you to the court."

"That's all I am?"

He cuts a look at her.

"An asset?" she says. "For the court."

The waitress brings their order to the table—she sets down the plates of beans and corn tortillas and spiced eggs.

"Gracias, señora." The marshal dips his head.

"De nada." The waitress smiles, she tucks her hair behind her ear.

Lauren picks up a warmed tortilla, breaking off a small piece.

The waitress heads back toward the counter.

Whicher forks up a mix of eggs and chili and pinto beans.

"I have a brother," Lauren says. "Anthony. He's sixteen."

The marshal lets his eyes rest on hers a moment.

"Both my parents are dead. He's all I have. I guess I'm all he has, too, for what it's worth."

He takes another forkful of food. "Go on," he says.

"Mom died when Anthony was only two. My dad was a heavy drinker, he died in a car wreck, ten years back. I've taken care of Anthony since he was six years old. I'm thirty-five. I've never been married. No kids. I'm a former accountant," she lowers her voice, "for the Coletti family…"

"For the mob…"

"For businesses owned and controlled by them. In Chicago."

He nods. "Right."

"You," she says, a note in her voice.

Whicher looks at her.

"I want to know about you."

"Ma'am? I'm not on trial."

She angles her head.

He puts down the fork. Sits back a fraction in the seat.

She stares at him.

"I'm thirty-eight," he says. "I grew up in the panhandle, Briscoe County, Texas." He shrugs. "You won't have heard of it, Quitaque."

"Married?"

"Nope."

"Brothers, sisters?"

He shakes his head. "I joined the army out of high school, ROTC. Graduated in eighty-six." He shifts his gaze to the window. "I served with Third Armored Cavalry. Led the battalion scout platoon. Toured overseas, the Gulf War of ninety-one. Joined the Marshals Service a year later."

"WITSEC?"

"No ma'am. I'm a criminal investigator."

She watches him, her face entirely still.

"I was close to Fisherville when your train got hit," he says. "Driving back from Florence SuperMax. I have the clearance, the security clearance." His eyes meet hers. "You again."

She draws a long breath. Lifts the mug of coffee, takes a sip. "I studied for a bachelor degree while my dad was still alive. Accounting. Somebody needed to take care of the family. I got a job at a decent firm. Or so I thought."

The waitress returns to the table.

She sets down two plates of cinnamon pancakes and brown butter.

"Can I get you some more coffee?"

"Thank you," Whicher says. "We're good."

Lauren pushes eggs into a fold of corn tortilla. "I worked hard, harder than anybody else, got noticed. Moved up. I kept on going…" Her voice trails off.

"What happened to Anthony?"

Her face changes. "My brother is off-limits."

"He's under protection?"

She shakes her head. "Nobody can know about him."

Chapter 15

Glimpses of I-25 show from the taxi—scant vehicles moving among the orange traffic drums.

The fall of snow is constant as the taxi works its way into downtown, windows dark in the low-rise office units.

Sidewalks are deserted, storefronts unlit, doors closed on the shopping malls.

"Bus station's up on the right," the taxi driver says. "But I don't imagine you'll be going any place."

"I called ahead," Whicher says. "They got some lines still running."

The taxi driver shakes his head.

Lauren DeLuca sits rigid in the seat alongside Whicher.

Rental car offices are closed, nobody looking to lease out till the storm eases.

The cab pulls in at a curb piled with dirty snow.

The marshal pays the man, Lauren steps out.

She carries her case toward a glass-front bus station—foot long shards of ice hanging from the roof.

AN AMERICAN BULLET

⁂

Inside the Greyhound bus, the heat is cranked. At the back, looking out through misted windows, Whicher eyes the few cars and trucks on the interstate.

A radio plays snatches of news on the worst winter storm to hit the Mountain West in years.

Lauren sits by the window.

Eight other travelers are on the bus, none of them seated close.

"I don't know how you think this is going to work," Lauren says. "Look at it."

Traffic's slow moving on the single-wide lanes, road crews out in both directions.

"You cut a deal with a federal attorney, the Marshals Service expect me to get you where you need to go."

"You think it's that simple?"

"You made a deal. All I'm saying. A man died already. Just to get you this far."

Her eyes widen. "They found Corrigan?"

He looks at her. "They found him."

For a minute, neither one of them speaks.

Whicher listens to the whine of the drivetrain, the growl of the diesel engine—noise coming up from the road.

"No free rides," he says.

Heat steals into her eyes. "I never said there was."

The marshal look off down the length of the bus. Three hours to Denver—three hours ahead of them, at best.

He pushes back in the worn leather seat.

Beneath his suit jacket, he feels the Ruger in the shoulder-holster. "I told you I took a guy out to Florence ADX, yesterday morning? I was headed home, I took the call about your train."

"So you said."

"They picked him up with human remains in the trunk of his car. Burnt human remains. Cutter Maitland. An enforcer for the Chicago mob."

She stares out of the window of the bus.

"He made a deal with the feds to plea-down," Whicher says. "Agreed to testify for the government. But then he skipped out. They picked him up again in Dallas. He'll spend the rest of his life in the highest security prison in the country."

She shakes her head.

"He reckoned me and him were no different…"

"I'll honor the terms of my deal."

"All the way up from Texas," Whicher says, "the son-of-a-bitch told me we were just working different sides. Him for the mob. Me, an enforcer for the law."

She looks at him. "And did it bother you?"

"It don't bother me none. I guess. So long as too many folk don't get confused."

She folds her arms on her chest. "You see everything in black and white?" She leans a fraction to look at him. "Don't you ever get confused?"

"Maybe."

She leaves her eyes on his. "Are you confused now?"

A beat passes.

Another.

"How long," he says, "did you work for them?"

"Twelve years."

"All that time keeping books for the mob?"

"That's not the way it started," she says. "I was naive."

"Y'all were busted?"

"Three of us, from my office."

"Anybody else cut a deal?"

She shakes her head. "FBI have been investigating the Coletti family for years. They decided on a different approach; forensic accounting. They offered me immunity, a new identity, relocation out of state."

"In return for testimony to convict."

Lauren nods.

"What kind of level?"

"All the way up to the top."

Whicher gives out a low whistle.

She glances at him sideways. "It's really only blind luck? That I get you?"

"Deaf, dumb. Blind."

"At least I know," she says. "That I can trust you."

The bus rumbles forward, through the dull, gray of the morning.

The marshal lets his eyes blur on a line of orange traffic drums out of the window.

"And I'm truly sorry," she says.

Whicher looks at her—sees the water welled at the corner of her eye.

"Everybody says to keep your distance—I hardly even talked to Marshal Corrigan…" Her voice catches in her throat.

"Whatever testimony you have," he says, "I hope it's worth it."

"You mean, worth a man's life?"

⚜

Inside the grand hall of Union Station, Whicher sits on a tall-backed wooden bench.

The waiting room is run down, tan painted walls detailed brown.

The ticket office is closed, kiosks boarded up. He studies signs left over from the fifties; Pullman, Rock Island, Sante Fe.

Every major road east is blocked or severely disrupted. A thousand miles to Chicago, fifteen hours straight. The bench is hard, the grain of the wood worn smooth from long years of use. He stares at the high, arched windows, caked with snow.

At best, the roads will be a crawl—narrow corridors cleared with salt trucks and plows. Any breakdown, any wreck, they'd be trapped for hours.

All the airlines have pulled their schedules; flying conditions are way too bad.

The marshal watches the street door—opening every few minutes, people coming in, going out.

The Amtrak service is due in half an hour; the California Zephyr, still running, despite the snow. Nineteen hours. All the way to Chicago—the train running all night, all through the next day, arriving the middle of the afternoon. In time to make it to the court the following day.

The marshal takes in the folk in the waiting room, around twenty, all told. Mostly couples, older couples, not in any kind of rush. One group that might be college friends, three young women, two men.

A handful of single men are traveling, some with backpacks, two others dressed for business, no luggage. Nobody looks out of place.

Whicher shifts his weight on the seat. The only people out of place are Lauren and him—in ill-fitting coats that don't belong to them.

He tells himself they're just a man and a woman waiting on a train. A winter's night in Denver, tickets out of a machine, nobody knows who they are.

"You alright?" He looks at Lauren sitting beside him.

He feels a flicker of warmth in the smile she gives.

She holds his eye a moment. Puts her hand on top of his on the wooden bench.

⁂

Standing by the ticket machine, Jerzy Belaski allows himself a single glance straight at her. He turns away, stifling a yawn.

Only ever a matter of time, he tells himself.

Following the Greyhound bus had been child's play.

The drop-off in Denver was outside the rail station. They'd gone inside. They hadn't come back out.

He'd ditched the stolen Chrysler, found a side entrance, checked with a rail employee—the only service coming through was headed east—bound for Chicago.

A block out from the station, he found an outdoor store,

bought a backpack, bought another winter coat, nondescript, fawn.

In a service-alley, he transferred the gun and the parka into the backpack, slipping on the new-bought coat.

Lauren DeLuca had never seen him before.

The guy in the hat wouldn't recognize him; on the train he hadn't seen his face.

He takes the ticket from the machine, crosses the terrazzo floor.

At a wooden bench on the side, he settles. He takes out his cell phone, opens it.

Two missed calls.

Coletti.

Two messages.

He reads the first—*I'm sending people. Where are you?*

The next; *Why didn't Jimmy call? Call me NOW.*

He stares at the waiting room floor, thinking.

Some disturbance registers in his senses. As if eyes are turned upon him.

Somebody looking at him.

Had the guy in the hat started to look?

⼈

A cluster of lights move beneath a road bridge—flashing, wide-set, pulsing left to right.

Lauren DeLuca shelters beneath the roof that spans the platform.

Whicher listens to the sound of clacking rails above the muffled noise of the city.

A train horn splits the night air.

The locomotive approaches along the base of a high-rise office building—plow blade mounted to its front—the blue and silver paintwork of the cars just visible.

Pieces of packed snow fall silent from the wheels to the ground.

The train slows, the sound of the engine shakes the air. The California Zephyr pulls in to Union Station, brakes squealing.

Doors on the lower floors of the cars open. Attendants step out, holding their jackets in the bitter wind.

A handful of passengers step down from three of the cars.

The Denver travelers move toward the train, the marshal picks up Lauren's case.

They walk fast to the nearest open doorway.

A carriage attendant holds out his hand.

Whicher pulls two tickets from his pocket.

The attendant checks, waves them onboard.

Looking up and down the platform, the marshal nods.

Nobody following behind.

Chapter 16

The coach car seat is pushed as far back as Whicher can get it. All the carriage lights are dimmed, people trying to sleep as best they can.

The sound catches his attention first, high pitched. Metal on metal.

He pushes himself upright. Feels the train start to slow.

Lauren's asleep in the seat beside him. Beyond the window, outside in the black, snow still falls.

He checks his watch—just before midnight.

Five hours out of Denver.

The marshal raises his seat to the upright position, feels the retardation of the train.

A voice comes on the Tannoy; "*McCook...*"

Lauren stirs, her face registering the sound.

Whicher stares out of the window, at lights now showing, track-side lights, buildings looming from the dark.

"*Next station is McCook, Nebraska.*"

Lauren keeps her eyes closed.

Whicher thinks of getting up, of going forward—to the

head of the car, to where there's hot coffee.

He checks around him, nobody's stirring. He's awake, now—he needs to stay awake.

The lights beyond the window slow. He looks at Lauren, sleeping, mouth part open, blond hair in disarray. He lets his gaze rest a moment on her face, feels the stir in his pulse.

Reaching for his hat, he stands. He starts along the central aisle-way, among the dozing passengers.

At the connecting corridor he finds the table set with flasks of coffee.

He takes a cup, pours himself a measure, adds cream.

The train slows to a complete stop.

Whicher takes his cup to the window, looks out at a station building—lit up. It's twenties-era, in dark brown brick. Behind it, a street runs parallel.

Store fronts crowd an intersection—grain elevators line the track to the east, picked out in the train yard lights.

No passengers are waiting to board.

He can't see anybody getting off.

A connecting door opens—an attendant enters the corridor.

Whicher nods.

"Problem up the line," the attendant says. "Conductor's saying twenty minutes. They've got a frozen switch up ahead."

Whicher takes a sip of coffee. "We're waiting here?"

"A storm like this, it can take a while."

"What is it, ice?"

"Could be packed snow," the man says. "It'll stop the rail from moving if it's deep."

Whicher looks out of the window.

"They get a crew out with a bunch of blow torches, they'll free it," the attendant says. "It can take time, if it's the middle of nowhere. If you want to get off, it's okay. If you want a smoke. Or you want to get some air. We're not going to be moving."

Whicher fits a plastic lid to the coffee cup. He steps through the connecting door, heads back into the coach car.

At the end of the aisle he can see both seats are empty, his coat spread out where she was sitting.

He moves down the car, looks around, he can't see her. At the end, he passes through the next connecting door.

She's nowhere in sight.

Cold air is streaming in, the train door is open—a group of college-age kids standing on the white covered platform.

He stares out of the train, alarm rising.

"What are you doing?"

A female voice.

He spins around.

She's coming out of the next coach car.

"I had to use the bathroom." She studies him a moment. "I woke up, the train had stopped."

"I went to get coffee," he says. "There's a problem up ahead on the line."

Lauren stares out of the door at passengers starting to walk around on the platform, pulling on coats. "Is it okay to get off?"

He doesn't reply.

"Do you think they have a phone in there," she says, "a call box?"

The marshal shrugs.

She gazes into the night air, at the falling snow. Lowers her voice. "Look, I'm not allowed to see people. But I can speak with them. I promised to try to call somebody."

"It's late."

"It won't matter." She rests her eye on his.

"Who?"

"I'm not supposed to discuss that," Lauren says. "Not even with people like you."

Whicher breaks off looking at her, to stare out into the frozen Nebraska landscape.

"If I called from here…" Lauren says. She makes a gesture at the empty country stretching off into the black.

Twenty-four hours, Whicher tells himself. Twenty-four hours since they broke the trail.

"Nobody's going to know," she says. "We're in the middle of nowhere."

The marshal steps into the open doorway of the car. "Five minutes," he says. He climbs down from the train.

⚘

The station waiting room is four glazed-brick walls, scuffed seats, no staff, no ticketing. The windows are track-side, looking out onto the line.

In a wall-recess at one corner is a payphone. Whicher checks there's only one way in and out.

The place is empty, just the two of them inside.

Lauren crosses the room, her footsteps echo from the vaulted ceiling.

"Do you think…" She inclines her head at the phone. "Do you think you could give me a moment?"

"I'll be right outside."

He steps out, stands in the lee of the station wall, out of the wind. Scans the intersection that forms a 'T' with the main street north, away from the track.

A stop light hangs from an overhead cable. But nothing's moving on the road.

On the white-over platform, groups are standing around, smoking, walking up and down.

The marshal watches snow swirling in the train yard lights. A parked freight load stretches to the distance, beyond the grain elevators, into the dark.

He squares his hat, steps around to where he can see through the window into the waiting room—Lauren's inside, speaking into the phone.

He moves away from the building, feels the wind against his exposed skin.

Glancing over his shoulder, he sees her putting down the phone.

She's not making a second call.

She crosses the room, steps outside, looks around, sees him. Pointing a finger at the train, she starts to walk back across the platform.

By the side of a coach car, Whicher sees an attendant, cigarette trailing from his hand.

Lauren reaches the open door of the train, she climbs on.

Whicher motions to the crew man. "Any word on that hold up?"

The man peers at him. "We should be moving shortly, sir. Conductor says there's another train ahead on the line."

"Another train?"

"Freight load," the man says. "They need to get the switch working, get the other train through before we head on up."

The marshal nods. "Guess I'll take a walk," he says. "Then turn in."

He moves along the length of the train all the way to the back.

At the end, he stops. Takes off the Resistol, shakes snow from it. Sucks down the cold air.

A truck is out on the street, it slows at the intersection. The marshal watches it a moment, turns around, heads back.

At the door to their car, he knocks his boots against each other, climbs on.

He enters the carriage.

The lights are dim.

Their seats are empty.

⁂

"Mister Houghton? Sir, this is Gail. I have a marshal here, that needs to speak with you." The female attendant listens on a carriage intercom phone. She studies Whicher's badge, a frown across her brow. "Yes, sir. A marshal."

Ten minutes.

For ten minutes he's been up and down the train.

Lauren's case is stowed exactly where it was in the baggage rack. There's no sign of her anyplace, he's checked the bathrooms, been in every car.

She's nowhere on the platform, not in the station.

The attendant nods, puts down the receiver. "Sir, you can go forward, the conductor's up with the engineer…"

Whicher hustles along the car, snatches open the door to the next carriage. He strides on toward the head-end of the train.

A suited man in an Amtrak cap steps into the far end of the corridor.

"Are you the conductor?"

"I'm about to give the word to pull out of here," the man says. "Dispatch at Commerce City want us moving east—we need to get up the line, we need to leave…"

Chapter 17

Two blocks up into town on Main Street, Whicher surveys the few stores fronting onto the road. Beyond the stone columns of a bank are businesses, an old movie theater, a Masonic lodge, a bar still open. He eyes the cars and trucks angled in at the curb.

At the train track, flashing lights from a police cruiser streak blue across the snow in the yard.

Forty-five minutes.

Forty-five minutes she's been gone.

She's not on the train, he's searched every space, every crew room, every sleeper car and roomette—McCook police and the train staff in tow.

Lauren's nowhere.

The image of her is in his mind—finishing up her call, stepping out of the waiting room, crossing the platform, climbing onboard.

He saw her get on.

He runs down the sloping street, hands burning from the cold.

Five minutes and the train is leaving.

He reaches the intersection with the track-side road. Enters the station waiting room, checks it's empty. Shuts the door.

Unzipping his coat, he fishes out a number from his jacket. He crosses to the payphone.

He keys the number, lets it ring, over and over.

The call picks up.

"This is Whicher."

The marshal listens to his own voice echo back off the bare walls.

The clock above the door in the waiting room shows one o'clock in the morning.

"McBride."

"She's gone," Whicher says. "About an hour ago. She disappeared. I think she's walked."

"Where are you?"

"Nebraska."

"Did anybody—intervene?"

"I don't know. I don't think."

"Is there a chance you could find her?"

Whicher stares through the window at the train in the falling snow. "Maybe. Law enforcement are here…"

"What've you told them?"

"Not much."

"Don't tell them who she is," McBride says.

"Can we arrest her?"

"You can arrest her—she's giving immunized testimony, she can't up and walk."

"We're in the middle of nowhere in a full-out storm. She has to be someplace inside. Some hotel, motel, she can't be out-of-doors. Local cops are going to know about whatever places there are."

"You think she's run, you think she's run out? You think somebody could have gotten to her?"

Whicher pushes back the Resistol.

"Jesus Christ," McBride says.

⚔

One hotel worth the name.

Three motels, a couple of bars, according to the chief of the watch, a police sergeant, name of Tierney.

The rail yard is empty, the Amtrak train gone—only the police vehicles remain; a cruiser plus an all-wheel-drive Tahoe.

Whicher stands with Lauren's case at his feet.

He stares at the snow, still falling, drifting.

Sergeant Tierney jogs across from the cruiser. "We got about a dozen streets classified priority," he says, "inside McCook city-limits."

The marshal looks at him.

"Emergency routes to keep clear," the sergeant says. "Along with two highways. The road crews have done what they can, but getting around's not going to be easy."

Whicher indicates the sergeant's Tahoe; "We get in?"

Tierney nods, climbs in behind the wheel.

Whicher sets Lauren's case in the back seat, eases into the passenger side.

The officer at the cruiser gets into his vehicle, reaches for his radio.

"I have two patrol officers on watch," the sergeant says. "They'll head in separate directions—one out onto the highway, past the airport, to check on a motel bar and grill. The other's going to head west, to a motor court. It's by a trailer park. There's a golf and country club hotel, also—but it's pretty damn unlikely…" Tierney moves the shifter into drive, pulls out from the yard. "We could use some photo ID."

"No can do."

"Good lookin' blonde," the sergeant says. "Fits a lot of description, depending on how drunk you are. A name could help."

"She won't be using her real name."

"You want to let us have it anyway?"

Whicher gazes out along the bleak street. "Orders," the marshal says. "Can't do it."

The sergeant nods. "I got a twelve-hour shift, I may as well spend it looking for a mystery woman as any other way." He drives a couple of blocks past the grain elevators, hits the blinker, steers the Tahoe up a ramp onto a bridge.

Whicher takes in the sign on an overhead panel—Blue Star Highway.

The bridge crosses the rail line. Snow is newly-plowed, piled high at the sides of the road. "What's down here?"

"Economy motel," Tierney answers. "I already called, checked with 'em. They say no lone females, they don't think they have any young blonde women checked in. We can find out anyway."

Satellite business parks sit to either side of the highway.

Gas stations, mall developments. Warehousing, building supply.

Whicher stares at the leafless trees around the street lamps, snow clinging to their frozen branches. He thinks again of the phone call Lauren made; no way she could've known the train would stop in McCook for longer than listed on the schedule—even if she called someone, who could've gotten out?

He turns to Tierney. "Are any of the highways drivable—out of here?"

"Red Willow, I reckon only the main routes," the sergeant says. "West, over in Furnas, it's probably worse. The weather reports are saying the storm's moving east, I guess we'd have to call the state troopers."

"Don't call them yet."

"A night like this, I don't see where a person could be."

Whicher nods.

"It's like a needle in a haystack," the sergeant says. "Inside of a goddamn snow globe."

Two hours.

Two hours she's been gone.

⚰

Jerzy Belaski sees the headlights approach from the highway—a single set of headlights turning in.

The room lights in the motel are switched out.

Gun in hand, he watches through the window, through a gap in the drape.

The car is a black and white Chevy Impala. Light-bar across its roof, the words *Police Department* detailed on the door.

It pulls in to the motel lot, parks in front of the check-in office.

Belaski stands, edging up against the cold glass.

The stolen Ford Taurus is parked around in back—out of sight from the road.

The door of the patrol car opens. A driver steps out.

He's dressed in uniform, all black. He puts on a cap, starts over toward the lit office.

Before he can reach it, the check-in clerk appears, silhouetted at the office door.

The clerk calls out something to the cop—he steps from under a porch roof, out into the snow.

The two men exchange a word together, then fall in step.

Side by side they start to walk toward the room.

Belaski half-turns. "Get in the bathroom," he says, over his shoulder. "Someone's coming."

He pulls the gap in the drapes closed, moves to the bed, rips back the cover and the sheets. Kicking off his shoes, he throws his coat on a chair.

A knock sounds at the door.

He puts the suppressed SIG in the small of his back, in the waistband of his pants. Pulls his shirt and sweater loose, covering it.

"Sir." Another knock. "Sir, this is the night clerk. I'm sorry for the disturbance—I have a police officer here, he needs to ask a couple questions."

Belaski roughs up his hair, stares through the dark at the door.

Another knock, louder.

They'll have a key, they'll come in anyhow.

"Who is it?" he calls back.

"Police. Sir, you need to open up in there. This won't take a minute."

Belaski pulls the bed cover half-off. "Wait. Wait, hold on…"

He positions himself by the door.

"Alright," he calls. "I'm opening up."

He unfastens the lock with his left hand—right hand at his hip, close to the gun.

He looks out. "What's going on?"

The cop steps forward. "Sorry for the disturbance, sir. You checked in here an hour or so ago? That right?"

"Yeah. I guess."

"This is the only room," the clerk says. "The only one we've let tonight."

"Are you alone?" the cop says.

"Yeah."

"You're traveling through?"

"Headed for Denver," Belaski says. "The weather got so bad, I had to just quit."

"You mind opening the door?"

"I got nothing with me," Belaski looks down at himself. "I had to sleep in my clothes." He steps away from the door, opening it wider.

The cop turns on the light. "You checked in on your own?"

"I told you," the clerk says.

The cop steps in, sweeps an eye over the room.

Belaski feels the SIG against the muscles at the base of his spine.

"Alright, well," the cop says. "I'm sorry we had to bother you tonight, sir. We got a situation is all. But I want to thank you for your cooperation."

Belaski nods.

The cop glances across at the bed, turns, starts to walk away.

The clerk spreads his hands. "Police department called," he says. "They said they wanted to know any late arrival."

Belaski shrugs, steps forward, closes the door.

He waits, listening. Turns off the light.

Thirty seconds pass, a minute. He puts a finger to the drape, eases a gap.

The cop is back behind the wheel of the Impala. The clerk returning to the office.

The Impala backs around, drives off the lot, out onto the highway.

Belaski glances over his shoulder. "Alright," he says. "You can come out now. They're gone."

Chapter 18

A crimson disc of sun creeps over woods to the east of the city. It's coming on eight in the morning, daybreak, the depths of winter on the plains. Outlying Nebraska lies buried beneath feet of driven snow. From the second-story window of the law enforcement building, Whicher sees both highways out of town.

A couple of hours sleep he's managed—restless on a police department couch. Lauren DeLuca has simply vanished into thin air. No sign of violence, nothing out of place. No blonde seen running in the snow. No blood on any tracks.

The marshal stares out at the highway east, vehicles moving on it, now—lights trailing into the distance.

Down at street-level, a car catches his eye, a police vehicle turning in from the strip.

He takes his hat from a desktop, puts it on. Buttons the white shirt at his throat, fixes his necktie in place.

Everything they could have done, they've done—short of putting out a stop order, making it public. They've searched in every locale known to city police. His gaze shifts to the window, to the fire-like sky. Sun rising indifferent across the fields, above the winter sticks of wood.

A muffled voice sounds from somewhere in the building.

"Marshal?"

Whicher steps out into a hallway.

"Marshal are you up there?"

He hears a sound from the stairs.

Sergeant Tierney is half-way up, hand wrapped around the metal banister. "Somebody had their car stolen last night—they just reported it. Taken from a house on East 5th."

"Where the hell's that?"

"Right over from the train station," the sergeant says.

The marshal runs a hand over stubble at his jaw. "The station?"

Tierney nods. "Real close. Like a few hundred yards…"

"We get over there?"

The sergeant taps his pants pocket. "I already got my keys."

⚔

A brick road is just visible beneath the scrape of ice and snow and dissolving salt. Sergeant Tierney steers the police Chevy past a white-over truck lot.

Whicher eyes the motionless hulks, standing frozen.

Tierney swings the SUV into a tree-lined street.

Board-side houses line the road beyond a post and rail fence.

"This is East 5th?"

"This is it." The sergeant pulls over at a run-down house, the driveway empty.

He shuts off the motor. The two men step out.

The front door of a screened-gallery opens.

A woman appears, wearing jeans, a sweater, a wool scarf.

Whicher steps onto the pristine snow in the driveway.

"Aileen Brennan?" Tierney says.

The woman folds her arms across her chest. "I already told the police department all the details."

"Yes, ma'am," the sergeant says. "The vehicle is a Ford Taurus?"

She nods. "A GL Sedan."

Tierney takes out his notebook. "White in color. Eight years old." He reads off a license plate number.

"They broke in the back door," the woman says. "They took the keys from the kitchen."

"You didn't hear it?"

"Not a thing."

Whicher looks at her. "It was parked here on the yard?"

"No."

"No?"

"My husband parked it at the curb," she points out into the street. "It's been leaking oil, messing up the driveway."

"How far away from the house?"

She indicates a spot thirty yards off.

"Is your husband here?" Sergeant Tierney says.

"He went to work. A neighbor had to give him a ride."

"Last night," Whicher says, "what time y'all turn in?"

"I don't know," she shrugs. "Ten, ten-thirty."

"The car was still here then?"

"Rod went to look out," she says, "my husband. He wanted to see what was going on with the storm. He came down this morning, there was glass on the kitchen floor, the door was unlocked. He couldn't find anything missing. Then he saw it," she says. "He saw the car was gone."

⁂

Steam rises from a cup of coffee on the plastic-topped desk in the police department. Whicher dials the Albuquerque number. He glances at the door to the office; it's shut.

The marshal checks his watch—Mountain Time in New Mexico, an hour behind Nebraska.

The call answers.

"McBride."

"Sir, it's Whicher…"

"I'm guessing you don't have good news?"

"We searched all night, we found nothing," the marshal says. "Till thirty minutes back. Somebody reported their vehicle stolen. Taken close to the rail yard, overnight."

"A car?"

"Police here say they don't get auto thefts—I want to put out a stop order."

"If somebody attacked her," McBride says, "why take a vehicle?"

The marshal puts a hand to the cup of coffee, turns it once. "I can't rightly say. But somebody broke in a house to get the keys to a car."

"What time was it taken?"

"Sometime between ten-thirty last night and seven this morning. It's a white Ford Taurus, eight years old, nondescript, not the kind of thing worth stealing."

McBride stays silent at the end of the line.

"It'll be covered in snow," Whicher says, "including the plates."

"You think there's any chance she could still be there?"

"We checked every place anybody could think of."

"If she's gone, you think there's any point in you staying? She may be dead already..."

The marshal leans forward, takes his weight on his elbows.

"Where are you now?" McBride says. "You might as well go ahead and tell me."

"Nebraska. A place called McCook."

"Give me the license plate of the car, I'll get the stop order put out."

Whicher stares at the desk.

"And I'll need your number there," McBride says. "I'll have to get back, I got to make some calls."

⊥

Out on the sidewalk, Whicher leans into an ice cold wind. In his pocket a pack of razors and a can of foam from a druggist on Main.

Beneath a hard blue sky, the store owners are out with shovels—clearing the wide, stone paving.

At a diner on the corner, the marshal orders breakfast—scrambled eggs and biscuits and country ham.

He sits a long time. Thinks of Lauren DeLuca. Thinks of a long night, mind turning, going over everything—the train stopping, people getting off and on. Lauren wanting to make a call.

Nobody had attacked her; nobody could've been there.

Not a single person knew they'd be on that train.

She must have walked.

He thinks of her in the Denver station before they set out; placing a hand on his—letting it linger.

Remembering the feeling. Was she just waiting, all along? Looking for a chance to come her way?

The stolen car didn't fit; Lauren DeLuca was white-collar, an accountant—would she know how to break into a house to find the keys?

Maybe she knew a lot of things.

He swirls coffee grounds at the bottom of his cup.

Calls the waitress for the check.

⦇⦈

Footsteps in the corridor pull him out of a half-sleep.

Whicher sits up.

Sergeant Tierney is at the door. "There's a call for you." He points at a phone on the desk in the corner. "You want to take it in here?"

The marshal stands, shakes himself awake.

Tierney squints, "Line three," he says. He turns on his heel.

Whicher pushes the door closed. The police department washroom had been cold to shave in, dozing in a back office better than no rest at all.

He picks up the phone.

"Is it snowing out there, marshal?"

Whicher looks out of the window.

"There's a ticket waiting for you at the airport," McBride says. "At McCook. They're flying today unless it comes in bad again."

"Flying?" Whicher says. "Flying where?"

"I'll get to that," the inspector says. "I just got done talking with Sheriff Dubois, back in Las Animas County. She sent the canine team up to Millersburg? This morning they found the body of Officer Kyle Guillory in the woods."

Whicher glances at the deer camp coat on the back of the chair. Guillory's coat.

"He was underneath a lot of snow," the inspector says. "Close to a hunting cabin, a family place. They searched the whole area, they found tire tracks up some side-road in the forest. There was a bunch of drag marks, they sent the dog team in, they found a second body."

The marshal takes a turn around the room, phone clamped against his neck.

"There was no ID on the second victim," McBride says. "They lifted fingerprints, they had FBI run them through IAFIS. Half an hour ago, they got a hit on a Jimmy Scardino."

"Y'all know who he is?"

"I don't. But FBI in Chicago know him—he's linked with organized crime."

Whicher waits for the inspector to go on.

"So there's more than one person involved here, somebody dragged this guy into the woods…"

"There's at least two," Whicher says.

"You know that?"

"They used Guillory's unit to come at us, at least two people were inside."

McBride grunts into the phone. "Colorado State Patrol found this guy Scardino's car about ten miles away—by the side of a highway, a Toyota pickup."

"That was us."

"Come again?"

"I found the pickup," Whicher says. "It was in the woods when they took off. We drove it to a highway, to get out, to get away from Millersburg."

"They're throwing everything at this," McBride says, "that's for damn sure. They've killed two peace officers—it looks like they got to your witness last night. But here's the next problem we have; she has a younger brother—also under protection. You need to head for the airport, right now. We need to move the brother. Today."

Chapter 19

Outside the one room terminal building at McCook municipal airport, a truck sprays de-icer on the wing of a twin-prop plane. The liquid flares, showering against a sun high in the sky. No cloud. No precipitation. Nothing forecast till late in the afternoon.

On the seat beside Whicher is Officer Kyle Guillory's winter coat, neatly folded.

Lauren DeLuca's been gone twelve hours.

The marshal stares into the glare of light from the white-covered ground beyond the window. Tries to bring to mind anything he knows about his destination—Rapid City, South Dakota.

⤞

Two hours later, FBI Agent Janice Rimes stands in arrivals at the regional airport in Rapid City. She looks up at him, five-three in a pair of Timberland boots.

"Do you want to get a drink?" She's swamped inside a mountain fleece jacket, black ringlet hair, an asymmetrical face. Her eyes are bright, tough. "I mean, you look like you could use one."

She grins at him, lop-sided.

The marshal eyes her from under the brim of his hat.

"I'm not saying you look like a lush. You look like you could maybe use a shot. Know what I mean?"

He doesn't answer.

"Where you from? You know, you have melting snow on that big hat?"

"Texas."

"You're going to freeze your longhorns off out here."

"I noticed that."

"So, no drink, no coffee. You all ready? You want to roll?"

"I look ready?"

She runs her eye fully up and down him. Twists her mouth. "Let's roll anyway."

⁂

Agent Janice Rimes steers the Chevy Cavalier down a loop road away from the city airport. "Your boss is coming up," she says, "to South Dakota."

Whicher glances at her.

"McBride," she says.

"You know when?"

"This evening. Flying in from New Mexico."

Whicher scans the snow laying either side of a plowed highway. The road skirts south of the city, retail parks and sub-divisions just visible beyond the frozen trees. "He's not my boss."

"Whatever," Rimes says.

"This here situation is a one-off."

"Well, he's flying in, I'm supposed to take you out, find the brother."

Beyond the roadway, the ground rises in long sparse grades—condominiums dotting the outlying hills.

"Tell me about him," Whicher says.

Rimes signals, moves lanes to pass a slowing logging truck shifting down for the drag.

"FBI offered protection back in Chicago," she says. "Under the victim support program. Marshals Service ran with it, Anthony being young it was a struggle to get him placed."

"Is he a witness," Whicher says, "as well as being related?"

"That, I don't know."

"You spend any time with the kid?"

"Almost never."

Whicher looks at her.

Rimes shrugs. "They told him where he could relocate—the places they could find for him. He picked this. Chicago FBI made contact with our field office. We're responsible for the western quarter of the state. We said okay."

The marshal lets his gaze run out to the Black Hills, thoughts forming, stringing themselves together; like a chain pulled from dark water.

⋏

Fifty miles west of the airport, a forest road runs through high woods—dense pine on the hillside throwing day-long shade.

Snow is in the road, a bank fallen from a cut through the rock. It's spread, piled thick, covering the asphalt for thirty yards.

Agent Rimes slows the car, moves the shifter down on the transmission.

"Think we could get through that?" Whicher says.

"There's no other way up."

The car hits the snow on the road. The wheels start to spin.

The grade is steep, the vehicle sinks, Rimes comes off the gas, bangs her hands against the wheel.

"Tell me you got a snow shovel?" Whicher says.

"In the trunk." She lets the car stop. Moves the shifter into park.

Whicher eases out from the passenger seat, steps around to the back of the car. Opening the trunk hatch, he sees the folded snow shovel, takes it out.

Rimes lights a cigarette, steps out to stand by the hood.

Whicher opens out the shovel, starts to clear snow from under a front tire. "How much further?"

"About another ten," she says.

"Ten more miles?"

"The county was looking to keep all the roads open…"

Whicher digs around the tire, body warming, sweat breaking at his brow. "How high are we?"

"I don't know. Six."

"What makes a kid from Chicago want to live out on a horse ranch in the Black Hills of Dakota?"

Rimes takes a draw on the cigarette. "How do I know?"

Whicher moves around to the other side of the car, the smell of smoke sharp against the dense sap in the air.

"Chicago are going nuts over this," Agent Rimes says. "The sister's considered a flight-risk."

Whicher drives the tip of the shovel hard against the road.

"FBI and the DA suspect her of concealing evidence. Plus possible concealment of assets."

"Assets?" Whicher says. "As in—money?"

Agent Rimes puts the cigarette to her mouth. "As in." She takes a pull.

Whicher pauses, looks up from the wheel. "The DA and the Chicago FBI thought she might try to run?"

Rimes stamps her feet up and down in the road.

The marshal scrapes the edge of the shovel against the tire.

"People I've talked to in Chicago think she could've stashed away enough to make a go of it," Rimes says.

"People?"

"Bureau people. If she has money, she could wind up anyplace."

Whicher lets the thought sit.

"She could make another life." Rimes grins. "Someplace warm."

The marshal stands, steps back from the hood. "You want to give it a try? Keep the revs low, inch out."

"Tex," she says. "I'm from South Dakota."

He tips back his hat.

"We know about snow. Driving in snow."

"Y'all know how to handle a shovel?"

She winks at him, flips her cigarette onto the ground. Gets in behind the wheel.

"Why hold back evidence?" Whicher says.

"Insurance, maybe?" The FBI agent puts the car into drive. "Something to bargain with in case she needs it in the future."

She raises the revs, the tires grip, then spin.

She lets the car roll back, tries again, the same maneuver three times, four.

She shuts off the motor, steps out.

"You carry chains?" Whicher says.

Rimes spreads her palms. "It's out of the pool at the law enforcement center. I don't know."

Whicher walks back around to the trunk.

Underneath a liner is a jack, a wheel wrench, a spare tire. No chains. A length of rope is coiled by the wheel arch, a tow rope.

Rimes looks at him over the roof of the car. "Do you think she's dead?"

Whicher doesn't answer.

"I'd hate to be the one that has to tell Anthony…"

⋏

Whicher stretches the tow rope between both hands, holding out a foot-long length. "Put your lighter under that."

Rimes fishes out her cigarette lighter. She sparks a flame, holds it under the mid-point of the rope. "Tell me about the sister?"

The marshal watches black smoke then flame taking hold of the nylon strands.

"You know, there was quite the rumor mill about her," Rimes says. "She's hot, right? Half the guys on the case in Chicago took more than a professional interest…"

Whicher pulls the rope into two pieces. "You ever meet her?"

"I went up to Chicago," Rimes says, "to pick up Anthony, escort him here. I didn't meet her, but I saw her."

"Is Anthony safe?" Whicher says.

The FBI agent presses her lips together.

"I mean, right now?"

"Nobody in the office has been able to speak with him." Rimes looks around. "It's not easy country out here. You can't just whistle a person up. As soon as I heard Anthony had to be moved, I telephoned this morning. I spoke with the owner of the ranch."

Whicher eyes her.

"Anthony wasn't there—I mean, not to hand, not at the ranch. They said they'd have him call back."

"That's how y'all left it?"

"My boss told me to come get you, cowboy."

Whicher thrusts the melted ends of the rope into the snow. "And he didn't get back?"

Rimes steps to the car, leans in, picks the radio off the hook on the dash.

Whicher moves to the front of the Chevy, squats at a wheel.

A static hiss bursts from the radio.

"Dispatch," a voice says.

"Agent Rimes, FBI. Can I get a line to my office?"

"Switch to channel two," the dispatcher says. "I'll try for you."

The marshal threads a length of rope through the wheel's alloy rim. He pulls the rope over the tire, against the tread.

The radio's silent, nobody picking up.

Whicher threads the rope through the next open lug in the rim.

"Nobody's answering," Rimes says. She replaces the radio transmitter. "I can try 'em again, later."

The marshal weaves the rope around, ties off the ends. He moves on to the next tire, starts over again.

"That a rope chain?"

"Looks like."

"Pretty neat."

"Army trick," he says. "You want to get in? See if we can get this moving?"

He finishes lashing the rope to the tire and rim.

She starts the motor, shifts into drive.

The tires bite, pull the Chevy forward, the car picks up momentum.

She drives thirty yards to where the road's clear again.

Whicher runs forward, throws the shovel into the trunk.

Rimes pushes open the door, leans out. "Nice goin', Tex."

He stoops to the front wheels. "I'll get these off, case we need 'em again."

"Tell me something," she says. "Chicago told us you

picked up Anthony's sister out at the Raton Pass. The train she was traveling on collided with a car?"

The marshal works his fingers into the cold, wet rope.

"Some folk think it might not be what it seemed," Rimes says. "Folk in Chicago."

Whicher strips the rope out from the tire. "You going to fill me in?"

"Maybe it was a set-up."

The marshal stops. He leans out, where he can see her. "You know?"

"No," he says. "What the hell's that supposed to mean?"

"The train colliding. Like it did. Maybe she had somebody park a car across that rail line. Maybe it was her set the whole thing up?"

Chapter 20

Janice Rimes stares out from behind the wheel—focused on the climbing, twisting, two-lane.

In the passenger seat, Whicher thinks of thirty hours with Lauren DeLuca. Thirty hours trying to keep her alive.

Beyond the windshield, glare and shade mark the road ahead. The marshal searches in his mind, back along the trail of moments with Lauren; snatches of conversation, images flashing half-seen—striated, like the light through the trees.

Ahead is a junction with a forest track—a galvanized sign standing proud at the side of the road: *Tigerville—Mystic*.

"That a place?" Whicher says.

"It was. An old mining camp." Rimes cuts him a look. "Beyond Mystic, where we're headed."

The road crests a rise before leveling. A quarter-mile section stretches out.

White-over mounds mark the stumps of trees where the ground has been logged. A crossbeam and twin uprights form the gateway to a property—a ranch.

Agent Rimes slows, lifts a hand from the wheel. "Right

there…"

"Anthony lives out here?"

"They have horses, a bunch of trails," Rimes says. "People come up to ride."

She turns the car from the road, steers through the lodge pole gateway.

Through the steep-sided gulley, a low sun throws shadows across the slopes. Boulders lie among the patches of scree and snow. Where the gully opens out, the Ponderosa are cut to form enclosed pastures—high meadow surrounded by forest, all of it blanketed white.

"They have campgrounds," Rimes says, "cabins for rent. Ranching, logging."

Whicher tips back his hat. "Quite the place."

"Maybe it makes him feel safe."

At the far end of the clearing, a group of buildings surround a big house made of stone. Cars and trucks are parked among log cabins and a scattering of barns. A few hundred yards to one side is a separate settlement—smaller cabins, with steep-pitched roofs.

"Those are rentals," Rimes says.

"Who else knows about Anthony up here?"

"You mean, among the ranching folk?"

The marshal nods.

"The place takes in delinquents, troubled kids. The county has a program, they pay to place 'em here." Rimes steers between the heaped snow at either side of the track. "A few kids come from out of state. They'll live and work on the ranch, helping out. Anthony's just another one of 'em, so far as the ranch staff know."

"Nobody knows he's in the witness security program?"

She shakes her head. "Plus they're used to law enforcement types coming out, from time to time."

Whicher looks at the side of her face.

"Us coming won't seem strange."

"Who else knows about him," the marshal says, "here in South Dakota?"

"The people in my office."

"That's it? Nobody else?"

"If somebody gets a relocate, the absolute minimum number of people get told."

Whicher thinks of Lauren, thinks of what her brother would be like.

He studies the buildings through the windshield, looks for people. Notices the flakes of snow now descending through the air.

人

Inside the log-lined office, Galen Coburn pours hot coffee—eyes hooded in his weathered face. The ranch owner is lean, around fifty, dressed in work jeans, suspenders, a wool shirt, a slate gray hat.

The marshal scans the Whitetail antlers hung at the walls.

"Fixin' to blow in again," Coburn says. He hands a mug of coffee to Janice Rimes. "We're going to be getting more snow."

Whicher studies the darkening sky at the window.

The FBI agent steps closer to the fire burning in a stone hearth.

"Anthony's out at the lake," Coburn says. "About eight miles from here, up the valley. We have an ice-fishing party coming in tomorrow."

"Sounds horrible," Rimes says.

Coburn grins, pours a mug of coffee for Whicher, hands it to him. "You can fill your boots with northern pike. Yellow perch, walleye."

"Yeah," Rimes says. "No thanks."

"We're not expecting Anthony back tonight. The camp has to be prepared."

"You can't call him?" Whicher says.

Coburn shakes his head. "Cell coverage is zip, you might have noticed."

Rimes shivers. "You don't have radio?"

"Mountains and trees," the ranch owner says, "don't work real good for radio. The two-way sets will work here and there, but I'd need repeaters to cover all of the acreage I got."

Agent Rimes takes a sip of hot coffee.

"I can't raise them out at the lake," Coburn says. "That's a part of the deal out here, why people like it—it's a place to get away."

Whicher pins the ranch owner with a look. "I need to see Anthony, Mister Coburn."

The man frowns.

"I'm afraid it's real urgent."

"Has something happened?"

"I can't answer that, sir. I just need to get on out there. We find him, we'll be leaving directly."

The ranch owner takes a pull at his mug of coffee.

"There be a problem with that?"

Coburn puts his head on one side. "We've had a lot of snow the last few days. A winter storm comes through this kind of height, it'll nail pretty much everything. The trail out to the lake has three to four feet of pack snow on it. No way you're going to get a vehicle through."

"How'd Anthony get there?" Whicher says. "How's your ice-fishing party getting out?"

"Horseback," the man answers.

Rimes looks at Coburn. "How about snow mobiles? ATVs?"

"Don't use 'em. Don't much like 'em."

"Seriously. You got to ride on a horse?"

"Yes, ma'am," the ranch owner says. "Or I guess you could walk. Does this all have something to do with Anthony's sister calling?"

⋏

Whicher stares across the room at Galen Coburn.

Janice Rimes sets down her mug. "You spoke with her?"

"A couple hours since," Coburn says.

"You spoke with Anthony's sister? You took the call?"

"It came through to our front office," Coburn says. He spreads his hands. "But they put her through to me."

Whicher feels a dryness in his mouth. "Did she give her name?"

"Yes, sir. She said her name was Lauren." Coburn's brow creases. "She wanted to speak with Anthony, wanted to know was he here."

Rimes's face is drawn. "Has anybody else called?"

"Not that I know…"

"What did you tell her?" Whicher says.

"I said he was out at the lake."

"You told her where Anthony was at?"

"I said he was out at Elk Lake, that she could leave a message…"

"Did she do that?"

"No, sir."

The marshal looks at Agent Rimes. "What's the absolute fastest way out there?"

She looks to Coburn. "How about logging roads?"

The ranch owner tugs at the collar of his shirt. "There's a logger runs a way up from the back, from the Rochford Road. I can't say as you'd get up it…"

"You need to take the car," Whicher says to Rimes, "get on back down the hill. Call the sheriff's office, get somebody—see if you can get up there."

"How long's it take to drive?" Rimes says.

"If the road's open," Coburn says, "around an hour, I'd guess."

"You think it's going to be blocked?" Whicher says.

"It's just a logging road, it's barely used."

"Y'all have a horse to fit me?"

"A horse?" The ranch owner puts back his shoulders. Runs his eye up and down the marshal. "Yes, sir," he says. He dips his head. "I reckon we do."

⊥

Eight miles west, in a fenced clearing off the ice-bound lake, Anthony Delano checks the generator; the gasoline tank is almost full. He wraps a gloved hand around the starter handle, pulls on the cord. The motor spins, it catches into life.

Across the white clearing, two mares lift their heads from a bale of hay—ears angled toward the sound.

Anthony nods to them. "What? It's just a generator."

Standing in the lee of a rough board shelter, he watches the generator run, bedded in the snow in its steel frame.

Gnarled icicles hang from the edge of the shelter's tin roof. He breaks one off. Taps it against an upright timber. It doesn't break.

Tossing it out into the snow, he studies the mares eating—happier outside than in.

From the shelter, he takes a piece of number-nine fence wire, steps out to an insulated stock tank.

Bending the wire into a hook, he plunges it into the water—stirs it, the surface already starting to re-freeze.

With the hooked wire, he picks a submersible heater from out of the snow. He lifts it over the side of the tank, lowers it down in the water.

He checks the earth strap—it's firm against the spike in the ground. Taking the electrical cord, he plugs it into the generator.

They'll drink more if the water's not too cold.

Satisfied, he steps back into the prevailing wind, off the lake.

He cuts another bale of hay, carries an armful to the wall-mount feeder.

AN AMERICAN BULLET

They'll stay hydrated. Food, water, shelter. They'll be okay.

He watches the mares eat, snow on their backs, no sign of it melting; their coats conserving nearly all of their body heat. His face splits in a grin—horses filled him with wonder, and always had, he felt better just for being around them.

Stepping from the shelter, he feels the wind on his face.

At the stock tank he hooks the heater out with the wire, holds it, dripping.

Steam is rising from the element, it's hot already. He lowers it back to the bottom of the tank.

Beyond the paddock, above the tree line, the mountain rises in jags of snow covered rock. The air is dense, opaque—more snow is coming, he's learning to read the signs.

He turns from the shelter, strides down toward a cluster of six cabins—their camp at the side of the lake.

Woodsmoke streams from four of the chimneys. By a rick fence is a stack of cordwood, he needs to check the stoves, keep them fed.

Against the white land and sky he sees a red and-black-clad figure—a man approaching, Will Jacobs, the senior guide at the ranch.

Jacobs spots him, gives a wave, points over at the cabins. He's dragging an ice-fishing sled, leaning forward—clumsy-looking in padded jacket and bibs, knee pads above his waterproof boots.

Anthony hurries to the wood pile. He lifts the tarp cover,

pulls out four lengths of seasoned pine.

He carries them flat against his chest.

By the porch of the first cabin, the cookhouse, he knocks his boots against the step.

Jacobs approaches at the edge of the frozen lake, breath clouding around his head.

Anthony sets down the wood. "What's it like out there?"

"Getting cold," Jacobs says, "real cold, if you're out of the sun." He drags the sled the last yards, ice around his beard and mustache, fleshy face red with the wind.

Anthony pulls off his gloves, tugs the woolen hat from his head. He runs a hand through his thick blond hair—getting long, he tells himself; a couple of the ranch girls are starting to tease him. Not a good idea to draw attention. Not now, not of any kind.

He studies the guide's fishing sled, piled with gear; a gasoline powered auger, a shelter, a tank of spare fuel.

Jacobs lifts out the augur. "This thing's heavy. Even dragging it on the otter." From the bed of the sled, he gathers up a bundle of wire pegs topped with orange flags.

"You get a few places marked?" Anthony says.

Jacobs grunts. "A few." He kicks at the hitch pin on the sled—squats, loosens the rope, wrapping it around the marker pegs. "Damn things are going to blow away, this wind."

"Did you cut some holes?"

"A couple."

"They won't freeze up?"

"They might. I put covers on 'em." Jacobs lifts a box-unit from the sled. "Let's go on in. The GPS is working, but the depth-finder battery gave out, I need to get it charged."

"I'll start the generator," Anthony says.

The guide looks at him, puzzled. "Ain't I hearing it already?"

"That's the water tank. For the horses."

Jacobs grins. "I swear you think more of them than you do any of us."

Anthony runs around to the back of the cabin, to a lean-to shelter made of triple-ply.

Opening up the slat-door, he stoops to the generator, checks the visual guide-mark on the side of the tank. He pulls on the starter handle—it fires. He flips the doors closed, heads back around to the front of the cabin, picks the firewood from the porch.

He wipes his boots, steps inside.

The cabin's warm, but dim after the outdoor glare.

He opens up the stove, feeds in wood—sparks fly up the chimney on the wind.

The depth-finder is already plugged into an outlet, charging. Jacobs is at the gun case on the cabin wall—its door open. He takes out a scoped hunting rifle.

Anthony shrugs off his coat. "What're you doing with that?"

The guide carries the rifle to the window, raises it to the glass. "Just checking…" He looks into the scope, angles his head, sighting through the lens. "I heard something out there…"

"Out on the lake?"

"A while back." Jacobs lowers the rifle. He turns from the window, looks at the younger man. "Everything alright?"

Anthony nods.

"It's nothing to worry about, kid."

"Well, what did you hear?"

The man frowns. "Just sounds. Noises on the wind."

Anthony stuffs his hands in the pockets of his bibs.

"Coyote, most like," Jacobs says. "But it could be a wolf. Fish and Wildlife say they got a report about a large adult male. I don't know if they're right."

"I didn't think they had them," Anthony says.

"Wolves?"

"In the Black Hills."

"They'll come through from out of state, from time to time. Out of Wyoming. Maybe Montana."

Anthony watches the guide work the bolt on the rifle. "Is it a problem?"

"Maybe," Jacobs says. "With the horses out there. In Montana, one was taken by a wolf in the fall. Maybe it's just coyote." He levels the rifle out of the window again. "But keep your eyes and ears open. If it is a wolf, a shot across the bows might scare it off." He takes down the gun. "You know? That's all. No need for any killin'."

Chapter 21

A cold wind cuts through the dog-hair stand of sapling pine. Whicher bunches his shoulders, fastens the wool coat tighter at his throat.

Galen Coburn sits his mare ahead on the forest trail, the horse picking its own way through the snow.

The marshal feels the rub of the saddle against his thighs. "How far you reckon we've come?"

The ranch owner turns his head. "Four miles," he says. "Around that."

Whicher grips the saddle horn, the mule-hide covering stiff beneath his gloves. He shifts his weight. "Reckon we could go any faster?"

"The horses are working hard enough," Coburn says. "I don't want 'em sweating, not out here. Not in this."

Whicher thinks of Agent Rimes—trying to make it up the logging road to the lake.

A clump of ice falls through the branches of a tall ponderosa—the quarter horses prick up their ears.

He studies the trail—the snow on it not deep now, not

feet-thick like it was a mile back in the last clearing.

"How's your horse feel?" Coburn calls back. "Her feet going down alright?"

The marshal thinks it over.

Coburn twists in the saddle. "Mine's getting a little trouble. We need to stop a minute."

"Sir, I need to get to that lake."

"Then you need to do what I tell you." The ranch owner takes a gloved hand from his horse's reins. He points to a spot of level ground. "Pull up ahead there. Over by those blackjack pine."

Whicher's mare follows the hoof prints of the lead horse.

Coburn slips from the saddle.

The marshal puts a hand to his foot, the lug-boots borrowed from a ranch hand tight even in the over-sized stirrups. He pulls one foot free, then the other, swings down.

"Tie your reins on the tree," Coburn says.

"Something the matter?"

"They'll get snow balling up—it messes with 'em."

Whicher lashes his mare's reins to a low growing branch.

Coburn takes off his elk-skin gloves, fishes out a pick from his winter overcoat.

Raising the fore-leg of the horse, he works the pick around the underside of its hoof. "You mind if I ask you a question?"

Whicher pulls off his own gloves, breathes warm air onto his fingers.

"Cold?" Coburn says.

The marshal nods.

"Work your hands into her coat there. Up on her back."

Reaching out, Whicher pushes his fingers slowly into the matted hair. Feels the warmth, leans in close to the horse's body. "Nice tip."

"So, I get to ask a question?"

"You can ask," Whicher says.

"Is Anthony in some kind of danger here? You and Agent Rimes coming out like this, sure as hell gives me cause for disquiet." He looks at the marshal.

"I can't tell you anything about Anthony."

"But is the boy in danger?"

"We're out here," Whicher says. "We're doing this, ain't we?"

Coburn puts a finger and thumb into the packed snow beneath the mare's foot. He prizes out a clump of white, throws it into the trees. "It melts then re-freezes," he says. "Worse if they're shod."

"They're barefoot?"

"These are—it's better in snow." The ranch owner puts down his horse's foreleg, moves to the hind. "I have to think about the other kids, the other people on this ranch. You know? I mean, if Anthony's some kind of risk, I don't want 'em exposed."

Whicher nods.

"Agent Rimes might have said something; warned me." Coburn cuts him a look.

"Take it up with her," the marshal says. "Or better yet, take it up with her boss."

He stares down the side of the hill, through the sapling

pine, to a stand of leafless oak. Bare branches black and tangled in the winter light.

Could anybody really get up here?

Could Lauren really have called?

⋏

Big flakes are tumbling from a dead-looking sky—the tops of trees moving whip-like in the wind.

Jerzy Belaski eyes the fall of snow between the tall pines. He steers the Nissan Pathfinder up the forest road.

No tracks are on its pristine surface—no vehicle has been up or down.

Lauren DeLuca's silent in the passenger seat. Her face still, the color drained.

Seven hours straight driving.

Seven hours since ditching the stolen Ford. All the way up from Nebraska, the roads choked with snow, with highway crews, with the fallout from the storm.

Belaski peers at the bend ahead, the road disappearing into high timber.

The rental office in North Platte had been happy to hire out the all-wheel-drive Nissan—they never could've made it in a regular car.

"This better be the place," he says.

No response.

Lauren Deluca stares out of the windshield, mouth shut firm.

He glances at her. Then at the new-bought map in his lap. Only one road to Elk Lake—steep, narrow, covered with snow.

He thinks of goading her, tired of her silence.

Then breaks off, sudden.

Beneath him, the wheels of the Nissan are starting to slip.

※

The clearing ahead is a half-mile wide—a dipping gully between dense-grown thickets.

Whicher's horse steps along the channel made by Coburn's mare.

"You need to get up here, take the lead," the ranch owner says. "My horse is getting worn out making a path."

The marshal twitches on the reins, leans his weight forward.

Galen Coburn pulls up, steps his horse to one side. "Let her get in front—give her her head. She knows the ground, she can feel it. Just let her do what she needs to do."

The marshal lets the reins go slack, grips the horn of the saddle as his mare pushes by.

Snow is up to her shoulders, a banked white mass.

Cold and wet seeps through the fabric of Whicher's pants. "What kind of country is up ahead?"

"Steep," Coburn answers.

"Like this? Exposed?"

"Through woods, mainly."

"Think we can make it?"

"So long as the horses hold out," Coburn says. "We'll reach the plateau in another couple miles, the land's flatter up around the lake."

The marshal cants his head as wind scours the frozen surface of the gully—whipping ice crystals into the air.

He clutches at his hat, tries to hide his face in the collar of his coat.

The mare rears, launches herself. Whicher stays low to her neck.

If Janice Rimes could get up the logging road, there'd be a way out, at least.

"You think we're going to have to come back this a-way?"

Coburn keeps his eyes down, focused on the hollowed-out path through the snow. He doesn't answer.

⁂

A wisp of steam rises from the top of the stock tank. Anthony dips a finger into the water—now tepid.

Switching off the generator, he unhooks the heater unit. He heads under the tin roofed-shelter, snatches up a fork, grabs more dry hay.

"Come on over here," he calls out.

One of the mares turns her head to look at him.

He makes a series of clicking sounds.

The mare's head dips, she starts to lope toward him.

Anthony walks back slowly.

The second horse turns, follows suit, feet dishing in the snow.

He sets the hay down alongside the stock tank. Puts his hand into the water, keeping it under, showing them; "See?"

He takes his hand from the tank, holds it out.

The lead mare puts her muzzle to it. He feels her hot breath, the rough rasp of her tongue.

He puts his hand back into the water.

The horse takes a step forward. Tries a drink.

A voice calls out behind him. "*Anthony…*"

The horse stops drinking, raises its head.

"What?" Anthony calls back, irritated.

Will Jacobs is standing at the cookhouse cabin. "So, you got a minute?"

Neither horse is drinking, now.

"Come on ladies," he says, "you need this." The young man shakes his head, steps away from the tank.

Jacobs squats at the ice-fishing sled. "I'm taking the otter back out while the light's still good." He sinks to his knee pads, checks the hitch-bolt is through the loop of nylon rope. "The depth-finder batteries are charged now. I want to mark up a couple places on the far side of the lake."

Bitter wind rakes his face as Anthony approaches. "Could it wait?"

"I want to check it out, I might even cut a couple of more holes." The guide settles the augur in the bed of the fishing-sled, orange marker flags nestled beneath it, half covered with fresh snow. "You want to come?"

"I want to stay with the horses."

"Everything alright?"

"I want them drinking."

"They'll drink," Jacobs says.

"Are you going to be long?"

"I don't know. An hour."

"Should I get some food cooking?"

Jacobs nods. "You could do that. There's a propane

cylinder in back if the one in there gives out. Say, Anthony?"

The young man looks at him.

"Long as you're keeping an eye on the horses, keep an eye out for anything bothering them."

Anthony studies the man's face.

"I'm just sayin'."

"I'd do that anyway."

"The rifle's in the gun cupboard. There's a key on a hook under the drain board." Jacobs looks at him.

Anthony nods.

"Watch for signs they're uneasy," the guide says. "They'll know before you."

⁂

Light is filtering, growing through the canopy of pines; the logging road is headed out from the cover of the woods—into open ground.

Belaski touches the back of a hand to his forehead, it's filmed with sweat. "Son of a bitch. This is bullshit."

The Nissan breaks from the tree line, windshield filling with dull, white flakes.

Straining his eyes to make out the route, he flicks on the wipers.

There's just a white-covered expanse, drifting snow—flat land, leafless trees.

At the far side of the clearing, a pine thicket stands ragged—he can make out a line of fence posts, no wire, no rail.

"We get our asses stuck, I might just put you out." He

glances at Lauren. "Leave you here—to freeze to death."

The Nissan plows forward—a scraping sound rising from beneath the chassis.

Belaski grits his teeth, pushes down on the gas.

"That little jerk better be out here…"

He eyes the sky above the thicket, snow in the air, wave after wave descending.

Lauren's face is set hard, as if she's alone, as if nothing of him touches her existence.

"I guess your brother really bought that he could disappear," Belaski says. "It might have worked…" he pauses, mid-sentence.

From the corner of his eye, he sees her angle her head a fraction.

He turns.

Her eyes look into his.

Some force lights them, some internal force. Belaski feels a surge down deep in his blood.

"About three months after he came here, he got bored, you know, a little lonely?"

She breaks off looking at him.

"Maybe he started to relax a little. Believe that he was going to get a free pass."

The wheels of the SUV slip in the deep snow, then bite. Wind hammers against the Nissan's side.

"He started calling up a few old friends from the neighborhood—in Chicago. A couple of times he even called up his girlfriend, his ex." Belaski shakes his head. "Your brother's whereabouts have been known a while.

You'd be surprised how easy it is to find a person. All it takes is one thread."

He stares into the darkness of the thicket, trails of snow and ice streaming off the outer branches of the trees.

An opening is showing—the line of fence posts run toward it.

"You see a thread dangling," Belaski says, "catch hold. Start to pull on it—little by little, all it takes…"

Chapter 22

Deep in the woods the air hangs heavy, slowed from the winter onslaught, cold and eerie.

The horses' ears are up. They find their footing swiftly, despite the rocky ground.

Whicher leans back in the saddle, pulls off one glove. Unfastens the heavy wool coat.

A heightened sensation is upon him—instinctive, a thing he's come to recognize. Ten years back as a combat scout—countless situations since, in law enforcement.

Maybe it's the light; strange, fractured through the pines. The high, keening wind in the tops of the trees.

Ahead, Coburn points to a dead trunk laying horizontal at the side of the trail. "We get around that fallen yellowbark, we got about another quarter-mile."

The marshal feels the rocking motion of the horse steady beneath him. He listens to the creak of saddle-leather, the bit jingling at the mare's mouth.

"We're going to have to ride back this way." Coburn twists his neck, looks up into the sky, into snow sifting through the trees. "I can't see any way around it—the logging road's going to be out."

"You don't think Agent Rimes could make it up there?"

"There's no reason anybody'd clear it," Coburn says. "There's been no timber harvest in a while." The ranch owner looks back over his shoulder. "We need to find Anthony, feed the horses, get 'em to drink. Then turn around and head back out—we need to be gone from here before we lose the light."

Whicher slips his hand inside his coat, reaches down, feels for the Ruger in the shoulder-holster. He takes it out. Eyes the big revolver, settles it into an outside pocket of the coat.

⁂

At the camp ground, Anthony sets the bucket of bran mash down to stare at the newly-arrived vehicle.

An SUV is pulling up in front of the cookhouse cabin, windshield wipers going—only the swept section of the glass clear of snow.

The ice-fishing party is slated for tomorrow, coming out on horseback. He glances at the leaden sky. Jacobs hasn't mentioned anybody coming out.

Walking toward the vehicle, Anthony raises a hand.

It's hard to see inside.

Nobody is getting out.

A man is staring at him from behind the wheel.

Beside the driver is another figure. Smaller.

The driver's door is opening. The man steps out.

He's wearing a winter parka, his face sharp, like a hawk. He's out of place—not a rancher, or a farmer. His eyes are hard as he stares, a tight smile beneath the hook of a nose.

"Anthony Delano?"

The young man's never seen him before. A feeling starts to tick inside. Countless times he's imagined a stranger—turning up, asking for him, a certain look in his face. From dreams he's woken, afraid—only to realize he's still safe, still hidden, far from Chicago.

"My name's Corrigan. I'm a US Marshal."

Snow is falling in Anthony's eyes as he blinks. "Is something wrong?" He studies the man, feels a dryness in his mouth.

"I'm from the witness protection program. I need you to step on over here. If you don't mind?"

The smile is gone.

The man takes out a leather badge-holder. He opens it. It shows a star in a circle.

"Your sister is in the car with me." He half-turns, gestures with a thumb.

Anthony stares at the windshield.

"We have to move her," the man says. "We're in a situation here, kind of an emergency. We have to move her, we need to move you too. Hell of a time to do it, in the middle of a winter storm, but there's no choice."

The passenger door is opening, now. Anthony sees his sister stepping out.

She's wearing a big coat, a man's coat. The wind whipping hair across her face.

"It's alright," she says.

One of the mares lets out a whinnying sound. He turns, looks at the horses.

Turning back, he sees his sister staring at him.

"Sometimes this happens," the man says. "In witness security." He nods at the vehicle. "You want to get in the car?"

Anthony takes a step toward them. "What, we just, go?"

"We need to get down this hill," the man says. "Get back onto regular roads. Before we're cut off."

"Is somebody coming out here?"

The man, Corrigan, puts his head a little on one side.

"Is somebody looking for me?" Anthony says.

"We think there could be."

"Everybody told me it was safe."

"We'll keep you safe," the man says.

Anthony looks at his sister's face.

"I'm sorry," she says. She looks away. "We need to just go."

She steps back into the car, pulls the door shut.

"Don't bring anything," the man says, "just come exactly as you are. Leave it all. We have to vanish. Just as if we were never here."

᛫

Out on the frozen lake, Will Jacobs holds the ice-auger upright—resting the weight of the motor on the steel screw-blade.

He stares at the SUV maneuvering at the cabins—turning now, backing—headed out.

He hoists the auger, carries it to the otter, dumps it in the bed of the sled.

In his head, he rewinds the last minute—he was setting up the shelter trying to get out of the wind. He got done with that, he'd dragged the auger out of the ice-sled—he straightened up to get a pull on the starter, he noticed a vehicle, an SUV.

From the far side of the lake, he couldn't tell much, except that he had no idea what it was doing there.

He grabs the nylon rope, starts to pull the sled over the surface of the ice.

A man had gotten out.

Anthony'd gone over.

They were talking. Then somebody else got out of the vehicle—smaller; it might've been a man or a woman. Blond hair. A big coat.

Anthony'd gotten in the back seat.

Jacobs pulls harder on the otter, breaking into a stumbling run.

The vehicle is almost gone already—it's out down the line of the rick fence, at the opening to the far thicket.

"*Wait…*" he calls out.

No way they're going to hear him.

The SUV keeps on.

It's in the tree line, now.

It's gone.

⸷

Down at the foot of the logging road, Agent Janice Rimes shelters beneath the trees by her car. For fifteen minutes the

Pennington County Sheriff four-wheel-drive has been gone. But she can hear it now, motor rumbling, descending back out of the woods.

She curses under her breath. Watches the vehicle emerge from the forest, steer down to the apron where the logging road meets the regular highway.

The driver, Deputy Mathis, slows to a stop, drops the window. "No way," he says.

The FBI agent slips out a cigarette.

"No way I'm getting all the way up that."

Rimes sparks a flame. "Somebody made it."

Mathis nods. Wheel tracks are clearly visible; something's gone up. "The tracks keep on going," he says. "But we got no way to know how long they've been there."

"It can't be that long."

The deputy puffs out his cheeks. "Through the trees, it's not real bad," he says. "The road's a little protected by the forest. But after a mile or so, it goes through a clearing. Snow's been drifting in there, deeper than the hood of this thing."

Rimes looks off through the failing light. "You're really sure you couldn't make it?"

"That's horrible snow, soft as all hell. I'd be wasting my time."

She pulls on the cigarette.

Mathis checks the Forest Service map on his passenger seat. "Logging Road 57," he says. He reads the note attached. "Designated high-clearance-vehicle use only. Six miles long. In poor repair at high elevations…"

"Somebody went up there," Rimes says.

The deputy turns to look at her out of the driver window. "Even if they did," he says, "I can't believe they'd make it all the way back down."

Whicher sees the group of cabins laid out beyond the ponderosa—a tree-lined basin, a flat expanse of snow and ice.

A man is pulling something toward the cabins. Dragging something. Some kind of sled.

Galen Coburn puts his horse into a canter.

The marshal follows across a glaring field of white.

Coburn turns back in the saddle, shouts at Whicher, "*Don't get your horse on the ice…*"

The man at the lake drops the line to the sled, he's running now. "*Anthony just got in a vehicle,*" he calls out.

Whicher reins in his mount, sees fresh wheel-marks—churned up snow.

Coburn bring his horse to a halt.

The man runs the last yards to the cabins. "I was out cutting holes," he says. "I looked up, I saw a vehicle…"

"Jacobs," the ranch owner says, "this here's a US Marshal."

"What vehicle?" Whicher says.

"I didn't see it come in," the man answers, flushed, "it just appeared. I looked up from cutting a hole in the ice. I saw an SUV. I saw a guy get out. Anthony came over. They were talking. Then somebody else got out."

Whicher eyes the wheel tracks.

"Next thing you know, Anthony was getting in the back seat, they drove away."

"How long?" the marshal says.

"Five minutes," Jacobs says. "The time it's taken me to get across the lake…"

Coburn turns his horse in the blowing snow. "We can follow 'em down the logging road."

Whicher pins Jacobs with a look. "Was Anthony acting any way strange?" he says. "You think he might've known somebody would be coming out?"

The guide only stares back, wordless.

"I can't believe anybody made it up here," Coburn says.

The marshal thinks of Janice Rimes. He looks at Coburn. "You know how to shoot?"

"What kind of a damn question is that?"

Whicher starts to take out the Ruger to give to him.

"You need a gun?" Jacobs says. "There's a scoped Springfield right in the cabin."

Chapter 23

Behind the wheel of the Pathfinder, Belaski checks the rear-view mirror. Anthony is seated in back, the kid's eyes fixed on a spot six inches in front of his face.

So far, he hasn't asked questions.

Lauren De Luca's silent in the front passenger seat.

Belaski focuses on the trail—already it's worse than it was coming up. Beneath the cover of the pines it's drivable. But where the trees thin, snow has drifted, it's piled deep.

He steers around a turn in the logging road—light streaking through the canopy of branches. The road is headed out onto open ground, now. He snorts air through his nostrils. A bloom of heat spreads inside.

Last thing to do is bog down.

Momentum. Put on more speed.

In the back seat, Anthony clears his throat. "Is it alright to ask where we're going?"

"Right now, the number one priority is getting out of these hills." Belaski glances up in the rear-view. "We need to get back on the road network."

The young man nods.

"I have to check in with my boss—there'll be a couple of safe houses or locales we can use. It's his call, not mine."

They'll wait till they're alone, Belaski tells himself—wait before they try to speak; he won't give them that chance.

"We'll be okay," he says, "just do what I tell you to do." He flexes his grip on the wheel, eases his foot down on the gas.

The SUV breaks from the tree line—plowing into exposed space.

Snow shoots from beneath the fenders, they're slowing—Belaski feels it, he pushes down harder on the throttle pedal.

He grips the wheel. The Nissan bucks and squirms, tires biting, slipping, biting again.

A little fast.

They're almost through the clearing, pine trees closing back in.

Beneath the canopy, the logging road drops in a steep descent, he remembers struggling to get up it.

Their speed is high, the track cambered, canted sideways—the road distorted, as if the land beneath has slipped.

Too fast—they're headed down too fast.

He whips his foot off the gas, feels his stomach lurch, feels the wheels break loose in the snow.

Touching a foot on the brakes he feels the Nissan snap sideways. Belaski turns the wheel, the edge of the road rushes—trunks of pine accelerating from the gloom.

He stomps the gas, "*Fuck...*" tries to power out of the slide.

They hit the edge—for a split second the motor roars in mid-air.

Lauren screams, her arms come up.

Glass and pine explode inside the cab.

A low branch punches out a window, a sickening impact.

Before the white world switches black.

Chapter 24

The Park Ranger Ford Explorer chews its way along the fire road across the back of the hill. Maddie Cook thinks about the partial message on the radio—a call-to-assist, the sheriff's department requesting a unit to Elk Lake.

The message sounded like the tail-end of a multi-agency request.

She listens for any more coming in from dispatch.

Radio coverage is sketchy this side of the hill, a known drop-out spot, shielded from the mast on the plateau.

The fire cut is little more than a cleared path between trees. A forest crew grubbed it free of dog sapling, the back end of summer. It's flat. It runs practically on a contour line.

Beneath the old-growth trees, the pack snow is firm, the Ford's winter tires gripping. She'll be alright.

A call-to-assist was likely somebody reported missing, somebody getting into difficulty. She gives a shake of the head.

People set out with no respect for conditions. A winter storm like this, you'd have to have a screw loose.

She thinks of her son—wonders if the school bus is running, if it'll get him home. She's left pot-roast. All he has to do is put it in the oven.

She smiles, thinking of him. Can't help it.

The radio stays silent. Static bursts, nothing more.

The woods are thinning, the fire road reaching a junction up ahead.

She knows she's coming to Logging Road 57.

57 runs all the way up to the plateau, right up to the side of Elk Lake.

At the bottom it's likely blocked, between the Rochford end and about half-way—she thinks of open pasture, the snow would be deep there, most likely that's the reason for the call.

Up on the plateau she can check out what's going on. The radio signal will be strong—she can get a heads-up.

She reaches the end of the fire road, makes a left at the junction with 57, to head up the hill.

She shivers despite the warmth in the cab; the road here more open to the sky, the snow worse, wind able to sweep along it. Nice enough in summer. In winter, not so much.

Nobody's likely to be up here, Maddie thinks. In fifteen years on the job, she's learned who's going to be where, and when.

In the depths of winter there's places in the forest you can drive all day, hardly see another person. No loggers. The trail's are closed to riders, it's not hiking country, not if you're sane, not in this.

She keeps the Ford working its way up hill, low gear, moving steady.

Rounding the bend is a traverse of 57—where the subsoil's gone.

She sees two men.

Plus an upturned vehicle—off the road.

The vehicle's on its side, smashed against the trunk of a Black Hills spruce—two wheels hanging in the air.

One of the men is on his hands and knees—the other standing in the road, doubled over.

She lets out a low whistle.

Lets the big Ford slow.

⋏

Belaski tries to keep from vomiting, hands gripped around his legs, above his knees.

Behind him, Anthony's dazed, sucking down air.

Belaski hears the engine note, lifts his head—stares downhill, down the track.

An SUV is at the bend in the forest trail—a Ford—a light bar fixed across its roof.

He glances uphill at the Pathfinder—Lauren's slumped against the side-pillar, covered in shattered glass, pinned against her seat by a branch.

He turns back to the SUV—pain thrumming inside his head.

The vehicle's stopped. It's just waiting in the falling snow, wipers flicking back and forth.

He puts a hand inside his coat pocket, closes it around the butt of the SIG.

The driver's door opens.

A woman steps out. "Are you folks alright?"

She's wearing a brown uniform—bib jacket, lug boots.

"Is anybody hurt here?"

If she has a weapon, she's making no attempt to get it. Concern is in her expression—but no alarm.

Her chestnut hair blows loose around her face.

"My sister's trapped…" Anthony calls out

The woman shifts her weight. "You have somebody trapped?"

Belaski's mind races, calculating; the way he learned in schoolyard fights.

The woman starts to walk up the track.

Squinting as she approaches, Belaski sees the embroidered badge on her coat; *National Park Service*.

He studies her face.

She pauses, looks at him.

He stands, breathing hard in the snow. *She has no idea who they are.*

"Let me take a look," the woman says. She starts forward again—then stops, suddenly.

Her face turns uphill—she stares at something—up the logging road, her mouth part open.

Belaski twists around, ignoring the stab of pain in his neck.

Two riders are at the head of the track, men on horseback. He sees the outline of a rifle across the first man's back. Recognizes the red and black plaid coat of the other rider.

A sensation rips through him—he snatches out the gun from his pocket.

Pushes himself upright behind the woman.

Puts the gun against her head.

⁂

Coburn wheels his horse in the middle of the trail. "That's him," he says, "that's Anthony down there…"

Whicher takes in the two men and a woman stumbling down the hill to a Parks Service SUV. One of the men is young, blond—the other man holding something that looks like a gun.

Whicher takes out the Glock, racks it. "*US Marshal,*" he shouts. "*Drop your weapon…*"

The gunman shouts something at the woman—she gets into the vehicle, into the driver's side. The man raises his gun arm.

Whicher digs his heels into the flanks of the mare. The horse takes off.

Two shots snap out.

The marshal flattens to the mare's neck, holds the Glock clear of her head, fires—three shots, in quick succession.

The horse pulls sideways, bolts.

The shooter fires back, Whicher clings on—the horse is in a flat gallop, he yanks the reins, tries to pull her back.

Her head snaps sideways, feet skidding in the snow. He clamps both arms to her neck. A shot cracks; louder, flatter—Coburn, behind him.

The mare is skidding, her legs splayed. Whicher shifts his weight as she slides, tries to turn back up the hill.

Ripping the stirrups from his feet, he grabs the horn of

the saddle, swings a leg across her back.

He jumps, hits the snow—rolls, winded.

The mare charges back up the hill.

Whicher scrambles behind the trunk of a tree. The rumble of a motor reaches him—the SUV.

He fights for breath, levels the Glock, edges out, stares down the iron-sight. He can just see the blond kid get in the front passenger seat, the gunman getting into the back.

He breaks off, turns to Coburn, on the hill. "*Stay there,*" he shouts, "*don't come down.*"

The ranch owner's horse is stamping, turning, Whicher's mare already gone.

The marshal breaks cover, the SUV is starting to back down the hill.

He braces his arm, draws a line—*he can't shoot*—the gunman's in the rear, the woman and the young man up front.

In the corner of his eye he sees a vehicle—off the road, crashed.

The SUV is backing and backing.

Whicher starts to run down the hill, boots hammering the snow.

He stares at the crashed vehicle—a Nissan Pathfinder, over at forty-five degrees.

The SUV disappears around a bend.

Whicher checks for the tell-tale smell of gasoline. A low branch is piercing the Nissan, he sees the outline of a head.

Blonde hair.

He steps to the high-side of the vehicle, opens the door.

Lauren DeLuca.

He takes off his hat.

A tear is sliding down the side of her face.

She lifts her head, blue eyes wincing in pain.

"Alright," he says, "it's alright…"

She's trapped behind a thick branch.

Her mouth moves, but the words are too quiet.

He lowers the gun, leans in closer. "Don't try to talk."

"No," she mumbles. "No, no, no…"

Chapter 25

Belaski covers the woman driving as she backs the Ford down the hill. Anthony's beside her—the pair of them covered with a six-inch sweep of gun.

He stares up the logging road, looking for the first sign of pursuit.

Two hundred yards.

Two hundred yards and nobody's come.

"What's your name?"

The woman's trying to steer, trying to back down the road, not look at him. "Maddie."

"You need to get us off this hill." He looks into her eyes, brandishes the gun. "What're you doing here?"

She swallows, focuses on reversing, face coloring with the effort. "I heard a radio message."

"What message?"

"The sheriff's department."

He stares at her.

"A call-to-assist," she says. "I thought it was some lost hiker…"

Belaski's eyes snap back onto the logging road.

Churned up wheel marks are in the snow at the side.

"Wait," he barks, "what's that? Wait, stop."

Her eyes cut to his. She comes off the gas.

Anthony cranes his head around to look into the back. His face is pinched, eyes glistening. Blue eyes, *like hers,* Belaski thinks.

A dark bloom passes over the young man's brow. "Who are you?" he croaks.

"Who the fuck do you think?" Belaski looks at the woman. "Are cops coming up this hill?"

"I don't know."

He shows her the muzzle. "Maddie? One thing; don't piss me off, don't play dumb." He angles his head at the windshield, at the side-shoot leading off into the forest. "What's that track?"

"A fire road," she says.

"To where?"

"Through the woods."

"Is that the way you came?"

She nods.

"You need to get us off this hill," Belaski says. "You get us off, I won't have to shoot you."

She lets out a held-breath.

Anthony looks into the side of her face.

Belaski raises the gun, moves it closer to the woman's head.

"Alright," she says. She slumps forward, reaches for the shifter—moves it from reverse into drive.

Still no riders.

Belaski stares at the empty stretch of road.

He leans in, up close to the woman's ear. "We don't make it out of here," he says. "The first bullet in this thing is for you."

⁂

At the bottom of 57 on the Rochford Road, Janice Rimes sits in the Chevy sedan.

Mathis, from the county sheriff's office waits in the four-wheel-drive Tahoe.

The FBI agent chews a fingernail, watches snow thicken on the hood. Every instinct tells her; take it wide. But nobody's come down the logging road—it doesn't look like anybody could.

The snow is feet thick, fresh fall still coming.

The tracks on 57 could be innocent; properties were up that road, there'd be animals to check on, to feed. She stares at the only thing marking out a road exists beneath the deep white powder; a post and rail fence. Wind scours the edge of the tree line. Lumps break and fall from the branches.

Nobody going up. Nobody coming down.

She thinks of the marshal—if he's found Anthony with Coburn, they'd likely turn around, head straight back for the ranch.

She slips another cigarette from her pack, thinks of putting out a call for help.

Witness security demanded the fewest number of people in the loop.

She stares at the blowing snow.

Feels her stomach twisting.

⁂

Whicher hurries up the steep grade of the logging road, cold wind at his back.

At the side of the crashed Nissan, Galen Coburn works the branch that's piercing the cab.

"There's a side trail," the marshal calls out. "Through the forest, across the hill."

"Are they gone?" Coburn calls back.

The marshal reaches the vehicle, glances in at Lauren—trapped inside, her face pale and still.

He wades into the deep snow at the edge of the road. "They're gone."

"Alright," says Coburn. "Then put your weight on this."

Whicher works his way along the side of the Pathfinder.

"I'll get inside," Coburn says, "try to get the end of the branch off of her. We need to get her out."

Through the tangle of low limbs, Whicher takes up position.

"She's going to freeze to death," Coburn says, beneath his breath.

The ranch owner hauls himself up the bank, back onto the logging road. He holds open the door of the SUV, clambers in over the sill.

"Alright—push now," he calls out. "Give it all you got."

The marshal flexes his back, heaves his weight against the limb of the tree—it moves a few inches.

"Hold it there…" Coburn calls.

Whicher grits his teeth, locks out his legs. Muffled sound comes from inside the cab, he feels his pulse climbing.

"*Keep pushing,*" Coburn yells.

The marshal heaves harder, feels the muscles in his legs and arms and back start to burn.

"*Alright, she's free…*"

He hears movement.

"You can let go…"

The marshal eases back on the branch.

Coburn climbs from the cab, reaches in, arm extended, trying to pull Lauren out.

Whicher scrambles up the bank as she climbs free, gets herself over the sill.

She sits in the snow.

The marshal studies her, he can't see blood.

He turns to Coburn. "How do we get down this hill?"

The ranch owner looks off along the descending track. "It's miles that way," he says. "You get down to the end it's just a mountain road, most likely snowed up."

Whicher thinks of Janice Rimes.

Coburn turns his face toward the marshal. "Best thing we could do is head back up to the lake."

"We need to call for help."

"It's only a half a mile or so," Coburn says. "We get up there, we'll at least have shelter, there's the cabins, food, we got wood for the fire. Even if the storm gets worse we'll be okay."

"We need help." Whicher looks at Lauren.

"Maybe so," Coburn says. "But there's no way we're going to get it."

Chapter 26

Belaski sits in the back of the Parks Service Ford Explorer, lizard eyes unblinking. "That thing on?"

The woman half-turns.

"The radio?" he says.

She nods.

No messages, no calls, no traffic. Zip.

So far, there's no sign anybody's coming after them.

Belaski sucks in air over his teeth; the guy on the horse had been the marshal—the big bastard from the train. The Marshals Service must have figured Anthony to be at risk, they must've sent the son-of-a-bitch.

He eyes the deadfall at the side of the forest track.

The woman ranger, Maddie, is silent at the wheel.

"How much farther does this go?"

"A couple more miles," she says.

Anthony, in the passenger seat, angles his head, stiff in his winter outdoor gear. He smells of something, Belaski thinks—some kind of animal. He holds the SIG between the pair of them, finger curled at the trigger. "How many?"

"Five or six."

"Then what?"

"It connects with another logging road."

Belaski stares at her eyes in the rear-view mirror. "Is it going to be blocked?"

She dips her head. "I don't know."

"Where's it go?"

"Down the hill. Back down to the main road."

"You a cop, Maddie?" Belaski says, mind speeding. "National Park Service. That be law enforcement, or are you just a guide?"

Her eyes flick up in the mirror.

"Stop," he says.

Her foot comes off the gas.

"Stop here." He raises the gun.

She brakes the Explorer to a standstill.

Silence fills the cab, there's just the sound of the motor idling beneath the hood.

"Get out," he says.

Nobody moves.

The woman sits in the driver seat, both hands wrapped around the wheel.

"Maddie? Did I just tell you to get out?"

She reaches for the door, opens it. Pushes it wide. Climbs out, her body rigid.

Anthony sits frozen.

Belaski opens up the rear door, steps after her. "You carry a gun?"

She stares, her face blank.

He looks into her eyes.

She nods.

"Take out the gun, throw it over here."

She pulls up the bib coat. Reaches down to her duty belt.

"Careful," he says.

She pops the restraining strap on the leather holster. Eases out the semi-automatic P229.

"Toss it over here."

She swings her arm, lets go the butt of the pistol. It falls into the snow.

"You wearing a radio?" he says. "Open your coat, let me see."

She unfastens the coat.

"Take that off," he says.

She unclips the Motorola two-way transceiver. Drops it.

"Take out your cuffs," he says.

She only looks at him.

"Those handcuffs. Take 'em out."

She unfastens the leather holder on her belt, takes out the stainless-steel cuffs.

"Walk around to the passenger side."

She takes a breath. Steps forward, around the hood of the big Ford.

Anthony watches, mouth gaping.

"Get out," Belaski says.

The young man flinches.

"You want to eat this plus a bunch of glass, it's all the same to me. Or you do what I tell you." He levels the gun.

Anthony opens his door, sits forward. Unfolds himself

from the Ford. All the air seems gone from his body. "I don't know anything…" His voice chokes in his throat. "I don't know a thing about any of this…"

"Maddie," Belaski says. "Put the cuffs on him."

The woman's eyes drill his.

Belaski gives a shake of the head. "Put your arms out, hands together," he says to Anthony.

Maddie Cook takes a pace forward. Fastens the cuffs around the young man's wrists.

"Alright, now you put him in the back there." Belaski jabs the gun at her, then at Anthony.

She walks slow to the tail gate, opens it.

The space inside is big, dark, the glass panels blacked, rear windshield the same.

In the bed of the trunk is a canvas carry-all, tire chains, assorted tools. At one wheel-arch is a ten gallon gasoline tank—ratchet-strapped to a chainsaw.

"Get in," Belaski says.

Anthony sits at the edge of the trunk, cuffed hands in his lap. His face is sick-looking, he swings his legs up, snow falls from his boots.

"Lay down."

The young man lets out a breath.

"Close it up," Belaski says.

Maddie brings the hatch door down, thoughts racing behind her eyes.

Belaski grabs her shoulder, pushes her out into the middle of the fire cut. He walks her ten yards from the Ford. Raises the pistol.

"Jesus God, no…"

He thumbs back the hammer.

"*Please…*"

He holds the barrel straight at her midriff.

"Ninety-nine times out of a hundred, I'd shoot you down, right here. But there's something you're going to have to do for me." Belaski looks off into the forest, at snow tumbling from the leaden sky. "If you don't freeze to death, you're going to walk out of here."

She stares, unmoving.

"You need to get a message to a woman named Lauren DeLuca."

Maddie looks at him, mute.

"You tell her a message from me. You tell her, it's time for her to do the right thing. If you make it out of here alive, law enforcement are going to want to talk with you…"

She doesn't answer.

"They'll talk to you. About this. About me. About what happened here."

She gives the faintest nod.

"You tell them the message. For Lauren DeLuca."

"Who are you?"

"She knows who."

Maddie stares at him, round-eyed.

"You pass the message; it's time to do the right thing…"

Chapter 27

At the campground on Elk Lake, Whicher stands in the lee of the cookhouse cabin, holding down his hat in the wind.

By the ice-bound lake, Galen Coburn dismounts his quarter horse.

He holds the reins of his mare, his face tight and red from the cold. "I don't know what the hell is going on," he says, "I brought you out here, I didn't ask questions. You said you needed to get to Anthony, I took you at your word."

The marshal nods.

"Anthony was placed in my charge," the ranch owner says. "We turn up, some maniac's crashed his car into a tree, Anthony's taken at gunpoint—with a park ranger…"

Whicher cuts him off; "Can we make it back to the ranch before nightfall?"

Coburn's horse steps sideways, picking up her feet. The ranch owner grabs her high at the bridle.

"We're a sitting target here."

"Why the hell are we a target?"

Whicher takes a pace back, into the shelter of the

cookhouse wall. "I'm not at liberty to tell you that."

"People shoot at me, I'm not allowed to know who they are?"

The marshal watches three horses by a slat-board shelter, his mare among them, still saddled. "I don't make the rules, Mister Coburn."

"You expect folk just to do whatever you want?"

"I have to go talk to her."

Coburn rubs a leather-gloved hand across his chin.

The marshal gestures with his head toward the cabin.

"You think she's hurt?" the ranch owner says.

Whicher doesn't reply. He eyes the snow driving in over a tree-covered hill.

"I suppose you're not about to tell me who she is?"

"You suppose right."

Coburn gives a shake of his head.

"I'm sorry for what happened," Whicher says. He looks over at Will Jacobs, the ranch guide attending to the group of horses. "If there's any way of getting back before nightfall, I'll call law enforcement, we'll get the hell off of your property. I give you my word."

"We need to get the horses fed, get 'em watered. Before we can do a damn thing."

"There's still time?"

Coburn casts a weather-eye at the darkening sky. He tugs at the bridle on the horse. Doesn't answer.

⁂

Janice Rimes steers down the cleared highway, headed south. She smokes a cigarette down to the filter.

No point staying at the bottom of a snowed-up logging road—no word from the marshal, no word from anybody else.

Head back to Rapid City—she can call in to the office, see if anybody had an update. Forty minutes, she can be there. She steers the car along the twisting road.

Ahead is a junction, where a county two-lane leads back up into the hills. Beyond it, a truck stop, RVs and campers huddled to one side in a lot.

She slows the Chevy—the road is flat-looking—she stops.

It's white over. She shakes her head. Bad enough last time, trying to make it up to Mystic.

She scans the sky. Grinds the cigarette in the ashtray. Better to stay on the main routes, head down through Merritt.

Her foot comes off the brake pedal, she gets on the gas.

The tires slip then spin before they grip.

Don't stop again, she tells herself.

She drives past a snow-bound field, on around the curve of a long, wooded hill.

The nose of a vehicle appears suddenly at the exit of a forest road—a big white SUV.

She gets off the gas, swerves into the center of the roadway.

The SUV dives on its brakes.

It skids slowly, stopping at the highway's edge. Light bar and a green stripe along its side. The words, *U.S. PARK RANGER.*

Rimes gives the driver an irritated glance—a park ranger

ought to know better than to hare out from an iced-up turn.

Something about the man's face strikes her—hawk-like, his eyes intense.

She shrugs it off. Eases back on the gas pedal. Steers the car back on-line. Continues south.

⁂

Lauren DeLuca sits on a wooden chair, the marshal's coat down around her waist. Flames from the wood stove light the dim interior of the cabin, her blonde hair is tinged with a sheen of red.

Whicher closes the door to the cookhouse. He studies the side of her face.

She said her head hurt. And her neck.

She holds herself entirely still in the straight-backed chair.

Walking up to the campground from the logging road, he'd been silent with her—unwilling to let her talk.

She was stiff, limping, no doubt in shock. He'd told her to follow Coburn, the ranch owner leading, with his horse, Whicher guarding the track from the low side—listening for any sound of a vehicle, any sign the shooter was coming back.

"So, that was your brother?"

Lauren stares into the stove.

"Down there," Whicher says. "Down that hill."

Her eyes blink, she gives a slight nod.

"The guy with the gun was who?"

He waits a long time for her to speak.

She stares at shifting pieces of burning wood behind the glass door of the stove.

"I don't know," she says, finally.

Whicher crosses the room, leans against a kitchen countertop.

"He said he got on to the train at Denver," Lauren says. "Our train. The same time we did."

Denver.

Twenty-four hours back.

Nobody knew they were catching a train.

They'd ridden a bus from Pueblo, bought tickets for cash. They'd sat in the Union Station waiting room, on high-backed wooden benches. With a handful of other passengers. Nobody knew they were there.

"At McCook," Lauren says, "when the train was stopped—he just appeared. He came up out of nowhere."

She stares into the fire.

The marshal folds his arms, watches her.

"You were outside," she says, "off the train, somewhere. I don't know where."

Whicher thinks of prowling the snow-covered rail yard—waiting for the night crew to clear the line.

Lauren lets out a breath. "He came up to me. He said; 'Tino Coletti sends his regards'..." Her voice trails off.

"Tino Coletti?"

She stares at the rough plank floor. "He said Anthony's whereabouts were known." She looks up. "He told me the place where he was staying."

"This place?"

"He told me the name of a ranch. In South Dakota, the Black Hills."

Whicher glances at the window as wind rattles the shutters against the cabin walls.

"I knew Anthony was on a ranch…" Lauren nods. She wraps her arms around her sides. "He said Coletti's people knew where Anthony was—either I got off the train with him—or they'd have him killed."

The marshal turns toward her.

"He was carrying a gun," Lauren says. "Holding it so no-one would see." She mimes the action, placing her fist close to her chest. "Just here," she says, "inside his jacket."

"You got off the train?"

"I tried to play for time…"

"Describe it," Whicher says.

She brushes back a strand of hair behind her ear. "It was dark. There were no lights. He made me run. We were at the back of some grain towers," she says, "he had his gun out. We went up some street. Then he broke into a house, he stole keys, he stole this car…"

"You waited? Then got in a car with him? Because he said they'd kill your brother?"

She swallows.

"They could kill him anyway…"

Lauren flinches.

"If they wanted," the marshal says, "if they already knew where he was."

"We started to drive." She looks at Whicher. "I realized I was making a big mistake. All I could think of was

Anthony…" The muscles tighten in her face.

"How come you weren't restrained in any way?"

Her eyes come up on his. "What do you mean?"

"Where'd that Nissan come from?"

She searches his face. "A rental car office."

"A rental office?"

"In North Platte," she says. "This morning."

"Y'all drove all that way?" the marshal says. "To North Platte in a stolen car. All of that time, just the two of you? You didn't try to get away?"

A sound is in her throat, muffled. "You don't know these people. You have no idea what they're like."

"You thought you were giving your brother some kind of a chance?" The marshal walks to the window, stares out into the blowing snow.

"I told him I have something," Lauren says.

Whicher watches the tree line, wind battering the limbs of the pine.

"Nobody's told you?" she says. "About me?"

He shoves his hands into his pockets.

"I have money. A lot of money."

"Mob money?"

"I offered him a share."

The marshal steps from the window, crosses the room to the stove. Heat is strong against the side of his face. He takes out the Glock checks it over.

From a twenty-round box of .40 calibre Smith & Wesson, he reloads the rounds fired on the logging road.

"The world I lived in," Lauren says, "that's your life. A

deal. This for that."

He finishes reloading the gun, slips the box into a pocket.

"I told him I'd split the money with him. All of it." She shakes her head. "I was trying to play for time, for God's sake…"

"You tell him you got money?" Whicher says. "What's to stop him doing what he needs to do with you, and taking the money anyway?"

"I have to be there."

He looks at her.

"I have to sign. In person."

He holds her eye a long moment.

"I have to be there at the bank—sign paper. There's no other way you can get that money out."

Chapter 28

Maddie Cook holds the bib coat close to her body—her un-gloved hands stuffed deep inside her pockets. The waterproof boots are holding out, the bottoms of her pants wet and cold.

Walking beneath the pine and oak at the edge of the track, she follows her own wheel marks in the snow. Where the pine is close-grown, there's just enough cover to keep from sinking to her ankles. She can drop back further into the forest—but the trees are dense, progress will be too slow.

She thinks of the man, pointing a gun at her belly. *She could be dead already*, she tells herself.

She's alive. She'll stay alive.

She wonders about the woman. *Time to do the right thing.*

Her foot catches on a tree root—she trips, falls forward, to her knees.

Thrusting her bare hands into the snow, she pushes up as fast as she can. Her clothes can't get wet, she can't afford for that to happen. She stands a second, feels her hands burn with cold—thrusts them in under her coat.

She feels a tear form at the corner of her eye.

No, no.

Fuck you, no.

She won't cry. She won't let that in.

She thinks of the hook-nosed bastard with the gun, thinks of ramming it into his ugly face. Following it up with a baseball bat, like the one in her son's room.

She nods. Alright. Better. She works her painful hands into her pockets, moves forward again.

In her mind's eye she sees the track through the forest, sees its progress, thinks of features along the way, points she remembers. A stack of felled timber in a clearing—power lines to hill-top ranches. She pictures a stand of yellowbark pine that always catches her eye. A gulch of exposed granite, a burn from two years gone.

One foot after another. All she has to do.

Both of her feet are numb from cold—at least they're not wet.

Five more miles.

Five more miles till she reaches the logging road. The descent to the highway is at least another four. It'll be choked with snow, she knows—she tries not to think about the descent.

Her face is sore, pain throbs in both ears. Snow is working its way down her collar, melting down the back of her neck.

The logging road is exposed, wind scoured, it'll be deep in snow.

She glances out from under the canopy of pine.

The blond-haired boy was not much older than her own son. They'll have gotten down to the Rochford Road. They'll have driven down, snow or not, the SUV could get there, four wheel drive and winter tires.

The thought of the warm cab catches her just for a moment. She pushes it away.

She can follow tracks.

All she has to do. Put one foot in front of the other. Not rush, not think of cold and fear, not think of stopping. Not think about the feet she can no longer feel. Or the rawness of every exposed piece of skin.

She can walk the forest, walk the logging road, get down on the highway.

A sickening thought reaches her—will they keep it open? God.

Please, God.

Let it be open.

⚜

On 16 West, dirty snow is piled on the double-wide median. Belaski drives in frozen wheel ruts, staring out through the salt-encrusted windshield.

Off the highway, openings show every mile or so; single-lane roads and tracks into the forest—barely any are marked or posted—private, he guesses, access to ranches and farms.

You'll have to pick one, he tells himself.

He pushes back against the driver seat, flexes out his arms.

Some will lead to unincorporated settlements, to scattered houses.

Behind him, there's no traffic. Nothing moving up ahead on the road.

He lets the SUV slow, the note of the motor dropping. The highway's running north and east, through a wooded valley. A sign ahead reads; *Rockerville 2 — Rapid City 13*

An intersection is coming up, a road crossing. He studies the apron where the side-road meets with the highway. The churn of the plows has left a berm of thick snow. But road crews have cleared the intersecting exit and entrance-way.

He glances in the rear-view, comes off the gas.

He waits until the last moment.

For a split second, he thinks of the kid, Anthony, handcuffed in the trunk.

Nothing's on the road behind him. He sweeps off the highway—not fast, not too slow.

Momentum carries the SUV across the lumps and frozen ridges at the edge of the road.

He glances again in the rear-view. Nobody there to see him turning off.

He steers along a single set of wheel tracks hugging the center of the road.

No sound from Anthony behind the rear seats. *Silent*, Belaski thinks. *Some go silent.*

The wipers flick back and forth on the windshield.

Close to the highway would be best—just far enough, not too far. In Rapid City, he can dump the Park Ranger SUV—he can pick up a vehicle at a rental office, so long as he doesn't have the kid.

He thinks of Lauren DeLuca. She'd be scared for her

brother—maybe she'd already have it figured out.

He strains to pick up on any feature ahead; the road is starting to climb—rising steady, trees taller now, dense, blocking out the light.

He sees another opening—a track into the forest. A green shield on a wooden post shows gold lettering, the outline of a tree.

U S Forest Service.

No vehicle has passed there.

He turns the steering wheel, eases the big Ford down the side track.

The depth of snow is greater, he feels it drag beneath him. Fresh snow is blowing in, showering the hood.

The track follows the contour of the hill, the sky nothing but a dull strip of light between the trees.

Reaching a wide turn, the trail splits into two—one fork disappearing into dark woods, the other climbing.

He pauses. Higher up the hill, between the old-growth pines he can see a clearing—two cabins set back at its rear.

He picks the uphill route, drives the Ford through a bank of snow.

Steering off the track at the clearing, he pulls up by the cabins, stops, opens up the driver's door.

He steps out—the snow is mid-calf.

He wades through to the first cabin. It's padlocked, shuttered windows on two walls.

He checks the second cabin—it's the same as the first.

Crossing back to the Ford, he opens up the rear hatch.

Anthony blinks at him in the glare of light.

"Move your feet." Belaski reaches in to the chainsaw, unhooks the ratchet-strap retainer—frees it. Hoists it out.

Anthony recoils, his eyes go wide.

Belaski unscrews the filler cap on the chainsaw—there's gasoline in the reservoir.

He screws the cap back, flicks the switch to 'on', sets the choke.

He puts a knee on the engine cover. Pulls the starter cord, sharp.

It coughs, dies. He knocks off the choke, pulls again.

Anthony's face is white; "Wait, wait, what're you doing?"

The chainsaw spits into life.

Belaski whips it from the ground, guns it—thick oil spatters the glistening snow.

Chapter 29

In a back office of the federal building in downtown Rapid City, Janice Rimes leans against a metal file-cabinet, staring down into the wide street. Cars and trucks roll slow down St Joseph, the roadway is a river—full of frozen brown slush.

For a moment, she watches the halo of ice and snow swirling around a street lamp. The FBI field office is empty. She presses a knuckle to the double-glazed window, feels the chill against the glass.

So far, she's telephoned the Coburn ranch twice. Nobody's returned from Elk Lake yet, she's left instructions for them to call the minute there's news.

Mathis, from the sheriff's department, has been up there. They'd been surprised to see him, then alarmed, according to the deputy.

She turns from the file-cabinet, thinks of smoking another cigarette. Can't do it, not inside the office. She gnaws on a nail.

She can catch a smoke outside on the building's steps. She opens the office door.

From somewhere along the corridor is the sound of her

boss, Kinawa—the Rapid City senior agent. He's talking fast with somebody—one of the county attorneys, she thinks. She utters a silent curse.

Chicago FBI was lighting up Kinawa's phone. They'd done everything right—that seemed to be Kinawa's main concern; Rapid City had done everything by the book—she could hear him now, down the corridor, using the exact same expression—*by the book,* he was telling the attorney.

Anthony had been offered a choice of locations—he'd wanted the Coburn Ranch. The ranch was pre-approved, in full validation by the state. Rapid City FBI weren't expected to guard him, shadow him. Just keep tabs from a distance, check in, from time to time.

Rimes wraps a hand around the lighter in her pocket, taps the pack of cigarettes. Stepping from the office, she puts her head down, turns for the stairwell.

Her boss calls out, "Agent Rimes…" He breaks off with the attorney. "We need to talk."

Rimes lets go the lighter, takes her hand from out of her pocket.

She takes the few steps back down the corridor.

James Kinawa follows her into the office.

"What now?" she says.

"They don't think we're liable."

"Who don't?"

"Judge Thompson. And Reese Carter, the county attorney." Kinawa pulls at the cuff of his dark suit. Trim at forty, he's strictly vegan, runs ten miles every morning, doesn't drink, doesn't joke. "The WITSEC marshal from

Albuquerque will be here in an hour or so," Kinawa says. "The boss of the program, Inspector McBride."

Janice Rimes looks out of the window, to the skyline over the street. "That's if his plane can even land…"

"They're landing."

"Did you check?"

Kinawa grunts. "You need to drive out to the airport, pick him up."

"Me again?"

"Take a decent car."

⁂

At the head of the column of four riders, Galen Coburn stretches out a lead. The weather and the dark and fatigue are setting in; the temperature dropping, sun disappearing, snow descending despite the canopy overhead.

Will Jacobs at the rear of the group, rides a draft-cross mare, the Springfield rifle slung at his back.

Lauren DeLuca rides her brother's horse—Whicher behind her, his hands and feet numb, despite the boots and gloves.

In the pocket of the woolen hunting coat is the Ruger revolver. The marshal stares ahead at Lauren. A ribbon of white between the trees is the only marker showing the way along the track.

The horses keep their heads down, tread cautiously. The feel of the woods is deep and still, the air weighted with a primal silence.

"We make it back," the marshal says, "we can get out of these hills."

Lauren rocks a little in the saddle as she turns.

"We get to the ranch," Whicher says, "to Coburn's place."

"We need to find Anthony."

"Other people will handle that."

She stares at him through the dim light, swaying slightly with the motion of the horse.

"The sheriff's department," Whicher says, "the FBI."

She turns away again to face forward.

The marshal kicks his horse onward, rides up closer to Lauren on the track. "You have any idea what this guy might do? Where he might go?"

She only stares dead-ahead.

"You were with him when he rented that Nissan—he must've given a name?"

"He wrote it."

"He never said his name out loud?"

"He wrote it on the rental form."

Whicher glances at her. "The clerk didn't say it?"

"Once," Lauren says. "Once, I heard the clerk say it. He took a set of keys from a drawer in the office. He said something like, 'Farndale. Mister Farndale', or 'Farnday.'"

Whicher says the name over in his mind. "The boss of your WITSEC program is flying here."

She turns her face half toward him.

"One of his marshals is dead, he's going to want you moved just as fast we can."

She shakes her head.

"He'll want to know everything that happened."

"Not before we've found Anthony."

"You're a federal witness, you got a legal obligation."

"I have a brother…"

The marshal strains his eyes to see along the path of the track.

Lauren gathers the reins in her hand, stares straight ahead into near-dark.

"Before you disappeared last night," Whicher says, "from the station at McCook—you made a phone call." He looks directly at her. "Who were you calling in that waiting room, Lauren? Who were you talking to back then?"

⁂

Maddie Cook's hands are balled-up in her pockets, her face twisted with pain as she staggers down the logging road.

The fall of snow is relentless; reaching up to her knees. The sky above the trees has turned full dark.

Her son will be waiting.

Her son.

If only she can make it.

In her mind, she conjures an image of him—far from the forest, far from wind and ice and snow.

She thinks of their warm, bright kitchen, sees him padding around in his socks. Eating the pot roast she left for him. A wave of something breaks inside her—longing, a deep, dark sadness. The house might as well be a million miles further, might as well have ceased to exist. Everything was ceasing, everything inside closing down. She wills herself onward, head tilted to the onslaught of wind.

If she can just make one foot follow after the other. If she can just keep on going.

Somewhere along the frozen roads, a path leads through the bleak, blizzard of air. All the way back to her kitchen, to light, to warmth, to her son. She pictures wrapping both arms around him, holding his back—putting her face in close to his neck.

But the sky is deadened, black, filled with swirling snow. The temperature will fall fast, she knows it, though she can't feel it anymore. Too late for that.

She gazes at the dim white track before her, marked only with the ragged forms of trees at either side.

Step after step, she stumbles in the tracks of her own vehicle. Thinks of the young man, the boy in the trunk. She half-closes her eyes.

A rip of fear grips her, inside. *A flashing sensation.*

Is she passing out?

A speck of light—there again, then gone.

She raises her head, sees nothing but the blackened woods, dim ground, snow.

Steadying herself, she takes another step, another. Afraid of losing consciousness.

Light flashes again—in a different place; moving. She feels her breath escape her. Stops.

Specks of light are moving through the tangle of trees—flashing, winking, somewhere down below.

The highway.

People driving on a highway.

People still out; still moving. Cars can still drive.

She takes a breath, feels heat bloom behind her eyes. She sets her shoulder against the oncoming wind, lifts a numb leg, pushes forward, trying not to panic.

The lights are gone.

They were there.

But now they're gone.

Will they be the last?

Chapter 30

Through the glass-front office window, downtown Rapid City is lit up with cars and trucks. Belaski raises a cardboard cup of coffee to his mouth, breathing in a lungful of steam.

At the rental desk, a clerk punches numbers into a keyboard—checks something on a monitor screen. "We have a GMC Yukon, all-wheel-drive…the way the weather is…"

Belaski nods. "That'll be just fine."

"All-wheel-drive and ground clearance," the clerk says.

Belaski turns back to staring out into the evening traffic. Reflected in the window, he sees the clerk read the drivers license—a fake license, in the name of Gary Farndale—it matches the copied credit card, not hard to come by in Belaski's line of work.

"You'll take it for how long, Mister Farndale?"

"A week," Belaski says, not looking round.

"Seven days from today." The clerk's fingers flit across the keyboard, he stares at the monitor screen.

Belaski thinks of Anthony, back in the cabin.

Breaking in had been easy—with the chainsaw; cutting clean through the wooden shutter. He'd left him handcuffed, bound to an iron stove, no way he'd make it out of there.

It'd be cold, though, real cold. Belaski puts the thought from his mind. Of more concern is the stolen parks service Explorer—now abandoned, four blocks south at the back of a mini-mart.

He thinks of the ranger woman—if she made it out of the forest she'd tell law enforcement the message for Lauren DeLuca. She'd have one more thing to think about, Lauren. One more worry, on top of everything else.

"Sir?"

The clerk looks up from behind the counter as Belaski drains the last of the cup of coffee.

"If you'd like to step this way, I'll show you right to your car."

⤜

The cold and the blackness are twin entities, the only things left tangible, existing. Within the cabin, strange creaks break the silence. Things freezing, contracting. Anthony leans his chest against his drawn-up knees, rests his face against the fabric of his ice-fishing pants.

The dark is almost unchanging, now. The coldness inside like a living animal—shaking, trembling—wind the only sound that comes to him. Wind in the nearby trees.

His breathing is slow, he fights the creeping sensation, the shutting down. *Dead already*, he tells himself, if not for the gear he was wearing.

Hunger churns inside, then fades. The thirst is more frightening, his tongue is thick, at times he can barely swallow.

In dream-like moments, light appears. Moonlight breaking through the clouds, he imagines; filtering into the cabin, the outside world. No idea if it's still snowing, or if it's clear.

Snow would be better. Clear skies will mean the temperature in free-fall.

He tries to move his arms, but they're pinned against him.

His wrists are bruised and sore, the handcuffs a kind of torture. The binding to the iron stove is tight against his breathing, against his chest. He thinks of Lauren. At the lake. Did she know, then? She must have known. Why hadn't she warned him, why would she lead a man there?

The questions cycle, unanswered. Breath and energy slip away.

If he can last till dawn, if there's light, maybe he can figure some way out. Useless to think so far ahead, he can't imagine it. Even if he frees himself, he daren't go outside into the cold.

An image comes to him, unbidden—the city of Chicago, Lauren cycling on the lake front trail. Lake Michigan, vast, under a summer sky. Eight years old. Pedaling to keep up.

His golden sister. Big, sure, beautiful.

He leans against his knees, his breathing stopped in his throat.

Why had she betrayed him in the end?

ᛉ

AN AMERICAN BULLET

Light from the brazier fires is visible from the tree line—drums of flickering orange, the figure of a man beside the outline of a barn.

He's silhouetted against a crack of yellow light. The crack widens as the barn door opens.

Coburn shouts something up ahead.

A flashlight clicks on, pale beam moving in the tumbling snow.

Whicher glances across at Lauren, riding beside him.

She stares ahead.

Still she won't talk.

Chapter 31

Inside the log-lined office, Whicher stands shaking in the warmth, his whole body reacting as he grabs the phone from the desk. He fumbles the numbers on the keypad—the phone rings, it picks up.

"Rapid City FBI…"

"I need to speak to Agent Janice Rimes," Whicher says. "I'm with the US Marshals Service."

"James Kinawa," the man at the end of the line answers, "I'm her boss…"

Whicher stares out of the window into black night—a patter of ice crystals tapping against the glass. "Sir, do you know where Agent Rimes is at?"

"She's driving back from the airport. She's with an inspector from the WITSEC program."

The marshal nods to himself. "If you're her boss then you'll know what this all is about? Why I'm calling?"

"Yes, I do."

"The brother of a federal witness has been abducted."

"That's correct…"

"Have y'all had a report of a missing parks service employee?"

"Say again?"

"An officer from the parks service," Whicher says. "A ranger."

No answer.

"Mister Kinawa, I'm up in the hills at a ranch belonging to a Galen Coburn—I have the witness with me. The witness, but not the brother."

At the end of the line, the FBI man is silent.

"You hear me?"

"I heard you, yes."

"I have to get off of this hill before the weather gets any worse than it is. I need to get into Rapid City. But you need to call the parks service, find out if anybody's missing."

"I don't understand…"

"Just call them, find out if it's been reported. Call the sheriff's office, the PD, the state troopers—anybody you need to call—and find out. I'm coming down into Rapid City, right now. I'll be there as fast as I can." The marshal hangs up the phone.

⚔

In the SUV from the law-enforcement pool, Janice Rimes eases out from the intersection.

The man beside her nervously smoothes a short-cut salt and pepper mustache. He watches snow breaking up on the roofs and hoods of cars—slabs sliding off, crashing into the street.

Agent Rimes's cell phone rings—she looks at it in the center well, reads the number off the screen.

The crow's feet around McBride's eyes crinkle. "Go ahead and take it."

Rimes presses on the key to receive.

"Janice?" Her boss, Kinawa's voice.

She puts the cell to her ear.

"We heard from Whicher. He called from the Coburn ranch."

"Do they have Anthony?"

There's a pause before Kinawa replies.

Rimes glances at the inspector in the passenger seat—compact, a lined face, in his early-fifties, hair starting to gray.

She feels a sinking sensation in the pit of her stomach.

"They lost him," Kinawa says. "They lost him, but they have the sister."

"Say again? They what?"

"I don't know how, but they're with the sister. They're coming down here, the marshal's bringing her down. Anthony's been abducted," Kinawa says. "And from what we can tell, a female park ranger is missing…"

⁂

Jerzy Belaski shields the side of his face in the hood of his parka. Hands in his pockets, he heads along the sidewalk, boots sinking into freezing snow.

The federal building in downtown Rapid City is dotted with lit windows. He reaches the end of the block, turns the corner beneath the streetlamps.

Wind slashes at every exposed piece of skin. He hurries the few yards to where the Yukon is parked.

He can just see the federal building. Not much traffic is moving. A city truck pushes snow from a plow at the end of a street.

He opens up the Yukon, climbs in, starts the motor. Cranks heat.

Gone, now, he tells himself, *he would've been gone already.* If it weren't for the storm. He could've been clean gone with both of them—Lauren and the kid.

He thinks of her, pinned inside the crashed Nissan on the logging road. Law enforcement had her, they'd have to move her, now. But travel would be next to impossible.

He stares at the federal building. Lights glare from offices on three of its floors.

They had her, they'd have to move her. But they had to bring her somewhere first, while they figured out what to do, what to do about Anthony.

FBI were protecting the brother in South Dakota, they'd known about it, Coletti'd told him, even before he'd set out. Feds wouldn't want another agency involved.

Whoever was in that building had to come out sometime. He could wait.

Belaski watches the lights in the office windows. He pushes back in the seat.

⁂

Behind the wheel of the ranch truck, Galen Coburn steers along St. Joseph Street, the downtown roads only half-cleared.

From the back seat, Whicher watches snow blow sideways in the gaps between buildings, streetlights veined in the windshield, traced in ice.

Lauren DeLuca holds a hand to the bruising at her neck.

"That's it," the ranch owner says, "that's the place, right over there."

The marshal looks at the office block set back at the side of the thruway.

Coburn signals, turns from St Joseph onto Ninth.

Half a block down he pulls over.

Whicher unhooks his seatbelt, looks out over the sidewalk—no sign of anybody moving, just a few cars parked at the curb.

He takes the cell from the pocket of his coat, dials the number—it answers first time.

"We're here," he says, "we're on Ninth. We're about to come on in."

Lauren fastens the coat around her, puts a hand to the door.

"Wait," the marshal says.

She looks at him.

"Let me get out first." He takes out the Glock.

Coburn shuts off the motor, turns around to look from Whicher to Lauren and back again. "Just what the hell kind of trouble is she in?"

The marshal doesn't answer. He fits a swollen finger through the trigger guard of the semi-automatic. Checks up and down the street.

Opening the door, he feels the push of the wind.

He steps out. Nothing's moving, nothing coming, the

nearest parked vehicles over a hundred yards away. The vehicles are covered in snow, they've been there hours.

He takes a pace into the road.

"All right," he says. "Let's go, let's move out."

⊥

He sees the truck as it rolls in, sees it slow, sees it pull in at the curb. Sees the figure that steps from the rear door—a plaid coat, a Western hat. Belaski recognizes the man in an instant; the man from the train, the man who shot at him—the rider from the hill.

A second man steps out from the driver's side.

Belaski reaches into the footwell of the Yukon, picks the suppressed SIG Sauer off of the floor.

The far-side passenger door opens.

He levels the gun at the inside of the windshield—Lauren DeLuca steps out in line with the barrel.

He holds the gun directly at her—adjusting on instinct, raising the can-like muzzle for the yardage.

He'll take out the Yukon's windshield, but there's no time to stop, to get out, he'll be seen.

Two shots, at least, with a pistol three to kill her? Maybe more?

His finger curls around the trigger—ten pounds pressure on the first pull, down to four on the second and following shots.

He takes a breath, holds it.

⊥

At the top of a set of stairs into the federal building, Janice Rimes has the street door open.

Whicher moves the party of three off the sidewalk, they clip up the wide, brick steps.

Passing inside, into a corridor, Rimes shuts the door behind them.

Whicher knocks snow from his coat, puts away the Glock.

Janice Rimes studies Lauren DeLuca.

Galen Coburn jabs a finger at the FBI agent. "You owe me an explanation, ma'am—you place a minor at my ranch—somebody comes up looking for him with a gun?"

A moustachioed man in a heavy wool coat steps into the corridor. "Inspector McBride," he says. "From the witness security program."

Whicher touches a finger to the brim of his hat.

The ranch owner looks at Rimes. "Who the hell are all these people?"

McBride steps to Lauren. "Are you alright?"

Lauren turns to Janice Rimes—the two women lock eyes. "Are you responsible for my brother?" she says. "I want him found."

At the back of the corridor a man descends the staircase—thin, fast-moving. Japanese-American.

"The sheriff's department have taken a phone call from the hospital," the man says. "It's the park ranger, the woman. Sheriff's office say the hospital have her."

Chapter 32

Car headlights sweep along the crack at the bottom of the drapes in the motel room. Jerzy Belaski lays on the queen-sized bed, TV on—a football game, a night game, Miami—the crowd in T-shirts and jeans.

On the night stand is the SIG, plus his cell. He thinks of calling up Coletti, back in Chicago. Stares at the leather badge-holder on the bed—US Marshals Service—ID in the name of Dale Corrigan.

He could have shot them all—all of them, right there in the street.

Watching Lauren cross the road, he'd been itching—take her out first, then take the big guy in the hat.

But at the federal building, a woman was there on the steps. She had the door open, waiting for them. They'd return fire as soon as he took his first shot. They would've rushed him, come up the street; they could call down every cop in the city. One marshal was dead already, Corrigan. Belaski wouldn't hold back. But the play had to be right—no Hail Marys.

He lets his eye blur on the TV game, mind wandering back to the first night—in Fisherville, with the Amtrak train. Sitting five rows back, he'd watched the pair of them—Lauren and her escort, Corrigan. When the train collided with Jimmy Scardino's car, he'd watched the marshal get up, quickly leave his seat, leave the train.

Belaski'd followed him—nobody else had gotten off.

He'd waited till they were at the head of a car, stepped forward, shot him once in the back of the head. The suppressed gun inaudible above the noise of the train. He'd dragged the man beneath the train hitch, through the pitch dark, the few short yards into the woods.

Nobody'd seen him do it. It was black outside, lights blazing in every car, everybody focused on the collision up at the front.

He'd dragged the marshal into the woods. Took his ID, his badge.

Running back, he'd checked for blood on the ground. What little he'd found he'd kicked over with fresh snow.

By the time people were stepping off the train, getting down from all doors, moving around, a hundred-plus passengers, churning things up, you couldn't see a goddamn trace.

But back onboard, there was no sign of Lauren.

He half-watches a running play repeat in slow-mo on the screen.

From that point on, not finding her there, the whole thing'd been going to shit. Cops turned up, a fire truck, EMTs. He'd gone back in the woods. He'd found Scardino, together they'd dragged the marshal's body in deeper.

They'd made a fast decision, a pressure call; stay on the train if it got re-started.

If Lauren got back on, Scardino could follow in the pickup, the road followed the rail line, they knew it could work.

Belaski'd get her off of the train or shoot her. One of the two. Except that son-of-a-bitch had been there; right there.

Then Millersburg. More bullshit.

A pony-ass town, the middle of no-place.

Trailing them to the forest, to that piece of crap hunting lodge in the woods. The fat cop showing up just one more piece of bullshit bad luck. None of that should ever have happened. What choice had there been but to shoot him?

Belaski sucks in air over his teeth.

A US Marshal. Plus a cop. No coming back from that. He'd be looking at lethal injection.

If ever they got a hold of him he'd probably never make it to any court. They'd have their orders, he tells himself. Shoot on sight.

He nods.

Don't ever give them that chance.

♏

South of downtown, off of 16, the hospital on Cathedral Drive is close to capacity—Whicher watches staff deal with a steady flow of arrivals; falls and accidents from the storm compounding mid-winter illness.

The waiting area is over-heated, too hot, too dry. The

marshal sits with Lauren DeLuca on one side of a low table, Inspector McBride and Agent Janice Rimes seated opposite.

Through a glass panel in the door, the marshal watches an Asian doctor consult with a hospital nurse. The doctor finishes his conversation, runs a hand over the stethoscope at his shirt. He pushes open the door.

Whicher stands.

"You can't all go in," the doctor says.

"I need to see her," the marshal says.

Lauren gets to her feet.

Janice Rimes stares at her. "Sit down."

The doctor holds up two fingers. "Two. A maximum of two, no more. Officer Cook has second stage hypothermia. She's willing to talk—I'll allow it, in the circumstances. But not for long, and not all four of you, she doesn't need the agitation and stress."

Lauren takes a step toward the door.

"I told you to sit down," Agent Rimes says.

"Let 'em go in," the inspector says. "You guard the door, I'll cover the corridor."

"This is a hospital," the doctor says.

Whicher moves forward, "Nothing's going to happen."

He steps through the door, to where a nurse is waiting, Lauren following him in.

The nurse exchanges a look with the doctor. She puts her hand to a second door. "In here," she says.

Maddie Cook is laying in a hospital bed, a drip attached to her arm. Covering her body is a forced-air warming blanket, hooked up to a thermostat and hose.

She lifts her head an inch from the pillow.

The marshal turns to the nurse. "If you wouldn't mind, ma'am?"

The nurse looks at him.

"The conversation here is private."

The nurse steps from the room, closes the door behind her.

Whicher looks at the woman on the bed. Her face is reddened, blotched in places, her eyelids sore, swollen, her lips cracked.

Lauren crosses the room, lays the palm of her hand on the woman's shoulder.

Maddie Cook glances from Lauren to Whicher.

"I was there," the marshal says, "coming down the hill. I was the man on the horse."

Maddie's eyes slide off Whicher's.

"I couldn't just keep on firing…"

Lauren squeezes the woman's shoulder.

"You and a young man were taken hostage," the marshal says.

"My brother," Lauren cuts in.

For a moment, Maddie Cook just lays in the bed breathing shallow. "He put my cuffs on your…brother. We were driving through the woods. He made me stop, made us all get out. I thought he was going to shoot us."

Nobody speaks.

The only sound is the faint hum of blown air in the heating blanket.

"He told your brother to get in the trunk," Maddie says.

She looks at Whicher. "He wanted to know how to get out of the forest…" She stares at the ceiling.

"It's okay," the marshal says.

"They're in my vehicle…"

"Everybody's out looking for it."

"I didn't have much of a choice," the woman says. "I told him the track joined a logging road, then went down onto the highway."

"You think he went that way?" Whicher says. "The way you told him?"

"I could see they did. I followed their tracks."

"There must be all kinds of places in those hills?"

She lets out a breath. "No-one else was up there…"

"Cabins, camps, shacks," he says. "Could they have gone someplace else?"

She lays on the bed, eyes roaming the ceiling. "I saw their tracks go down the hill…" Maddie pauses, shifts her head on the pillow to look at Lauren. "After he made your brother get in the trunk, he made me get out." She swallows.

Lauren lifts a jug of water from a stand by the bed. "Do you need a drink?"

"No." Maddie closes her eyes. Opens them. "He told me the only reason he was letting me live was so that I could give a message. To a Lauren DeLuca. Is that you?"

Lauren nods.

Maddie runs her tongue over cracked lips. "He said—it's time for you to do the right thing."

Whicher looks at the woman.

"That's what he said." Her gaze shifts to the end of the bed.

AN AMERICAN BULLET

Beyond the open blinds on the sixth-floor window, powdered ice and snow swirl in the lit up air. Whicher crosses the room, looks out into an empty lot. "You think this man expected you to find your way out? The storm the way it is…"

"I think he didn't much care."

The doctor re-enters, looks at each of them in turn.

"I'm sorry," Maddie says.

Lauren leans in close, strokes the side of her face. "You did everything you could possibly do."

⋏

Half an hour later at the federal building on St. Joseph Street, Agent Janice Rimes is last into the lobby.

Senior Agent Kinawa leads Whicher, Lauren and Inspector McBride down a corridor to a small office. Janice Rimes pushes the door closed. She brushes by Whicher as she sits.

Kinawa crosses his arms over the front of his suit.

McBride, settling behind the desk, leans forward. "Lauren," he says. "We have to move you."

She doesn't answer.

"Soon as we can, we have to find a way, get you moving—get you far from here."

She gives a half-shake of her head.

"I have to get you to Chicago," the inspector says. "You have to be there in time for the trial."

"Find Anthony," she says.

"The trial starts Monday."

"Then find my brother."

"Anthony is the responsibility of South Dakota FBI," McBride says. "You, on the other hand, are mine."

Lauren's head drops a fraction.

"WITSEC has been protecting you these past months, lives have been on the line. One of my men is dead already—Marshal Dale Corrigan."

She presses her lips together. "My life is on the line, too."

McBride studies her a moment. "We think the people who parked the car across that train line in Fisherville were from Chicago. Police found the body of a man named Jimmy Scardino. Do you know him?"

Lauren shakes her head.

"He pretty much moved in your old circle."

She eyes McBride, now, a hot looking flush in her face.

Kinawa cuts in, "How did people from Chicago know you'd be on that train?"

Whicher raises a finger. "This man who kidnapped Miss DeLuca, and then Anthony—he already knew where Anthony was at." He turns to Lauren. "That right? They knew exactly where Anthony was hiding out."

Kinawa regards the marshal, stone-faced. "What do you mean to say by that?"

"What do you think I mean?"

Janice Rimes turns sideways in her seat. "What're you saying? That our security is compromised?"

"Are y'all saying WITSEC's is?"

"Look," Lauren says, "you don't know these people. They have friends everywhere…"

"You got off a train at McCook," Agent Rimes says. "You're in the middle of Nebraska, scores of people around you, all the other passengers from the train. But this guy manages to get you off, get you out of there." She gives a little snap of her fingers. "Like that."

Kinawa stares intently into Lauren's face.

"Galen Coburn?" Rimes says. "The man who owns that ranch? He says a woman claiming to be Anthony's sister called his ranch this morning. Wanting to know where he was, wanting to speak to him. Was that you?"

Lauren lets out a choked breath. "They knew," she says. "They knew Anthony was at the ranch…"

"How?" Rimes stares at her.

"He'd made phone calls. To Chicago. To some of his friends."

Agent Kinawa looks at Rimes. "Could he have? Could he have called back home?"

Rimes spreads her palms.

"Why co-operate?" Kinawa says.

"To save the life of my brother."

"You called the ranch, had Coburn tell you where Anthony was. Then went out there to get him."

"They were going to give the order to have him killed."

Janice Rimes leans back in her chair, head cocked to one side.

"Unless I cooperated—that was what they said."

"You show up," Rimes says. "And Anthony goes with you, just like that?"

Lauren stares at the edge of the desk, a muscle working

in the side of her jaw. "He knows…"

"He knows what?"

"That when it's time to run he has to *run*. Just run. No second guessing, no second chances."

McBride speaks; "You picked up Anthony, then the three of you drove down the hill."

Lauren nods.

"And the vehicle crashed?"

Agent Rimes winds a black ringlet of hair around her finger.

"The kidnapper escaped with your brother and Officer Cook," McBride says, "from the Parks Service."

"You know something?" Janice Rimes says. "There's a bunch of folk in the Chicago FBI office think you arranged that accident in Fisherville. They think you organized it yourself."

Lauren turns her face to stare at her.

Rimes shrugs.

"*I* organized it?" Lauren says.

"You got off the train at McCook—maybe that was deliberate, too."

Whicher sees the lick of flame building behind Lauren's eyes.

Inspector McBride smoothes his mustache, eyes clouded.

"I got all night, honey," Rimes says.

"What exactly are you accusing me of?"

Whicher leans forward in his seat. "Are we likely to be staying here tonight?" He looks at McBride. "In Rapid City?"

"We can't get anyplace else, till the storm clears."

"Do we know when that all could be?"

Kinawa answers; "The weather radar shows clear air tomorrow. Cold but clear, no snow."

"I want my brother found," Lauren says.

"We're searching for the Ford Explorer," Kinawa says. "All law enforcement units have been alerted."

Inspector McBride shakes his head. "All of this is supposed to be need-to-know only."

"They could be out of state already," Kinawa says. "Fifty miles from the last known sighting, at Elk Lake, and you're into Wyoming."

Rimes nods.

"Head north a hundred miles, you're in Montana."

"We don't know if they're still using that same vehicle," Whicher says.

"Nothing's reported stolen or taken," Kinawa says. "If anybody reports anything, we'll move right on it."

Lauren stares across the desk at the inspector. "Find my brother. You have to find Anthony."

"How about if they're still in the woods?" Whicher says. "Somewhere up in all of those hills?"

"You think we can search out in this?" Kinawa answers.

The marshal stands. "We need someplace to stay. I haven't slept in two nights, neither has she." He angles his head toward Lauren.

"You need to be moving again in the morning," McBride says.

"Do we have to stay here? In a goddamn office?"

"You find Anthony," Lauren says, "or you can forget about me as a witness. I'll retract every statement. I'll refuse to testify."

The three men study Lauren, in silence.

"Then they'll send you to a federal prison, honey," Agent Rimes says. "You'll go away for the rest of your life."

Chapter 33

The downtown hotel is from the nineteen-thirties—eleven floors, a view right across the snow-bound city.

The top floor is sealed off, no public access—uniform officers at the elevator door. The hotel is the highest building on the street, nobody can snipe down into it. Inspector McBride has a master room off the main corridor, Whicher occupying another, larger suite of rooms with Lauren DeLuca.

Food is coming. Hot food. The marshal thinks of eating, thinks of taking a shower, of laying on a bed for the first time in forty-eight hours. He thinks of sleep.

Opening up a set of sliding glass doors, he steps outside onto a roof-top terrace. Snow is frozen hard, the air clear, stinging.

Out beyond the city, on a ridge of hills, lights wink red on a distant antenna. Down the wide boulevard, the bars and restaurants are open, it's not yet late.

Skaters glide on an ice-rink in the main square. He thinks of Lauren—if she refused to co-operate, she'd be taken to

Chicago in wrist and leg irons. She'd be put on trial herself. He watches the ice-skaters moving in and out of the lights, circling, spinning. A crowd mills among the food stands. The faint beat of music drifts in the air.

Kinawa offered Rimes as a substitute for Whicher, as close protection. Inspector McBride refused—Lauren was his witness, till they delivered her to the Chicago court.

The marshal swirls a shot of whiskey in a cut-glass tumbler.

At the rear of the terrace, he hears movement.

Lauren steps out.

"Don't come up to the front," he says.

"Why not?"

"Just don't."

The sound of a passing vehicle rises from the street.

Whicher peers over the terrace rail—a city truck salting the road.

He turns back, looks at her.

Her hair is loose, freshly washed from a long bath. Fine blond strands move in the light breeze.

"You can be protected, Lauren."

She stands, in his coat, head angled, her features poised.

"But you can't back out."

She tilts her head at the night sky, at stars arching into an ink black dark.

"You cut a deal with the DA in Chicago. They'll have enough to nail you, you'll be in a prison the rest of your life. You'll never get out."

She stares across the tops of the buildings.

The marshal leans against the rail. He lets out a breath that mists around him.

"Find my brother."

"I'm not here to find your brother."

She closes her eyes.

Whicher studies her. He takes a pull at the whiskey, cut-glass rim like a sliver of ice against his lips. "For what it's worth," he says, "I don't think he's hurt."

She half-turns toward him.

"You're still alive, Lauren. How come? How come you're standing here right now?"

Confusion is in her face. He takes another sip of whiskey.

"If somebody wanted you dead, you'd be dead already. At Fisherville. It didn't happen. Then again at McCook."

Her blue eyes roam his face. She shudders.

Whicher pulls the brim of the Resistol an inch lower on his head.

He turns to look down on the street below, at the city truck rumbling on to an intersection.

"We were followed from Denver to McCook," he says. "They could have hit you anywhere along the route. If the Chicago mob wanted you dead before the trial, they'd have done it. Same goes for Anthony…"

She takes a step forward, closer to him.

"It happens," he says. "Happens every day of the week." He takes out the Ruger revolver from the shoulder-holster. "Somebody pulls a gun, shoots somebody. Why not just do it up at the lake?" He moves off the rail, stands facing her in the dark. "They want you alive. You and Anthony both." He stares at the side of the gun, balancing it, puts it back in the holster.

She steps close to him, closes her hand around his, on the glass. Stands silent. Eyes holding him.

He lets her roll the tumbler from his grip.

She takes a sip. "Can we go inside?"

She settles the glass against her chest, takes a pace back, slides open the glazed door.

Warm air rushes from the room.

He takes off the Resistol, follows her to the threshold of the suite.

At a polished oak cabinet, she takes a second tumbler, pours another measure.

"How come folk all have so many doubts about you, Lauren?"

She holds up the glass.

"I want to know what there is to know."

"Then you'd better come in. And close the door."

⊥

The room is well heated, the lighting dimmed low. Lauren settles in a vintage, rolled-arm couch.

Whicher crosses to the cabinet, takes the bottle, pours himself another measure.

A knock sounds at the door.

The marshal sets down the glass. "Who is it?"

"Room service," a muffled voice. "Sir, we have your food order."

The marshal takes out the Ruger, thumbs back the hammer.

Lauren watches as he opens the door.

In the small, outer lobby, a uniformed city cop stands with a night clerk. The clerk wheels a food trolley into the room. It's loaded with covered dishes, crisp table-linen. He sets out the food on an antique dresser. "Omelettes, French Toast, buttermilk pancakes. Two turkey clubs. And coffee in the flask."

Whicher holsters the revolver. "Much obliged."

The clerk dips his head, steps out of the suite.

The marshal locks the door behind him. "They're never going to let it go," he says.

Lauren pushes up from the couch.

"What is it you have that they all want?"

She takes a plate of pancakes and French Toast. Holds out her glass.

"You want coffee?"

"No."

Whicher fills her glass from the bottle of whiskey, knocks back his own drink, sets it down. He takes an omelette and a sandwich. Sits with her at a table, away from the window.

"There's money all over," she says.

The marshal cuts into the omelette, takes a forkful. "Money you set up?"

"Hidden accounts."

"But you have to be there? To get it out."

She nods, slices into a piece of French Toast.

"Answer me this," he says. "If you could disappear—if you could walk out of this room right now, with Anthony, tonight; the two of you? You have enough for that? Do you have enough hidden away?"

"Maybe I wouldn't." She takes a bite of the food.

He eyes her.

"Maybe I wouldn't leave the room."

The marshal looks away. "The only reason they have for wanting y'all alive is the money you stole. The money you took for you and Anthony."

She studies on him.

"They want it all back," he says. "Before they're finished with you. They get a hold of you, they'll go to work on you. On both of you. Till one of you breaks."

She picks the whiskey tumbler off the dining table, holds it in front of her, hands very still.

He sees the yellow-white skin tight over her knuckles.

"I asked you who you were calling from that waiting room in McCook?"

She nods. "I have a single living grandparent."

"Who?"

"My mom's mom."

"Why call her?"

"Because I'm scared."

The marshal lets the words sit. Continues eating.

Lauren takes a sip of her drink. "She lives on the west coast. She moved to San Francisco years ago, we keep in touch the best we can."

"And now you're scared?"

Her eyes cut away. "I'm supposed to testify against an organized crime family. I'm in a federal trial. I'm scared to die, I'm scared for Anthony."

"What did you say to her. To your grandmother?"

"I told her…that I love her. And that I don't know what's going to happen anymore."

⊥

Whicher stands under the steaming-hot shower in the bathroom, water pummeling his skin. Eyes closed, he lets the rush of sound fill his ears. Heat oozes, spreading, untying knots of muscle down his spine, stripping away the lack of sleep, the days in the grip of cold.

Officer Cook's duty vehicle. If they couldn't find it, couldn't find Anthony, couldn't find the man who took Lauren from the train—she'd retract.

She'd take the fall, so long as Anthony was alive; retract her evidence to protect her brother.

Time to do the right thing.

But if Anthony was dead, who knew what she'd do? He lets the warm water run into his mouth, after the whiskey.

For now she was holding out. One phone call could change all that. Losing Anthony would be like losing her own child—a twenty-year age gap between the two of them, she must have practically raised him.

He takes a last lungful of heated steam. Turns off the water, grabs a freshly laundered towel.

Stepping out onto the heated floor in the bathroom, he dries himself, runs a hand over his clean-shaved face.

He steps into his suit pants, fastens the Glock around his waist. Listens for a moment—no sound is coming from the apartment.

He towels his hair, grabs his shirt, carries it out of the bathroom.

She's in the lounge, standing—cut-glass tumbler trailing from her hand.

He glances around the room. "Everything alright?"

Her eyes come up on his.

The suite is silent, only a faint hum reaches him, heated air moving in the ventilator ducts.

She takes a step in the turned-down lights. Another. He sees the rise and fall at her throat.

Inches from him, breathing shallow, her body arcs, he feels her mouth on his, her arms around his neck.

⋏

She pulls him to her, tongue cold from the ice in her glass, mouth warm, traced with alcohol.

Her hands are on his back, fingers pressing into his still-wet skin.

He holds her, feels a surge—a charge run the length of his body.

Mouth on hers, he breathes. Lets his mind run blank. Puts his hands to either side of her face.

He pulls away.

Her eyes swim in his, suffused with heat.

He rests his forehead against hers, separating, inch by inch. Thinks of trying to speak, trying to tell her something.

She presses her face into his shoulder.

He stares at the cold, glass pane of window across the room—blackness beyond it, her body soft against him, molded. A sinking feeling sweeping over him. His eyes blur as he pushes his face against the side of her head. He tries to think of nothing. *Nothing.* Not loneliness, not the emptiness. The well of silent hours.

He closes his eyes. "I don't know what to tell you." His voice hoarse, thick in his throat.

"Just hold me."

He strokes her hair.

She's still now, finally. Tears wet on his bare skin. Breathing over and over.

"Just hold me, just hold me."

Chapter 34

In the orange glow of sunrise, Lars Karsten turns the corner of the city block, light streaking between the buildings, blading the snow-bound streets.

The mini-mart opens at eight. Supplies are coming in, a load of groceries if the truck can make it through.

He guesses the delivery should be there mid-morning, with the weather. He thinks of the pressed cardboard and packaging waste at the back of the store. Left out in the snow the night before, it'd need moving before the truck made it in.

He skirts a low wall, reaches the rear lot—entirely covered now, amorphous, under a blanket of white.

A panel van from a neighboring store is in there. Plus one other vehicle that wasn't there when they closed for the night. It's tucked in behind the panel van, right up next to the dumpsters. The recycling cage is behind it, the vehicle's blocking the damn thing in.

Karsten crosses the lot, stares at it—an SUV, covered in a foot of snow.

AN AMERICAN BULLET

He runs the edge of a boot along the frozen white powder masking the license plate. Walking down the side of the vehicle, he clears snow from the door.

In decals, he can read the words *U.S. PARK RANGER*.

He steps back. Reaches in his coat for his cell.

⁂

Five minutes pass before the police cruiser pulls in at the curb.

A uniformed officer is at the wheel—a woman beside him, dressed in plain clothes.

The woman climbs out first, takes a pack of cigarettes from the pocket of her mountain fleece jacket. She sparks one up. "You the manager?"

"Lars Karsten."

"It was you that called?"

The man nods. "Yes, I did."

The woman sticks the cigarette in the side of her mouth, runs a hand through her black, ringlet hair.

She steps forward.

The uniform cop gets out of the car, walks around the hood.

"I just got here," Karsten says. "I need to open up the store." He jabs a thumb over his shoulder at the mini-mart. "That thing's blocking access to the loading bay."

"Right," the woman says.

"I took a look, saw it belonged to the Parks Service."

"You think it's been here all night?" The woman eyes the piled up snow on the ground.

"I guess," says Karsten.

"My name is Agent Rimes. With the city FBI. Did you touch anything?"

"Excuse me?"

"Did you touch the vehicle yet?"

"All I did was move a little snow off of it."

"Good," she says.

"What the heck's it doing here?" Karsten says.

The woman nods. "That's mainly the question."

⋏

Belaski tries the rear tail-lift of the Yukon—it's frozen. He can't get it to shift.

He clears snow from the back windshield, peers inside, into the trunk space; big enough.

He steps away, crosses back to the motel, opens up the room. Nothing is left in there from the night before. He checks a last time, feels for the gun in his coat pocket, the suppressor unscrewed.

He pulls the door closed. Fastens the parka up to his neck.

Walking out, he leaves the lot, leaves the motel forecourt.

The snow-packed sidewalk follows the highway straight out of town—its surface a mix of salt and snow and dirt, but vehicles are on it, moving slow.

Breakfast, he thinks. Plenty of it. The diner from last night would be open now. He leans into a whipsaw wind.

A half hour is all it should take. Half an hour, eat breakfast, walk across the road, check the outdoor store he'd seen.

AN AMERICAN BULLET

Anthony would be alright. Wrapped up in all that winter fishing gear. He was out of the wind and snow in that shack; sheltered. If he couldn't get to Lauren, he was going to need him.

🙵

All the doors of the vehicle are open; nothing locked. Agent Rimes stands by the park ranger Explorer in the mini-mart lot, feet numb, in spite of the Timberland boots.

A basic visual examination has shown nothing to indicate a body. No sign an injured person has been transported. She's wearing black, nitrile gloves, she's made a minimum of contact. Nothing untoward is inside the vehicle—no blood, no mud, no debris from the ground.

A streak of brass colored light paints the snow in the lot. She leaves the doors open, steps away.

Turning toward the uniform cop, she calls over, "Officer Stevens?"

"Ma'am?"

"I need the radio."

The store manager, Karsten, watches her.

"Go right ahead," Stevens says.

She squints into the sun, trudges to the cruiser. Yanks open the door, slides in.

Shaking off the cold, she shudders, lifts the radio transmitter from the console.

🙵

On the top floor of the hotel downtown, Inspector McBride talks fast into his cell. It's the third call inside of ten minutes;

Whicher glances at him from his place at the picture window.

McBride nods as he listens, then clicks off the call. "Agent Rimes is going to wait down there," he says. "Kinawa's calling in a crime scene technician."

"At least we know they're not in that vehicle," the marshal says.

The inspector stands, walks to the window. "Maybe," he says. He peers out into the middle distance. "I have to say it's not looking real promising."

Whicher follows the man's gaze to the wooded hills beyond the city skyline. "No need to search the forests," the marshal says. "Or check on outlying properties."

"Kinawa thinks they'll be out of state, long gone."

"He thinks they have another vehicle?"

"No reports have come in," McBride answers. "Nothing's been stolen. They're going to check with the rental car places." The inspector shrugs.

"If that park ranger SUV was dumped downtown," Whicher says, "they could be in here now. Right here in Rapid City."

McBride eyes the younger marshal. "There's no sign of blood. He could've just shot the poor son of a bitch and dumped him someplace in the woods."

"He shoots Anthony, then drives to Rapid City?"

"Nobody would find the body, maybe not for months." McBride scowls. "If he's in here somewhere, we'd have no way of knowing about it." He runs a knuckle over the salt and pepper mustache. "If the guy drove into town, he could have picked up a phone, called for somebody to come get him. Kind of thing he might do if he was alone by that point…"

Whicher thinks about it. "You're saying you think he killed him?"

"Explain it, if he didn't."

The marshal turns to stare out over the rooftops, steam rising from flue vents and chimney stacks at the sides of buildings. "If the guy came to kill Lauren and Anthony, how come he waited this long?"

The inspector doesn't answer.

Whicher shifts his focus onto a neighboring roof, thick with snow. "The guy's boss wants them back alive."

McBride steps away from the window, takes his coat from the back of a chair. "The only thing I know is I want you gone today," the inspector says. "There's a break in the weather, I want you out of here, you and Lauren, headed east. We get her back to Chicago. In time for the trial. After that, she's the DA's problem."

"She's going to retract."

"You believe that?"

Whicher squares his hat. "Right now? I think she'd take back every word."

Chapter 35

Behind the wheel of the Crown Vic, Officer Stevens steers inside the ruts on the two-lane thruway.

Janice Rimes smokes a cigarette out the open window, box stores and strip malls whumping by.

Stevens lifts a finger off the wheel. "Right there," he says.

The FBI agent checks the glass-front strip of a rental car unit, the vehicles outside cleared from snow, from the caked-on salt of anything that's been on the road.

"Nearest rental place," Officer Stevens says.

Rimes takes a final draw on the cigarette, sails the butt end out of the window.

The Crown Vic slows, signals. Makes the turns at an intersection.

Stevens parks in the rental car lot, he shuts off the motor, hustles out.

Rimes zips up her coat. Stevens puts on his cap. They cross the lot to the big glass door of the office—push it open, wipe their feet on the mat.

A black woman is seated behind a counter. She's wearing

a roll neck sweater, her hair in braids.

Janice Rimes takes out her badge-holder, shows it. "FBI, ma'am."

The woman looks from one to the other of them.

"I need to ask you about rentals, any vehicles rented here yesterday. Or today."

"Did you get a look out there?" the woman says. "At the weather out there?"

"Excuse me?"

"Nobody's looking to rent right now."

"You didn't rent any cars?"

"The way things have been, with the storm, no. Yesterday, not a thing," the woman says. "Nothing so far today, but I guess it's early."

The patrol officer spreads his hands.

"I can check with the other office," the woman says.

"Where would that be?"

"It's just up the road—the corner of Mount Rushmore and Columbus."

Stevens shoots an eyebrow. "It's not that far."

"I guess," Rimes says. She nods at the woman.

The clerk picks up the phone.

The FBI agent watches traffic rolling into Rapid City, workers headed in, a string of big rigs headed out.

The woman behind the counter talks into the receiver.

Rimes turns to Officer Stevens. "How about crime scene? You think they're going to dig up anything?"

"If something's in there…"

The room goes quiet.

"Downtown rented a vehicle last night," the clerk says. "Nothing today."

The FBI agent leans in closer to the counter.

"A GMC Yukon," the woman says. "Yesterday evening around six—the guy wanted it for a week."

Rimes looks at Stevens.

"An Illinois state drivers license," the clerk says.

"Tell them," says Rimes, "tell them we're on our way…"

⁕

Streaks of sunlight hang in the dark interior of the cabin—Anthony's mind drifts, his eyes half closing.

He listens to the sound of his own breathing, feels the dryness of his throat, his swollen tongue.

Yards distant, just beyond the log-walls, beyond the ache inside his head, the world is moving. He tries to sit up—all his muscles are cramped, limbs like weights, his tail bone numb.

The wood stove at his back is drilled onto a concrete plinth, he can feel the bolt-heads with his fingers, feel the rough dry surface of the cement.

Waves come and go, waves of emotion. All night, feelings—fear mixed with anger, a bottomless well of despair. Sometimes, a strange kind of calm. Now it must be morning. But cold and dark still haunt him.

He tries to move sideways against the stove, to find a moment's respite.

His back is screaming, rippling with pain. Hunger comes and goes, sometimes intense, sometimes nothing. But the muscle spasms leave him fighting for breath.

All night he's had to think—to think of getting out, trying to free his arms, to rip his hands from the cuffs. Over and over, trying to dig his heels into a plank floor. Scrabbling, pushing with all his strength. Useless against the bolted-down stove.

The thirst is constant, now, racking every living atom.

He thinks of her again, tries to conjure her; the mother he can't remember, that he never really knew. A beautiful stranger. Gone, gone before she was even there. No memory, nothing save for photographs, a single video, her wedding day.

So many times he's tried to reach inside, to feel, to touch something—something he must have known, or felt, as a child. Two-years old, looking up into her eyes. If only he could summon it. Commune somehow.

He lets the thought sit. Somewhere out there—just in front of his eyes.

Maybe we'll be together. In just a short while. Together again.

He thinks of his mother's eyes—sapphire blue in the faded photographs. A shade that only existed in one other person; Lauren. He thinks of his father—was he with her now, with their mother? Free from everything, the misery that'd seemed to stalk him—the drink-pity-rage.

He'd never gotten over it—that's what everybody told him. Everybody in the family; if only he could have seen his father—known him, before.

He screws his eyes tight, tries to push away the thought. Thinks instead of Lauren—helpless, trapped in the front seat of the crashed Nissan.

His head slumps an inch between his shoulders. Why did the little they'd had get ripped away? He thinks of the day, a few short months back—police arriving at the yard, and men in suits. All of them, rushing up to the house. He'd stood in disbelief as they arrested her.

Lauren.

They'd put her in cuffs, they'd taken her away.

Nothing made any sense in the weeks that followed. Nothing anybody told him, nothing anybody said.

They were putting her on trial. All the evidence they had, they'd convict her, that's all they'd say. Organized crime. She'd be in prison the rest of her life.

He stopped going to school.

Stopped getting out of bed.

Stopped everything, those weeks. Till finally, one day, a black car rolled up to the house.

A man and a woman. From the FBI, they said. Lauren was going to cut a deal, they told him. She'd be cutting a plea.

But everything they'd ever known would be different.

New names, new lives, in new locations.

His eye follows a speck of dust floating in a shaft of cold sunlight. He wills it to stay, to float just as it is, suspended. Only cling on in the narrow band of light.

Chapter 36

In the car park beneath the federal building, Whicher waits with Lauren DeLuca—wind blowing powdered ice off the hardened-steel security bars.

A hum of street traffic echoes in the bare, concrete space.

He looks at Lauren. "They'll be here soon."

The morning air is chilled, now. Un-warmed by any sun.

She gives back the barest nod.

The marshal stares out into the street at vapor pooling above the slow-moving traffic. Feels only distance between them.

The hood of a police department cruiser pulls in view.

It swings in from the road, lines up on the entrance ramp, beyond the locked gate.

Whicher stares at its windshield, the sky reflected, etched wide.

"Tell them," he says. "Even if you don't mean it." He glances at Lauren. "You're a federal witness. Tell them you'll cooperate."

A uniformed driver reaches out of the cruiser window—he presses on a switch by the gate.

Lauren angles her head toward the car about to enter their space. Finally, she turns. Her eyes search the marshal's face.

The walls echo to the clack of a lock, the gate slides back on its runners.

The cruiser rolls in, parks.

Janice Rimes steps out.

The rear door snaps open—Inspector McBride.

The uniformed driver exits the vehicle—a patrolman, he glances at the blonde woman huddled in an oversize coat.

"Alright, Stevens," Rimes says, "you can go, now."

The officer strides across to the door for the main building, punches in an access code. Steps inside.

Rimes takes out a pack of cigarettes. Shakes one out. Lights it up.

Inspector McBride turns to Lauren. "We think it's him." He pulls a Xeroxed copy of a drivers license from his pocket.

Lauren stares at it.

"In the name of Gary Farndale," McBride says. "It's fake. But a good one."

She nods. "That's him."

"He picked the vehicle up at six o'clock last night," Rimes says. "At a car rental. Downtown. On Mount Rushmore and Columbus."

"Alone?" Whicher says.

Rimes's eyes are hooded. She takes a hit off the cigarette, blows a thin stream of smoke out of the side of her mouth. "The clerk said he was alone."

In the chilled space of the car lot, the only sound is traffic rumbling.

"Fifteen hours," Rimes says, "that vehicle could be anywhere."

"All law enforcement units have been notified," McBride says.

Janice Rimes clamps the cigarette to her mouth. "The parks service SUV was clean."

Whicher studies the FBI agent's face, unwilling to voice the question in his mind.

"There was nothing in it," she says, "nothing to see."

"You mean there was no trace of my brother?" Lauren says.

Rimes doesn't answer. She looks away at the floor. "They could tell he was in there," she says, finally. "But nothing more."

Inspector McBride turns to Whicher. "You need to get going. I have to leave. I have a flight back to Albuquerque, y'all need to be on the flight for Minneapolis, at noon. There's a half-hour layover, the connecting flight to Chicago should get y'all in around four-thirty. Agent Rimes will drive you to the airport."

Whicher nods.

Lauren only stares across the car park space.

Janice Rimes walks to the cruiser, opens up the front passenger door, reaches in. She takes out a set of nylon flexi-cuffs. "Hold out your hands," she says to Lauren. "I'm getting you across the city, to the airport." She looks at Whicher. "What you do with your witness after that is up to you."

"You get to O'Hare," McBride says, "Chicago FBI will take charge. It's their case, Lauren's their witness, our responsibility ends."

"Put out your hands," Rimes says. "Palms together."

Lauren stares straight ahead.

Agent Rimes takes a hold of her arms, fits the double-loops of white plastic around her wrists, pulls the ends of the straps through the zip-locks. "You have to cut these off," she says, to Whicher. "I'll let you have another set in case a bathroom break is unavoidable. You cut them off, wait outside the door. Put them back on right after."

The marshal fixes her with a look. "I know how to transport a person."

"Safety first," Rimes says.

"Agent Rimes will accompany you to the airport," the inspector says. "She'll drive you, see you to the gate."

"We'll take my car," Rimes moves toward an unmarked Jeep Liberty parked two spaces along from the cruiser. "It's my own private car," she says, "nobody can clock it for a law enforcement vehicle."

Whicher places a hand in the small of Lauren's back.

The FBI agent looks at him. "You're armed and ready? Right?"

⁂

Guns are lined floor-to-ceiling on the back wall at the outdoor supply. Belaski rests his full gut against the counter edge. *Assault rifle*, he thinks. Assault rifle could be good.

The breakfast from the diner sits like lead inside his stomach. He eyes an M16, an AR15. Spots the Heckler and Koch. If numbers started stacking up against him, an assault rifle would give him weight of fire. But better not to let that happen, better just to pick up the brother, get out someplace safe; Anthony would buy Lauren's silence. The further he could get from law enforcement, the better.

The store clerk is looking at him. "Sir?"

He pushes off the counter.

"Can I help you?"

"I need some handgun ammunition."

"Alright-y."

"9mm, hollow-point."

"Did you have a brand preference in mind, sir?"

"Nope."

"Well, we have a range on sale…" The clerk turns, taps a finger along the stacked boxes on the shelf behind him. "9mm, hundred-fifteen grain."

"I'll take a couple hundred," Belaski says. "Long as I'm here."

The clerk pulls down four fifty-round boxes.

Belaski eyes a saw-tooth hunting knife displayed beneath a section of glass in the counter top. "I could use a decent knife."

"That's a carbon-steel, military grade survival knife, sir."

"Looks neat."

"Finished in zinc phosphate. You got something needs cutting, that'll cut it."

"Break one out for me."

The clerk stacks the boxes of bullets, searches in the drawers beneath the counter. He takes out a brand-new, packaged knife. Takes it from the sheath, lays it on the counter top. "It comes with the ribbed leather handle on a five-inch blade." He flicks a finger against it.

"Bag it for me."

"Yes, sir. Will that be everything? I just need to see a driver's license on the ammo."

Belaski shrugs, takes out the license. "I got to pick up some other things in the store. Sleeping bag, a tarp, maybe."

"Yes, sir—Mister Farndale. Over on aisle ten you got your camping equipment. You have a good day, now. Looks like the snow is set to break."

Belaski looks at him. "They're saying that?"

"Yes, sir. Clear air moving in."

Belaski takes the knife and the boxes of bullets. Walks around the store, finds a rolled sleeping bag, pre-packed. He takes one. Moves along the aisle till he finds the tarps.

Up at the check-out, a cashier bags everything, Belaski pays the man in used bills.

He heads out, walks in snow at the side of Highway 16.

Cars and trucks are moving steady in both directions, now. Stores open, workers out with shovels, everybody in layers. *The kid would be cold.*

Back at the motel, he can pick up the Yukon—take off out of Rapid City, go pick him up. Take him, keep him alive. Half an hour he can be out of town, down the highway. He can get off in the woods, find the Forest Service road.

He stumbles along toward the cold horizon. Screws up his face at a new thought—*how about if the kid was dead?*

⅄

The sheriff's deputy coming on shift—Deputy Quinlan—rides 16 south, straight out of town.

AN AMERICAN BULLET

The shift is going to be a long one; two storm-disrupted days to make good, starting with a warrant to serve—non-payment of child support on a guy out in Hill City.

After that, there's a statement to take—a report of a vandalized vehicle, acid-attack.

Leaving the sheriff's office, somebody handed him a slip of paper—details on a vehicle, a stop-on-sight.

State-wide alert. Something serious, Quinlan figures.

He slows in traffic, approaching an intersection.

Alongside the highway is a run-down motel.

Quinlan glances into the forecourt. Sees a GMC Yukon parked in one of the bays.

His eye rests on it a moment.

The vehicle is thick with snow, no visible plate. He tells himself he ought to check it out—even if it's most likely nothing.

He hits the blinker. Waits for the stop light to turn.

Somewhere in his coat is the slip of paper. He searches for it, patting down pockets, trying to remember where it went.

The overhead lights flick to green.

Quinlan makes the turn, steers into the entrance-way of the motel lot.

He parks the cruiser. Searches in his jacket again. The slip of paper is crushed in the bottom of a pocket, beneath a glove.

He takes it out. Checks it.

The vehicle is side-on to him, a GMC Yukon.

It's the right year, right color. He unhooks the seat belt, pops the door.

Stepping out into the snow-covered lot he sees no-one. Nothing moving. He scans the motel, notes the couple of other vehicles also parked.

Along the front of the building, drapes are closed in three of the rooms.

He walks across to the rear of the Yukon. Squats. Brushes a forearm over the mound of snow.

He straightens at the tail hatch of the big SUV—looks from one motel room to another. Sees an office, a reception lobby. Watches for a moment. Stalks back to the cruiser.

Reaching in for the radio, he presses down on the button to send. "Dispatch?"

A static hiss.

"This is Deputy Quinlan."

"Dispatch, go ahead."

"I'm out on Highway 16—just south of the Indiana turn. At the White Fox Motel. The stop-order on the GMC Yukon? I got it right here. I'm standing looking at it."

Chapter 37

The clover-leaf for 44 to the airport is a mile out. Janice Rimes keeps the Jeep humming, Whicher in the rear, Lauren beside him in white nylon cuffs.

The sun hangs low in the sky—Rimes sprays washer-fluid onto the windshield trying to clear the salt coming up off the road.

A call comes in on the hands-free speakerphone clipped to the sun-visor of the Jeep. She presses to answer it.

A male voice; "Yeah, this is Stevens, calling."

"Officer Stevens?"

"From this morning. I was going to call if anything came in on that GMC Yukon..."

"Sure," Rimes says. "Go ahead."

"The sheriff's office has been notified of a sighting," he says. "Vehicle reported stationary—located Highway 16, south. Near to the Indiana Street intersection."

She flicks off the windshield wipers.

"Where?" Whicher says.

Rimes ignores him.

"It's in a motel parking lot," Officer Stevens says. "The White Fox Motel. One unit in attendance, back up pending."

"Any sign of a driver?"

"Nothing on any driver," Stevens says. "The message just came in. I heard it, I thought to call…"

Rimes stares ahead at the road.

"So, you want to do anything about it?"

"No," she says. "Not right now, I can't. I'll check on it later. I'll call back. But thanks. I appreciate it."

"Not a problem." Stevens clicks off the call.

"Indiana Street?" Whicher says. "Where's that?"

"Five, six miles…"

"We have to go there," Lauren cuts in.

The marshal looks at her.

"I have to know," Lauren says, her face animated. "I have to know if my brother is there."

"You're getting on a plane," Rimes tells her.

"I have to know if he's alive…"

"Law enforcement will see to it."

Whicher shifts his gaze to the traffic out of the windshield—feels Lauren's eyes on the side of his face.

"It's hours till the flight leaves," she says.

Rimes shakes her head. "I don't care if it is."

"If the car's been found at a motel, if they're there, if Anthony's there, I want to know, I need to be there, to see."

"I'm getting you to the airport. You're getting on that flight."

"You're responsible," Lauren says.

Rimes turns her face to the side.

"You lost my brother—Anthony was yours to protect."

Rimes straightens at the wheel. "Save it." She steers along the highway.

"If anybody wanted to know," Lauren says, "you'd think it would be you. You were supposed to keep him safe."

The FBI agent looks at Whicher in the rear-view mirror. The marshal sees the question in her face.

⁂

Deputy Quinlan stares down the rear side of the building at the single-floor motel. A row of rooms, no doors, just windows. Ten yards of dead ground to the perimeter. Pristine snow.

A six-feet high fence runs around the back, an evergreen hedge beyond it. Dense but not impossible to get through. There'll be cover to the rear, if they need it.

In a service unit at the near-end of the row, a woman in her fifties leans from the doorway. "There's nothing else out here."

The deputy holds up a finger to his lips.

She looks at him through outsize glasses. "I didn't see anybody," the woman whispers. "Not this morning."

Quinlan retraces his steps back.

"Folk get up, they'll come on in the breakfast bar," the woman says. "They need to give me the room number, before they can eat."

"Alright, ma'am." The deputy steps by her, through the door to a utility room. He squeezes by a cleaning cart. The woman follows into a corridor.

"My husband booked 'em in last night," she says, "I wasn't here."

"It reads 'single occupant' on the booking form," Quinlan says.

"Yes, sir. But there could be more than one person in there. It's not unknown for folk to lie."

The deputy keeps on walking through the deserted breakfast room.

"If their vehicle's still in the lot, they're probably asleep," the woman says. "The drapes are closed, it's not real late. They got the room till ten, before they need to be out."

Quinlan cuts through the entrance lobby to the main reception area—he ducks inside the office, stares through the big, plate window, out onto the motel lot.

"I've been running this place nine years," the woman says. "The most part, folks ain't much trouble. They'll check in late, get up early, get the free breakfast, hit the road. If they're still here around this time, it's probably 'cause they're asleep."

The deputy looks at her. "You got occupancy in four of the other rooms?"

"Yes, sir. Three retired couples. One single female."

"Can you call them?"

"Sure. The rooms have phones…"

Quinlan stares out of the window at his cruiser. If he can move it, block the exit—he'll make one less route for anybody to get away.

"I want you to stay inside right now," he says. "But I'll need you to get out real soon, you and all the other guests."

"Who do you think is in there?"

The deputy shakes his head. "Call through to the guests, one by one. Don't get 'em alarmed, ask 'em to come to reception, keep it quiet. Try to get 'em all out. More units are on their way, but we need to be careful." He un-clips the strap holding his semi-automatic pistol in its holster.

"Oh," the woman says. "Well, do I start calling now?"

The deputy steps back into the lobby. "Start with the older couples."

He pushes open the main door, leads with the gun.

⊥

Highway 16 runs a straight line to the south—stores and businesses scattered at either side of the roadway. Janice Rimes pulls onto the edge of a supermarket lot. "The next intersection is Indiana."

Whicher sits forward in his seat, studies the scene ahead.

"You get out here, you can walk," Rimes says.

The marshal cracks the door on the Jeep.

"The motel is going to be somewhere right after the intersection." Rimes turns, stares at Lauren. "The two of us stay right here."

"If anything happens," Whicher says, "y'all get moving."

The FBI agent looks at him.

"Get out of here," he says, "head for the airport. I'll meet you there. I'll find a unit, I'll get a ride."

"If Anthony's here, I want to see him," Lauren says.

"Don't push it," Rimes says. "Your brother has a direct connection with the case, that's the only reason we're doing this."

"We wouldn't be doing it at all, if you'd done your job…"

"In five minutes," Whicher says, "we need to be gone."

Lauren leans back into her seat.

"I'm going to head down," Whicher says, "take a look. Find out what's happening, that's it."

"Find Anthony. If you want me to testify…"

Rimes turns to face forward—she stares through the windshield, puffs out her cheeks.

"That's my price…" Lauren says.

"Go," Rimes says. "Damn it. Go, if we're doing this."

"Five minutes," the marshal says. "Five minutes and we're gone."

⁂

Whicher squares his hat, pushes wide the door. He steps out into the cold, hard, wind.

Moving fast along the sidewalk, he listens for the tell-tale pitch of sirens.

Traffic is rolling steady on the highway, residential roads lead east-west—to clapboard houses, stone-built properties.

Across the road is a gas station, a pizza joint nearside.

He crosses at the intersection, walks two more blocks by a carpet mart.

At the end of a line of trees, a sign is sticking up into the air—he sees the words written on it; *White Fox*.

Beyond the trees is a motel, a brand new GMC Yukon parked out in the lot.

Four more vehicles are in there, three together in a row, another off to the side.

A sheriff's cruiser is blocking the exitway.

Reception for the motel is at the near-end.

The rooms extend out from reception—in a single story, the marshal guesses around twenty, all in.

The nose of a second sheriff's cruiser is just visible by a hedge in back.

Whicher searches inside his coat, locates the Marshals Service badge and ID.

Despite the cold, he leaves the coat open. The Glock at his hip is just inches from his hand.

He stops short on the sidewalk.

A door is open at the rear of reception—a group of folk standing in a service-alley. White haired couples standing close to one another, a woman gesturing to them with her hands.

Whicher keeps on walking. At the end of the lot he makes a turn to where the first of the cruisers is parked.

Two sheriff's deputies are by the second cruiser, in back of the hedge.

Whicher holds out the badge and ID. "US Marshal—with the Rapid City FBI office."

The older deputy studies him, round faced. "Marshal?"

"Working with Agent Rimes," Whicher says. "On a witness protection case. We got somebody missing, we think they could be inside."

The younger of the two deputies steps forward, his hair cut high and tight. "Dispatch said to hold, they're sending the SWAT team."

"How long?"

"They're mobile, they'll be here in less than five."

"Y'all get everybody out?"

"We think," the older deputy says. "The owner's coming down, we got his wife in back of reception with all the guests. She reckons everybody's accounted for. But one of the rooms, the drapes are closed, the key's not where it's supposed to be…"

"How's that?"

"There's an outside chance the husband took a late deal—for cash. According to the wife. It could just be the room needed cleaning, the guy forgot to put the key back in place."

"Y'all tried calling?"

"We called, there's no answer. I'm guessing we're clear—but we want to be a hundred per cent."

⼈

At the edge of the supermarket lot, Jerzy Belaski sees the waiting vehicle. It's stationary with its motor running—vapor pooling, curling around the pipe.

A waiting vehicle.

Motor running.

Check inside, clock the people inside.

Always. Make sure. Evaluate the threat.

He studies the Jeep Liberty—metallic-gray finish, no markings, a South Dakota plate.

Something about it makes him slow to a stop.

He moves the store bag from under his right arm to under his left.

Standing on the sidewalk, he buys another moment—adjusts the bag beneath his arm.

Taking in the Jeep from out of the corner of his eye, a sound comes to him through the clear air—a motor, gunning, revving high.

Accelerating.

He turns a fraction, to see the highway.

An SUV is driving fast, cutting in and out of the flow of cars.

County Sheriff's Department.

No siren. But the flashers are popping on and off.

Belaski feels his mouth dry.

Somebody must have seen it—seen the Yukon.

Cars are peeling left and right, making way for the SUV.

He puts a hand in his pocket, closes it around the butt of the SIG.

Check first, he tells himself, go closer—make sure.

He walks forward, eying the Jeep.

Sitting inside is a blonde woman.

He stops. Angles his head and neck.

Heart pumping, he slips the gun to the edge of his coat pocket. Takes another half-step.

Lauren DeLuca is sitting in back. She's on the right-hand side of the vehicle.

A dark-haired woman is behind the wheel, the seat behind her empty.

Belaski scans the street, as if about to go across.

He grabs the handle of the rear door, rips it open.

Lauren's head snaps sideways.

The woman in front jerks, "Hey, what the hell…"

Belaski jumps in behind her, grabs her hair—points the gun in her eye.

Lauren recoils—he sees the nylon zip-ties at her wrists.

"Drive," Belaski says.

The black-haired woman blinks at him.

He tilts her head straight, throws his arm forward, releasing his grip.

Her head snaps down toward the wheel.

He grabs his bag from the sidewalk, slams the door.

Silence.

Just breathing.

"*Drive*," he shouts.

The woman steadies, braces her shoulders.

"Come on. Do it…"

She reaches down to the shifter.

Moves out of park, releases the brake.

⊥

Whicher stands in back of the motel reception, by the service-alley—he can just see three men getting out of the newly-arrived SWAT vehicle.

The motel guests are huddled in the wind—the woman at the head of the group staring up at him on the sidewalk.

He holds out the badge. "Ma'am?"

"My husband's on his way up…"

"I need to move you and everybody else—all these folk here. There's a gas station back up the road." He points north in the direction of the intersection.

AN AMERICAN BULLET

In the motel lot, the SWAT men are already dressed in tactical gear—the two regular deputies fastening on kevlar vests.

The woman moves out of the alley. "They got to wait on my husband," she says. "There's a room unaccounted for…"

The marshal jabs his arm up the road. "We need to go, now." He stares at the drapes of the room, still closed. "Lead everybody to the gas station," he tells the woman.

"What about you?"

"I got the rear."

She steps onto the sidewalk, starts up the road, waving everybody on.

Three older couples tread careful over frozen snow, the last guest, a younger woman, follows them out.

Whicher stays rooted, watching till the group has moved clear.

Ten yards. Fifteen.

At the far end of the lot, the buzz-cut deputy tracks behind the building, going in behind the hedge.

The SWAT team maneuvers—one man crawling on his hands and knees below the line of the windows.

Whicher looks back up the road to the group now hurrying up the sidewalk.

His hands are starting to go numb, he can't shoot if he can't feel them. He shoves them into his pockets, he can see the gas station—the sign for the pizza joint across the street.

Wind is raking his eyes, making them water. He peers farther along the highway, along the lines of piled snow.

The road is long and straight. Half a mile before any curve.

A surge of alarm breaks inside him.

He can't see it.

He can't see Rimes with the Jeep.

Chapter 38

The road out through the subdivision exits back onto Highway 16. Belaski guesses it around a mile from the motel.

The woman at the wheel eases the Jeep into the southbound lane. The surface of the highway is a mess of grit and salt—clear in its center, snow piled at either side.

Traffic's moving—Belaski glances at the speed dial; approaching forty-five miles an hour.

Lauren DeLuca sits as far as she can get from him in the rear of the Jeep, pressed up against the door.

He turns, stares at her a moment.

She glares back. Refuses to look away.

He breaks off, turns to the driver. "You a cop?"

"FBI."

"Where's my brother?" Lauren says. Her voice cold, flat.

Belaski glances at her. The back at the driver. "What's your name?"

"Rimes."

He smells the scent of shampoo in her black, ringlet hair. "Just Rimes?"

"Agent Rimes."

Belaski nods. "What're you doing with Ms. DeLuca, here, Rimes?"

The woman holds the speed of the Jeep steady. She doesn't reply.

"FBI?" Belaski says. "So, are you local? Or out of Chicago?"

"Rapid City."

"Right," he says. "The country cousins."

Lauren speaks; "Where's Anthony?"

Belaski half turns. He lets the muzzle of the SIG drop—to point at her belly. "How about we go get him? One thing," he says. "Either one of you tries something, you need to know there's not another living soul knows where Anthony is."

Beyond Lauren, out of the window, the land is flat, white with snow, a line of hills at the horizon. The Jeep speeds by a clapboard chapel, its low spire stark against the sky.

"Nobody knows where he's at," Belaski says. "Except for me."

Lauren's eyes burn him.

"I'm guessing he's not in that great of a shape," Belaski says.

Rimes speaks over her shoulder. "Why would that be?"

The highway is climbing, now, the Jeep cresting a small hill. To the south is a dark line, approaching forest.

"He'll be close to freezing to death," Belaski says. He keeps his gun arm low, below the line of the window. A diner catches his eye at the side of the road, a sign out in front of it; *Cowboy Pancakes—99 cents*. "He needs somebody

AN AMERICAN BULLET

to get to him real fast…"

Rimes shakes her head. "You have any idea what you're doing? Kidnapping a federal officer. Every cop in the state will come looking for you."

Belaski touches her cheek with the cold steel muzzle of the gun. "Then, you better hope they don't find us."

⋏

Running down the sidewalk in the churned-up snow, Whicher rips his cell from his pocket.

Down at the motel, a SWAT team officer holds a cut-down shotgun by the door of the suspect room. He shouts across the lot; "Clear. It's clear…"

Whicher stops, presses the key to call, clamps the cell to his ear.

There's no answer from Rimes—she's not picking up.

He holds out the Marshals Service badge, sprints to the nearest sheriff's department cruiser.

Running from the back of the motel building, the older deputy stares at him.

"I need your radio—right now."

Chapter 39

Belaski studies the surface of the Forest Service road; no new tracks in the snow.

He stares past Lauren at the ground fronting the cabins—unchanged since he left it.

"Pull in over there," he says.

The woman, Rimes, slows—she steers the Jeep into the clearing between the trees.

The last few miles she hasn't spoken; since he took her cell and threw it out onto the highway.

The cabins are undisturbed—the woods dark, deserted. "Alright," Belaski tells her. "Cut the engine."

She puts it into park, shuts off the motor.

He jumps out, steps level with the driver window, points the gun. *Some got the urge to talk*, he thinks, to sound off. More were like her. Silent, calculating.

Rimes's face is frozen, a rigid mask.

He opens up her door. "Get the hell out."

Eyes on him, she unhooks her seat-belt, slides out, stands in the snow.

"Lauren," Belaski says. "You want to help your brother? Get your ass out here."

He hears the rear door of the Jeep click open.

"Up in that cabin," he says.

Lauren gets out, steps forward, wading into the snow, her wrists still zip-tied together.

Belaski flicks the muzzle of the gun at Rimes. "Get on up there."

"*Anthony…*" Lauren calls.

"Shut your damn mouth," Belaski snaps.

Lauren claws at the edge of the cabin door, jamming her fingernails into a gap in the frame.

Belaski steps up, grabs the door, yanks it open. He levels the gun at Agent Rimes. "You're going to carry him out. You and her together." He pushes her inside.

The air in the cabin feels frozen, an ice house. On the plank floor, Anthony is slumped in his ropes, his back against the iron stove in the center of the room.

Lauren drops to her knees, reaches out, lifts her brother's head from his chest.

"You sick fuck," Rimes says. "You left him here? You left him out here all night?"

Belaski twists his mouth, drives the butt of the gun into the FBI agent's face.

Rimes staggers, falls backward into a pine table. She hits the floor, head cracking against the hard, bare boards.

Anthony looks up, blinking—his face gray, hands locked in the park ranger's steel cuffs.

Belaski steps to Rimes—she's not moving, her eyes are

closed. He pulls the big survival knife from his pocket, unsheathes it, moves across the cabin, behind the stove.

He squats. Puts the serrated top-edge of the blade against Anthony's ropes. Sawing back and forth, he slices through the fibers.

Anthony gives out a groaning sound.

Lauren leans in. "Alright. It's alright. Hold on. We'll get you out of here…"

Belaski watches Rimes, works the knife back and forth, pulling, twisting. The rope comes free.

Lauren stands, gets her hands on her brother's ice-fishing jacket, pulling in the folds of fabric, closing her fingers into a grip.

Anthony shifts his legs, moves his torso. He falls to one side.

"Come on," Lauren says.

Belaski steps around the stove, puts away the knife, the gun still out.

He reaches down, grabs Anthony, lifts him.

Lauren ducks a shoulder beneath her brother's arm.

He draws his legs beneath him—stands, unsteady.

Belaski lets go, walks to Rimes, still laid out on her back.

He kicks her in the kneecap. No wince, no reaction—no sign of pain in her face. "Get him outside," he says to Lauren. "Get him out in the Jeep."

Lauren staggers with her brother, hands slipping on his jacket.

Belaski reaches down to Rimes, holds the gun at the FBI agent's midriff.

He pulls at the bottom edge of her fleece jacket. Beneath it, fixed to the belt of her pants is a Glock 23 in a nylon holster. He takes it, sticks it into a pocket, pops the stud on her leather cuff-holder. He takes out the cuffs. Removes the key from the lock.

He crosses the cabin, steps out after Lauren and Anthony into the glare of light.

The smell of the forest is sharp in the air.

Lauren and her brother limp toward the side of the Jeep.

"Open up the rear," Belaski says.

Lauren stares back at him. "What? What for?"

"Just do it. He'll be fine." He steps from the cabin door, jogs to the driver's side of the vehicle. Rips the keys from the ignition.

Lauren's eyes drill him.

"I'll finish this," Belaski says, "then we haul."

He raises the gun an inch, strides back to the cabin.

"*Wait*," Lauren calls out.

Belaski steps through the open door, enters the room, crosses to Rimes, laid out flat.

He levels the gun at her head.

"*Wait*," Lauren calls behind him, at the door. "Jesus Christ, *wait*. Don't do that."

Chapter 40

The unmarked Crown Vic draws level with the White Fox Motel.

Whicher sees Kinawa behind the wheel.

The FBI agent spots him, brakes hard, pulls the car over into the lot.

The SWAT team have cleared the building. Quinlan, the sheriff's deputy, is taking a statement from the motel owner—nobody's reported seeing the renter of the room except for him.

The marshal watches Kinawa step from the Crown Vic. Through the open door of the cruiser is the sound of radio chatter—one transmission following the next.

The driver of the Yukon was booked in under the name of Gary Farndale—alone, nobody else accompanying him. No sign Anthony was ever there.

At the edge of the lot, the SWAT team stand stripped of vests and helmets, their body-armor stowed back in the trunk of their unit. Two of the team are pacing, smoking cigarettes. The handful of motel guests shelter in a room at the end of the building, the younger sheriff's deputy taking statements.

AN AMERICAN BULLET

Nobody can raise Janice Rimes.

There's no response from her cell.

Kinawa's eyes are sunken as he steps across the frozen lot.

Whicher bunches his shoulders, tries to huddle some heat back into his body.

"Two Jeep sightings," Kinawa says, raising his hand, holding up two fingers.

Whicher takes off the Resistol hat—ice cold air clings to his scalp.

"One vehicle sighted near the state line with Nebraska," Kinawa says. "The other, east of the city here, off the interstate—near the Air Force base."

"They get either one of 'em stopped?"

"The interstate sighting looks like an airman—right vehicle, wrong plate," Kinawa says. "The other sighting was from Highway Patrol. A trooper down in Lakota County thinks he saw a Jeep headed south."

"He couldn't confirm?"

"He was driving north—a median and a barrier between him and the south-bound lane. He found a gap, got turned around, but by the time he did it, the vehicle was gone."

The marshal looks at him.

Kinawa's face is grim. "He went down the southern stretch, couldn't see the vehicle, couldn't catch it up. But it's a country road, there'll be all kinds of places to turn off."

Whicher sets the hat back in place.

The FBI man stares at the motel. "It's an hour south."

"Y'all had no other sightings?"

Kinawa shakes his head.

The marshal listens to the garbled stream on the radio. "You think we were followed?" he says. "This morning? You think there could've been some way…"

"You were off-air," Kinawa says, "in an unmarked vehicle."

"Y'all call the phone company?"

"It takes time for them to pinpoint a cell."

The marshal nods. "Why take the Jeep? Why head for Nebraska?"

"Dammit, why didn't you just go straight out to the airport?"

Whicher eyes the FBI man. He points a finger at the motel. "The guy was in here; we had an even shot."

"Kidnapping a federal officer plus witness is our best-case-scenario, now," Kinawa says. "Worst case—might be double homicide."

The marshal lets out a long breath. "They were parked well back up the road in the Jeep, I told Agent Rimes to take off if anything happened."

"Janice Rimes doesn't disappear," Kinawa says.

Whicher scans the snow-blown area around the motel.

The FBI man walks back to the Crown Vic. He gets in the vehicle, slumps behind the wheel.

The marshal checks his watch, thinks of Inspector McBride—he'd be in flight, now, half way back to New Mexico. What to tell him? He stares back up the street toward the intersection and the gas station. He can just make out the lot of the supermarket where the Jeep had been parked.

Glancing across at Kinawa, he sees the FBI agent leaning forward in the driver's seat. His mouth is open as he listens to his radio.

Whicher steps toward him.

"Unit in contact," Kinawa calls out. "Nebraska State Patrol reporting a sighting—north of Redwood…"

"Where the hell is that?"

"Just across the state line."

"We need to get a message to them," Whicher says.

"The sheriff's office has been asked to field units."

"We don't know who's in that vehicle, there could be two innocent women in there," the marshal says. "They need to know to hold fire."

Kinawa starts up the motor. "Nobody's going to be backing off."

Chapter 41

In the rear-view mirror, the cruiser is a speck—Belaski checks his speed on the dash—pushing seventy on the county road, snow and ice and grit slipping to wet melt in the morning sun.

He eases his foot a fraction from the gas; the risk of crashing out too strong, he only needs to pull away.

Ahead, to the east, block shapes stand proud of the white horizon—rooftops, outlying buildings—the edge of a town.

The shock of seeing a State Patrol trooper is fading. He'd spotted the vehicle, an Interceptor, coming toward him; the officer behind the wheel seeming to look in as he passed.

He'd kept on going; the trooper keeping the same course in his rear-view.

Town.

Town could be a good thing.

He could drive in, switch it up. He checks the rear-view. Still the small, dark speck.

Lauren in back is half twisted around—looking over the rear seat-rest into the trunk space. Looking in at her brother.

AN AMERICAN BULLET

Belaski flexes his hands on the wheel, focuses on the road ahead—the churn of snow, fence lines, phone poles—threads across the bleak, plains land.

The first cop, still on the highway, back in South Dakota, he'd spotted him a quarter-mile off. Light-bar sticking up above the median. He'd found the first place to turn off, worked a way on south.

He could do it again.

He checks the cruiser—just a dot, now.

Posted signs on the county road show two state highways coming up ahead.

He eyes the outlines of buildings, bigger now. He could head into town, wait a spell.

He looks up in the mirror, catches Lauren, eyes fixed on him.

She turns her head away.

He could just shoot her?

Why not?

Just shoot her and be done.

Her and her brother—the two of them, put a bullet in both of their skulls. Photograph it with his cell, send a picture to Coletti. No star witness anymore, no conviction. Maybe not even any trial.

The town looks big enough, he could head in, lay up, get the hell out of sight.

He could shoot them both and ditch the Jeep. A lone man on foot, he could disappear, call for help, get a ride out.

He could do it, if not for Jimmy.

If not for Jimmy Scardino's death.

Bring them back alive, both of them, and everything might be forgiven.

Belaski checks for the Interceptor in his rear-view. Barely visible as he steers toward the town.

⁂

Wind is rattling down Main, relentless—straight off the miles of empty prairie. Sheriff Colton leaves his office, a brick two-story—right across from the town's old movie theater.

He struggles with his sheepskin coat, trying to put it on, trying to run at the same time.

Fifty yards up, across the main east-west highway, the lot of the police department holds one parked cruiser, plus a single SUV.

Colton runs as best he can along the snow-bound sidewalk.

He crosses the highway—dodging light traffic—trucks and rigs hauling loads, trying to catch the break in the weather.

The sheriff eyes the cluster of radio antenna on the roof of the Redwood PD. Last inbound message was via Nebraska State Patrol; a unit west of town in visual contact with a felony kidnap suspect. Vehicle likely containing hostages. *Hostages—in the plural.*

Two of Colton's deputies are out in the south of the county. At full strength they're only four men strong. The missing deputies are an hour and more away.

The sheriff crosses the police department lot, the flag in front of the building snapping in the wind.

He reaches the main entrance—pushes open the double door.

Inside, the tall, rangy figure of Chief Eriksson is at the front counter, talking into a cell. He spots the sheriff, raises a hand.

Colton takes off his hat.

Eriksson closes out the call. "I'm radioing all units…"

"How many y'all have on duty?"

"Six," Eriksson says. "Lieutenant Ganley's out of town, I have a sergeant and four patrol officers. The rest are off-duty, I'm trying to reach them now."

"Did the State Patrol call again?"

Chief Eriksson nods. "They're sending units up from Troop E—in Scottsbluff."

"That's an hour and a half," the sheriff says.

"South Dakota units have crossed into state—they can't find the vehicle."

The two men stand looking at one another.

"Now it's our problem…" Colton says.

Chief Eriksson rubs at the sleeve of his dress-shirt. "According to the last message, there's an FBI agent on the way down here, with a US Marshal in tow."

"Who the hell is in that suspect car?"

From the open door of a side-office, the voice of a dispatcher carries into the lobby.

"State Patrol reckon a federal witness," the chief says. "A witness under protection."

"I heard missing federal officer," Sheriff Colton says.

Eriksson scowls. "If we're going to stop the vehicle, we

need to cover the highway, plus the main axis routes north-south."

"No way we can get all the county roads covered off."

"Some of those roads must be snowed up."

"I can hold a line to the south," the sheriff says. "I'll put my two deputies out there, if you can get units to the east?"

The female dispatcher puts her head out of the office. "Chief?"

Eriksson spins around.

"State Patrol say their unit has lost contact with the vehicle. But they think it could be headed in here."

"Into town?" the chief says.

The dispatcher nods, eyebrows raised, still listening in on a head-set.

The sheriff peels back the sheepskin coat. He tightens his gun belt. "No way they're blowing in and out of here."

⋏

Concrete stands rise above the trees to Belaski's left; the main stands of a football stadium. He sees the tower of a college campus, surrounded by mid-rise buildings, more trees.

Loop-roads run in and out of the subdivision, he works the Jeep along a service road, a mall development to the north, commercial units, used car lots.

The cruiser's nowhere. Gone from sight.

He watches Lauren DeLuca in the rear-view, muttering something to her brother, in back.

"Quit yapping," Belaski says.

Lauren cranes her head around, catches his eye in the rear-view. "He needs to take a pee."

"Too bad. Let him piss in his pants."

He sees the flash of anger that passes behind her eyes.

"You get off?" she says. "Making people's lives a fucking misery?"

Belaski cracks a flat laugh. "You sell out on people, this is what you get." He shakes his head. "Cause and effect."

Ahead is a junction, a fork in the road—one branch leading toward housing, toward the town, the other leading east, back out to open country. He steers the Jeep up the left fork, headed for town. Checks again in the rear-view, looking back along the road.

Something—something is in the rear-view mirror.

The road curves, passes a disused barn, blocking off the view.

He sits up straighter.

Thinks of slowing, trying to get another look.

The road straightens, he presses down harder on the gas.

A side-street is coming up ahead. He steers left, accelerating into it.

Fifty yards up is another road—he makes a right. He's running parallel with the original street. He makes another right, at the next junction. A semi is parked at the curb, he cruises up behind it in the Jeep.

He pulls in, brakes to a stop.

He can just see past the semi to the road he turned in from.

From the back seat Lauren says, "What're you doing?"

The nose of a police cruiser rolls into view.

It passes the end of the lane.

Then it's gone.

Belaski holds the image of it, burned onto his retina.

One man.

Driving slow.

If it was following him—why drive slow?

⊥

Angled across the main road into town is a black and white police car. Kinawa slows the unmarked Crown Vic, Whicher eyes the two men approaching from the side of the road.

The taller of the two is in police uniform. The second man wears a sheepskin overcoat and Cutter hat.

Kinawa rolls the window. The warmth inside the car vanishes. "FBI," Kinawa says. "Your patrolman sent us through from the highway."

"Chief Eriksson," the tall man says—he gestures at the man in the sheepskin coat. "And this is Sheriff Colton."

"You the fellers out of Rapid City?" the sheriff says.

Whicher opens up the door, steps out. "Name's Whicher. With the WITSEC program."

A gust of wind scours snow into the air as Chief Eriksson studies him.

"What's the latest y'all have?" the marshal says.

"State Patrol had a unit following at distance," the sheriff answers. "They think they've come in here."

"They think?"

"Orders were to hold off, not get up real close. I have

deputies covering the county roads to the south, and southeast."

"Police units are in position," Chief Eriksson says. "North and west, at all the main strategic points."

"The trooper unit was pretty sure they came in here," the sheriff says.

Whicher scans the wide open streets of the town. "You're looking to lock the place down?"

Colton pulls on the brim of his hat. "If they came in, they're not going back out."

Eriksson looks from Whicher to Kinawa. "We'll find them, if they're in here."

"How close did the Patrol unit get?" Kinawa says. "Could they see into the vehicle?"

Eriksson twists his mouth. "They're saying caucasian male driving, plus a woman in back, possible blonde. We've got the main exits covered off. We'll see them if they try to leave."

The sheriff looks at Kinawa. "Who are these people?"

The FBI agent steps around to the rear of the Crown Vic, pops the trunk. "That Jeep Liberty is the personal vehicle of one of my agents. We can't get hold of her."

"Meaning what?"

Kinawa leans in, lifts out a bullet-proof vest marked *FBI*. "Meaning we can't raise her, she's not answering any calls, we don't know where she is."

"Who's the blonde female?" Chief Eriksson says.

"A federal witness," Whicher answers.

"My agent was with her," Kinawa says, "providing escort."

The sheriff scratches at his ear.

"We think the guy driving is most likely a mob guy," Kinawa says, "out of Chicago." He puts the vest on over his suit jacket, reaches in the trunk, takes out spare magazines for a .40 caliber Glock.

"The last contact we had was five minutes ago," Eriksson says. "Down near Fulton College." He gestures south, over his shoulder.

Kinawa buckles up the straps on the Kevlar vest. "Whoever this guy is, he's bad news. He could do anything if he's crazy enough to shoot an FBI agent…"

"We don't know he shot her," Whicher says.

"Is there any reason to believe she's in that vehicle?"

Chief Eriksson and Sheriff Colton exchange glances.

"The guy's not doing any more damage," Kinawa looks at Whicher.

"I've got a town to protect," Eriksson says, "plus the safety of my officers. I won't have them taking any risks…"

"We sure as hell don't want them getting out of here," the sheriff says. "The rest of the county is farm land, ranches—last thing we want is anybody holing up."

Kinawa takes out the Glock 23, checks it over. "We take no chances."

Whicher looks at each of the three men in turn. "We need these people alive."

Chapter 42

Behind the Redwood Police Department black and white, a State Patrol Interceptor pulls across the lot of a taco restaurant. It crosses the twin-lane carriageway, slowing to a stop behind the cruiser.

Chief Eriksson places a Xeroxed map onto a clipboard.

Kinawa steps forward. "I'm calling federal jurisdiction on this."

The trooper shuts off the motor on the Interceptor, gets out.

"You want to take this over?" Sheriff Colton says.

Whicher stares at the side of Kinawa's face.

"FBI has the legal jurisdiction."

"Marshals Service ranks with that," Whicher says.

Kinawa cuts him a look. "You have a problem?"

"With you running this? I sure as hell do. Y'all have the experience?"

"What do you have?"

"Command of an army scout platoon, USMS training on manhunts, outside of swarm tactics…"

"We're not going to be swarming anything," the chief says, "with the handful of officers we have."

The state trooper approaches the group, Campaign hat between his hands.

"Any chance of Scottsbluff sending up a helicopter?" the chief says.

"Too cold," the trooper answers. "Icing conditions."

The marshal glances at the sky.

Chief Eriksson holds a marker pen over the map attached to the clipboard—he rings four circles around the town. "This is where we have units—officers at each of these locales."

Kinawa studies the map fluttering in the wind.

"Lot of holes," Whicher says. "We need a stronger perimeter."

"We were asked to intercept," Eriksson says, "not contain."

"We don't have enough units to ring the place," Sheriff Colton adds.

"State Patrol can have units here in under an hour," the trooper says. "With specialized teams, SWAT, K-9."

"There's no time for that." Whicher turns to Sheriff Colton. "Y'all have two deputies to the south?"

Colton points to two spots on the map. "We've got 'em there looking for the vehicle—they'll be in place to pursue."

"Suspect was last seen south of town," the trooper says, "traveling north."

Whicher scans the town beyond the main drag. "How big is this place?"

Chief Eriksson answers; "We're about five thousand.

Plus the college population. But classes are out, it's holiday season."

Kinawa digs a thumb behind the bullet-proof vest. "What would you advise, marshal?"

"Assuming they're in here…"

"I saw them turn in," the trooper says.

Whicher looks at the sheriff and the chief, each in turn. "If they drove in here, what're the odds of them driving right back out? Is it all plains land, is it flat, what is it?"

"It's a mix," the chief answers. "There are woods to the south east…"

"My deputies are there," the sheriff says, "they'd spot 'em."

The marshal studies on the map. He looks at the trooper. "If you sit on the highway east of town, you can move up or down from there."

"Yessir."

"I've got more officers arriving at the PD," Eriksson says. "We need to seal off the southern end of town, stop people from going in."

"They may not even be down there," Whicher says. "We get the perimeter established, we'll go in and find out." The marshal looks at Kinawa. "You and me," he says, "in that…" He points at the unmarked Crown Vic.

Kinawa nods.

"Sheriff," Whicher says, "I need for you to ride shotgun on the flank. Take a man with you. Use a marked vehicle."

"How about Sergeant Hooper?" the sheriff says.

Eriksson inclines his head. "Hoop can do it. Hoop's a

good man." He turns to Whicher. "Listen, I want to ride along with you. This is my town, my ass."

"Chief, you need to be in the center, in contact with all units—you know this place, you can make the right call if we flush 'em out. If we find 'em, if we set 'em up, they're going to run, they ain't about to stand and fight."

"You don't know that," Kinawa says.

Whicher adjusts the Ruger in the shoulder-holster, pats down the Glock. "The gaps in the net are too big. We flush 'em out, we have to move faster than they move. Otherwise, they're gone."

⋏

A Honda sedan is coming up the street behind him—parked at the curb, Belaski watches through narrowed eyes.

He takes the SIG from the side pocket in the Jeep's door, places it in his lap, the muzzle pointed at the steering column.

The Honda fills his rear-view, he hears the motor on it, its tires deadened by the snow.

It's not slowing.

It's rolling on, drawing level.

He eyes the driver as it passes by—a white-haired senior behind the wheel.

The car keeps on till it reaches the intersection ahead—it makes a left, toward the town.

The cruiser was following.

It had to have been following.

They couldn't reach Rimes, they'd want the vehicle, want it found, want it stopped.

AN AMERICAN BULLET

He lifts his foot from the brake pedal.

Lauren DeLuca's staring at him in the rear-view mirror—electric-blue eyes boring into his.

He yanks down on the wheel, pushes on the gas.

The Jeep slews sideways, tires gripping as he steers out into the street.

Above the snowed-up roofs of the houses, the outline of the college tower stands alone against the sky. Belaski drives to the intersection, makes a left, following after the Honda.

He powers the Jeep up the road to the next intersection. Cranks the steering right.

"You saw that police car," Lauren says. "You saw it just as well as I did."

The Jeep drifts around the corner, sliding on re-frozen ice. "Yeah," Belaski says. "So, you want to go say hi?"

⋏

Whicher drops the magazine on the Glock, presses down on the top round—feels the spring push it back.

He checks the brass-jacketed round is snug, the magazine full, he refits it.

Holstering the semi-auto at his waist, he reaches in under his jacket, takes out the big Ruger revolver.

He opens up the cylinder. Spins it. Flicks it closed.

Mid-morning, a Nebraska town, the depths of winter on the Plains. Traffic's light, people going about their business.

He lets the gun rest against his leg.

Kinawa steers the unmarked Crown Vic, pausing the car at the mouth of an intersection.

Sheriff Colton and Sergeant Hooper from the PD are on their left flank—two-blocks over.

The marshal checks the side-street to his right, staring out of the passenger window.

Kinawa checks the block to the left.

Two streets over, the sheriff and the sergeant do the same.

Fifteen miles-per-hour, running parallel—between them they can cover four streets at a time. Fifteen minutes, Whicher reckons. Twenty minutes, tops, they can comb the southern end of town.

Kinawa holds the Crown Vic on the brakes.

"No sign up there," the marshal says.

"You don't think they're here, do you?"

"I guess we're going to find that out."

The FBI man looks at Whicher. "How come you have your gun out?"

"Army habit."

"If they're here, if we find them, I don't see how this could work out…"

The marshal doesn't respond.

"What's the guy have to lose—if he took down an FBI agent?"

"Don't go there in your head," Whicher says.

"He killed a US Marshal in Fisherville…"

"We don't know it's the same guy."

"Nobody's reporting any sign of Janice Rimes."

Whicher twists in his seat.

Kinawa's grip is tight on the wheel. "Whatever this

woman did, this Lauren DeLuca, her brother Anthony wasn't responsible for any of it."

"You mean to say something by that?"

The FBI man pushes on the gas pedal. "If we find the Jeep, this bastard doesn't get to leave."

Chapter 43

The black SUV rolling across the intersection has white letters on its door.

County Sheriff's Department.

Belaski stares at a man on the passenger side—he's wearing a Western hat, a sheepskin coat. His face is agitated—he shouts something to the driver.

The vehicle brakes, skids to a stop, three-quarters of the way across the intersection.

Belaski mashes down on the accelerator, the Jeep lurches forward.

Right fender in line with the back of the SUV, he grips the wheel, locks out his arms.

The Jeep strikes the back of the sheriff's vehicle—windshield shattering. Belaski stabs the brake, whips the gun from his lap.

He aims, fires six rounds through the passenger window—the bullets blowing out two windows on the SUV, smacking steel.

Both the men inside are ducked down—the driver hits

the throttle full-out.

The SUV heaves forward, tires spinning—it tears away from the intersection.

Belaski punches a hole in the Jeep's crazed windshield with the butt of the gun.

Lauren's laid out across the back seat, her knees drawn up.

Cold rage inside, Belaski stomps the gas, barreling the Jeep along the street to the next intersection, tires floating on the frozen snow.

He steers toward the tower looming over the roof line, heart-pounding.

Cars pass behind, horns blasting.

He stares through the fist-size hole in the fractured windshield, face numb in the cone of glacial air.

Animal speed is in his mind.

Speed and a raging pulse of violence.

He gets off the gas, brakes, feels the wheels slide, then grip.

At a dead stop, he pushes open the driver's door.

He jumps out, rips open the back.

Lauren DeLuca stares up at him.

"Get out."

She recoils.

He points the muzzle of the SIG an inch above her supine body. "I shoot your brother right here." He angles the gun at the seat back. "Or you get out."

He leans in grabs at her, pulling on her coat.

She scrambles, pushes upright, zip-tied hands on the seat, trying to swing her legs.

He pulls her off balance, rips her from the vehicle, dumping her out into the street.

"Get up…"

A voice calls out from behind him; "*Hey, what's going on?*"

Belaski spins around.

A man is standing by a wood-frame house, clearing snow from a driveway—shovel held in mid-air.

The man steps back as Belaski raises his gun arm.

Lauren struggles to her feet.

Jamming the muzzle hard above her kidney, Belaski pulls her forward along the snow on the sidewalk. "You can run or you can die, now. You can die here anytime you want…"

⅄

Whicher stares through the windshield of the Crown Vic at Sheriff Colton. He's at the rear of his SUV, weapon drawn, the back of the vehicle smashed up.

Aiming over the roof is Sergeant Hooper.

They're on the edge of the street, fifty yards from Janice Rimes's Jeep Liberty.

The Jeep's right side is bent up, body panels scraped, the front fender twisted.

A black and white patrol car is racing up from the far end of the next street.

It turns sideways, blocking the route out.

Kinawa brakes nose-on to the curb.

Through the side-window, Whicher sees two patrol officers and Chief Eriksson exit the black and white. Weapons drawn, they run behind the vehicle—level their guns across the roof.

Whicher gets out, stays low, crouching to the road.

The rear windshield of the Jeep is smoked glass, he can't see in.

Chief Eriksson snaps around to something—something over at Whicher's left.

The marshal whips the Ruger around—a red faced man is standing at the side of a house.

"*Get back,*" the sheriff shouts, "*get back in your house…*"

Shock is in the man's face, he stands, frozen.

Whicher aims at the Jeep, starts to run toward the sheriff.

The man at the house is still rooted.

The sheriff shifts along the side of the SUV, making a space.

"Are they in the vehicle?" Whicher says.

"Can't tell…"

The marshal puts away the Ruger, takes out the Glock from the holster at his hip. He grips the semi-automatic between both hands, runs forward, past Sergeant Hooper. "Cover me," he says.

Eyes on the windows of the Jeep, his heart is pounding.

The motor's running, but there's no seeing inside.

At the front-end, the windshield is crazed, shattered, a single hole punched through.

The man at the house calls out, "*They're gone…*"

Kinawa runs from the Crown Vic, crouched low, following in Whicher's footsteps.

Sheriff Colton calls to the man at the house, "*Get back— get back inside.*"

The door opens at another house, a woman in a bath

robe steps out. "I saw them," she calls out, "a man and a woman." She points up the street. "They ran up there."

The marshal sees footmarks in the snow on the sidewalk. He turns to Kinawa. "Come on, you and me…"

⁂

In the rear trunk of the Jeep, Anthony hears the voices above the thrum of the motor running—people are shouting, the sound sears through the pain in his head.

Lauren is gone.

The man is gone.

He needs to get out.

He twists his body in the cramped space.

Raising his arms, he gets his cuffed hands on the back of the seat. He hooks his fingernails into the cloth, summons all his strength, grips hard.

A wave of nausea breaks in him as he starts to pull himself up.

His grip fails, he falls back, strikes his head against the wheel-arch.

Pain splits his skull, he feels a tear form in the edge of his eye.

He draws up his legs, gets his feet beneath him—*he can push himself over*.

Sweating now in the thick clothes, he heaves, launches his head across the top of the seat.

He's halfway—but he's stuck, he can't fit, he can't make it over.

He can't move forward, can't get back.

AN AMERICAN BULLET

⚔

Two shots crack out in the frigid air.

Whicher stops, spins in his tracks.

He stares back down the street at Sergeant Hooper—gun arm locked on the Jeep.

Kinawa and Sheriff Colton are braced to fire; everybody rigid, their weapons trained on the stricken vehicle.

Through the rear side-window, he sees something—hair, a mess of yellow hair. His heart comes up in his mouth.

Hooper squeezes off another round.

"*Cease fire,*" Whicher yells. "*Hold your fire…*"

"*There's somebody in there,*" Sheriff Colton shouts back.

Whicher moves toward the Jeep, willing himself to see inside.

Eriksson calls from behind the black and white; "*What the hell are you doing?*"

The marshal feels the energy spiraling, spinning out of control.

He raises the Glock, holds it out front, reaches the vehicle—steps to the door.

Heart hammering, he grabs the handle.

⚔

The kid from the logging road is looking at him.

Anthony.

Eyes like his sister.

Looking back at him.

Alive.

He's alive.

Chapter 44

The parking lot of the college campus is covered in crisp, white snow, the buildings unlit, their windows dark. Nobody coming in, nobody going out. Belaski eyes the handful of vehicles—they're bunched near a stone-faced building at the side of a broad, brick tower.

He tightens his grip on the arm of Lauren's coat.

She pulls away, yanking against him.

"If I drop you right here," Belaski says, "I still get paid." He smacks the flat of the gun against her forehead, barrel hard against the bone. "If I kill you right in the lot…"

Her legs buckle, a thin line of blood races from her nose.

"Quit," he spits. "You slow me down, I'll shoot you." He raises the gun, points it at her face.

She flinches, turns her head away.

He pulls her off-balance, stumbling—gets her running, drags her on across the lot.

A set of stone steps leads to a double-height door inset with long panes of glass. He heaves her up the stairway, pushes open the door.

Inside is a lobby—a polished floor, a reception counter—a glass atrium to the side.

A woman in a white blouse appears, she takes a step back, eyes fixed on the gun he's holding.

She lifts a hand to her mouth. "Oh my God…"

Belaski pushes Lauren forward, leveling the SIG on the woman. "I want a car…"

The woman shakes her head.

"*I want a God damn car,*" Belaski shouts.

"I don't have one…" Her voice trembles. "I don't have a car…"

Lauren pulls away again—he whips the base of the gun into the back of her head.

She cries out, falls forward.

He catches hold of her, keeps her upright on her feet.

A door at one side of the lobby opens, a suited man steps out.

Belaski swings the gun around on to him. "I need a car—*now.*"

The man swallows, pats down his suit, reaches into a pocket. He pulls out a set of vehicle keys.

"Where?" Belaski says.

"In the lot," the man gestures with his head, holding the keys at arm's length. "A blue Ford Windstar."

"Put them on the counter."

The man steps across the polished floor, puts down the keys on the countertop.

Belaski shoves Lauren forward, snatches up the keys. He digs his fingers into her arm, turns her around, pushes her back toward the main door.

He pauses, stares through one of the long, glass panes.

Two black and white police cars are out in the lot—one at the far end, blocking the exit, the other slowing to approach the building.

A cop in black uniform is crouching by an ornamental clock.

Belaski pulls back from the glass pane, turns to the man at the counter. "Get over here." He points the gun. "Get over here and lock the door." He raises the muzzle in line with the man's chest.

The man hurries across the lobby, lifts a sliding latch on the door—he presses down on a button.

Belaski grabs at the handle, it won't open. "Where's another way out?"

The man turns, points to the lobby space beneath the glass-roofed atrium. "Past those stairs, down the side, down the corridor. There's an exit door at the rear."

"Alright," Belaski says. "The pair of you; get walking."

The woman's eyes are wild—she steps from behind the counter into the lobby.

Lauren pulls away again.

Belaski jams the gun into her belly, doubling her over. "I pull the trigger on this you'll die screaming."

"Please," the man says, "it's just here, it's right down here…"

The woman in the white blouse stares at Belaski. "Don't hurt her," she says. "Just don't hurt her."

⁂

Whicher picks a path through the trees at the back of the building—Kinawa, Sheriff Colton and an officer from the

Redwood PD in line behind him.

Through the gaps in the trees, the marshal sees a door at the far end—windows are set at regular intervals along the wall, all the rooms unlit.

He holds up a hand to stop, turns to the patrolman. "Let me use your radio…"

The officer un-clips the transceiver from his jacket, stretches out the coiled lead.

The marshal presses to call; "Chief, this is Whicher, what's happening around the front?"

The radio crackles into life. "The door's locked—but dispatch say they definitely received an alarm signal from here, it's the main building on campus."

"We're almost at the back entrance," the marshal says.

"We need to clear the building," Eriksson says.

"Y'all don't force the front. We'll go in here. How many people are in there?"

A static burst.

"Chief?"

"We don't know."

"Get on every exit, cover the windows," Whicher says. "I'm going in."

He hands back the radio to the patrolman.

Sixty yards off, a rear door is opening.

A face appears.

The sheriff calls out, "*Police—stop, don't move.*"

The man at the door is the shooter from the logging road—his arm comes up.

"*Drop your weapon…*"

The PD officer opens fire.

The face disappears.

The door slams shut.

※

Belaski points his SIG at the man in the suit. "Give me another way out."

The man stares back, white-faced. "There's a fire escape…"

"Where?"

He angles his head. "Along the front side of the building."

"What else?" Belaski snaps.

"An emergency exit. At the far end of the east wing." The man hesitates. "Or windows…"

"The windows open?"

"They're locked from the inside, but they'll open."

"Turn around," Belaski says. "We're going back the way we came."

Lauren looks at him. "You're never getting out of here."

He raises the gun, holds it in her eye-line. "Then neither are you." To the suited man; "Lock this, lock the door."

The woman in the white blouse holds her hands to her head. "The janitor has the key…"

Belaski flicks the gun at her.

Feels the cold rage rising, rippling inside.

※

Whicher crouches, runs the last yards to the building bent double—no cover beyond the trees. He reaches the door, flattens himself against the stone-block surround.

Kinawa, a yard back, runs for the opposite side of the doorway. Leaning in against the wall, he holds his pistol upright against his Kevlar vest.

Whicher holds the Glock 19 out in his right hand, reaches over with his left. He tries the door handle. It turns, clicks down. The door's unlocked.

The marshal glances at Kinawa. He pulls the door sharp, lets go.

Momentum swings it wide as he steps away from the wall.

Both men lean back, brace.

They strain to hear.

Silence.

One beat following after another.

Whicher pushes the Resistol onto his head. He gestures forward with the Glock.

Kinawa nods.

The marshal takes a two-handed grip on the gun, steps around the door, edging into the corridor from an angle.

He sweeps left to right.

Doors lead off at either side—the visible space is empty—thirty yards in, the corridor turns a corner, no way of seeing more.

He takes a pace inside, then another.

Kinawa moves in behind.

The marshal keeps the turn in the corridor dead ahead. He reaches the door to the first room, stops.

The walls feel solid, will they stop a bullet?

He steps past the door, to the far-edge of the frame.

Kinawa sets up in place.

The marshal tries the handle, the door's locked—locked solid.

Maybe they're in there, maybe not.

There's no time—he waves the FBI man on with his free hand.

Move on. Move up to the next door.

⚜

Back in the reception lobby, Belaski stares at the suited man. "Open this, open up the front."

The man stares back at him, uncomprehending.

"Unlock it," Belaski says. "Open it. You're going out."

The man takes a half-step, then turns. "What about…" he gestures to the woman in the white blouse, "Miss Robertson."

"You get to walk. She stays."

The color drains from the woman's face.

"What if they shoot me?" the man says. "Out there, the police…"

"Hold your hands high," Belaski answers. "Tell them I've got two hostages—one of them's a witness in a major trial."

The man's eyes shift to Lauren DeLuca.

"Tell them I'll deal," Belaski says. "I've got a federal witness, plus an innocent woman here." He points at Miss Robertson.

The man gives the faintest nod.

"I can be a witness myself—for the right price, a government witness…you hear what I'm telling you?"

AN AMERICAN BULLET

"Yes. Yes, I do."

"Then step out."

"I walk out? I walk out now?"

Belaski flicks the muzzle, "Get moving."

The man unlocks the mechanism. Pulls back the door.

⚹

Voices are up ahead.

Whicher touches Kinawa's arm, stopping him.

The sound of a man's voice echoes down the corridor—one man talking.

Whicher leans in close to Kinawa. "The chief and the sheriff need to know…"

The FBI man shakes his head.

"Go," Whicher breathes. "The sheriff's out there, let him know the position." He listens a moment—there's only silence now, under the hum of overhead lights.

Kinawa whispers. "What if they move?"

The marshal nods. "They move, I move."

⚹

Chief Eriksson holds his thumb down on the radio mic, free hand raised into the air. "All units, hold fire…"

The man walking down the steps in front of the main door is Vice-Principal Gillespie—Walt Gillespie. He's holding up both hands, his suit jacket splayed open, flapping in the wind.

The front door's already closing behind him.

Eriksson checks along the line of his men, their weapons

trained at the doors and windows of the building, none of them aiming at Gillespie, they all know him.

"Let him come down," the chief says, "don't go out…"

The vice-principal walks on, unsteady.

Last thing they need is an officer shot responding.

Gillespie reaches the foot of the steps, starts to walk out across the snow-covered lot.

Eriksson waves to him. "*Here. Over here.*"

At the far-end of the building, Sheriff Colton's moving in a wide arc, skirting the edge of the lot, behind a line of leafless birch.

Gillespie walks past the few parked vehicles.

He makes his way toward the chief at the back of the black and white.

"Paula Robertson's in there," he says.

"Who else?"

The man just looks at him, eyes bulging.

Eriksson hustles him into cover behind the police vehicle. "There's five cars parked here," the chief says, "who do they belong to?"

Gillespie peers out. "Apart from mine," he says, "there's Brian Thanet, the janitor, Terry Woodson, one of the lab technicians." He stares at the other vehicles. "Peter Carlsen from I.T. The Toyota belongs to a student, I think, I don't think it's staff…"

"What about Paula?"

"No, no, she walks in, she walks to work…"

"Five people in the building?"

"It's the holidays."

"That's all there is?"

AN AMERICAN BULLET

"From tomorrow, there'll just be Brian."

"You need to call everybody, get them on their cells," the chief says. "Tell them to stay where they are, lock themselves in their rooms, if they can."

Gillespie stares back at him. "That man in there is armed with a pistol."

"A pistol—did you see anything else?"

Sheriff Colton arrives at the back of the lot, behind Eriksson's car. "Walt," he says. "Jeez, are you okay?"

"He's got Paula Robertson and another woman in there," Gillespie says to the chief. "He's talking about negotiating, he says the woman in there is a federal witness."

Eriksson looks at Sheriff Colton.

"Horseshit," Colton mutters.

"That's what he told me to tell you."

The sheriff shakes his head.

Gillespie lets his hands fall away at his sides.

"No way that's happening." Sheriff Colton rubs his chin against the collar of his sheepskin coat. "That FBI agent, Kinawa, just came out the back of the building—he said the marshal's got himself right with them, right in there, just off of the main corridor—he can hear them."

Gillespie fishes for his cell, lights it up, starts to scroll the list of numbers.

"Hooper went in," the sheriff says, "I told him to head up the stairs in the back—see if he could get behind them, reach the front of the building from the upper floor."

The vice-principal finds the number to make the first call.

"Maybe we can take 'em by surprise," Sheriff Colton says.

Gillespie lifts the cell to his hear, takes it away again. "What about Paula?"

Neither the chief nor the sheriff meet his eye.

⁕

Whicher hears footsteps—somebody is in the corridor.

Kinawa steps around the turn.

The marshal lowers the Glock.

"They know we're here," Kinawa breathes. "The chief and the sheriff; they know."

For a moment neither man speaks.

There's been no more talk up ahead, no more voices.

Time is almost up, it's running out; Whicher feels it, senses it. "We have to go in."

Kinawa dips his head.

"They don't know we're behind them. We just get one shot."

The FBI man adjusts his grip on the semi-automatic.

Whicher moves off the wall, Glock out at shoulder-height. "Ready?"

The two men step to the end of the corridor.

⁕

Daylight is streaming from a glass roof—lighting up an open space, some form of lobby.

A staircase of concrete and steel blocks the line of sight.

Whicher sees part of the main front door; a reception

area, a counter—the back of a woman in a white blouse.

Moving a fraction, he sees the shooter side-on—he's holding a gun to Lauren's head.

There's no clear line; no shot.

Kinawa ducks beneath the staircase—opening up an angle.

The gunman snaps around, fires twice, noise exploding, deafening.

Kinawa falls to the floor.

Whicher holds the iron-sights of the Glock on the shooter—Lauren fully facing him now, the gunman behind her, the muzzle of his pistol against the side of her head.

"*US Marshal—drop your weapon.*"

Lauren's face is screwed up in pain, the man's arm wrapped about her neck.

"*Let her go…*"

The woman in the white blouse gapes across the lobby.

A groaning sound rises from Kinawa on the floor.

"Oh my God…" The woman stares. "There's blood pouring from his neck…"

The FBI man lets out a choking sound.

"*Drop your weapon*," Whicher shouts. "*Drop it, and let her go.*"

"He's going to bleed to death…"

The gunman's eyes fill with a strange light. He pulls Lauren in tighter—her face a mask; confusion, fear.

"*Please*," the woman in the blouse cries out.

The shooter leans his head over on one side.

"He's bleeding," she says, "he needs help, *now*."

"Put down the weapon," the marshal says.

The gunman twists his pistol against Lauren's temple. "A cop's life," he says, "got to be worth more than her life." His hawk-face splits into an ugly grin.

The woman drops to her knees, she lets out a sob.

"The building's surrounded." Whicher locks eyes with the shooter.

"You help him," the man says. "You get him out. You take him out of here…"

The marshal glances at Kinawa—in a ball on the floor. His knees are drawn up, both hands clamped at his neck, blood oozing between his fingers.

His gun's laying out of reach—in a corner by the wall.

Whicher turns to the kneeling woman. "*Her*," he says.

The gunman shakes his head.

"She takes him out—I stay."

"One chance," the shooter says.

Whicher takes a breath—bends slow, extending out his gun arm.

"What the fuck're you doing?" The shooter grinds the muzzle of the pistol into the side of Lauren's head.

The marshal lays the Glock down flat against the floor. "I stay." He straightens, raising up his hands. He nods at the woman. "But she goes. She takes him out."

Beneath the wool coat he feels the weight of the Ruger in the shoulder-holster.

The gunman stares at the kneeling woman, eyes alive.

Lauren pulls at the arm about her throat, choking her.

The gunman grips tighter. "Do it, then," he says.

AN AMERICAN BULLET

The woman looks to Whicher.

The marshal nods.

"I let you do this," the shooter says. "Tell them that—you *tell* them that out there."

She crawls on hands and knees across the lobby space.

Whicher keeps his hands high. "Let me help her. Let me help her get him to the door."

"Bullshit. She can do it, cowboy…"

Whicher looks at the man—looks right through him, thinks of the big revolver just beneath his coat.

"Alright, fuck it, do it then—do it, help her…"

The marshal steps along the side of the staircase to Kinawa, sees the impact mark of a round in the Kevlar vest. The second round has caught his unprotected neck. He's losing consciousness, bleeding out.

The woman has her hands over Kinawa's hands, pressing down on the wound.

Whicher reaches, gets a grip, heaves the FBI man from the floor. He gets his weight against his body, the woman still pressing against the man's neck.

Kinawa folds, the marshal catches him—they stumble, stagger to the door.

"Open it," the shooter tells the woman.

She takes away her bloodied hands, works the mechanism.

The FBI man's head jerks, his eyes are open, he tries to lock out his legs.

The woman pushes the door wide—she faces out, holds up both hands.

Whicher shifts into the line of the doorway—sees the

black and white PD cars, police officers, the tall figure of Chief Eriksson.

Kinawa grunts as the woman puts her arms around his waist.

The marshal eases off his grip, lets the man go.

Limping through the doorway, the pair step out.

Whicher turns around—the gunman's easing back into the lobby, eyes darting, trying to see outside.

Lauren dips—no warning—she kicks a foot between the man's ankles.

He trips, counters for balance.

Whicher snatches at the zipper on the coat—it snags halfway.

The man grabs at Lauren's hair, he smashes the butt of his gun into the base of her skull. "*Get in front of the door,*" he shouts to Whicher. He thrusts the muzzle back against Lauren's head.

"*Police…*" a voice calls from a Tannoy. "*Drop your weapon.*"

The marshal stands stock still.

"*Drop your weapon, step outside.*"

"Shut the goddamn door…" The gunman stares at him. "My name's Belaski—Jerzy Belaski. I'll trade, I'll give her up. You call the Chicago DA…"

The marshal looks into Lauren's face.

"You call. I'll give her up, they can have her. I'm not talking to anyone out there."

Whicher swings the door shut.

The shooter juts his chin toward the staircase. "Get over here…"

"What for?

"You're going to tell that bunch of hick fucks who I am," Belaski says. "But first we're going up. We're going up the stairs."

⁂

Whicher leading.

Belaski behind on the staircase with Lauren—an arm around her neck, his pistol at her head.

The marshal lets his arms dip a fraction.

"Keep your hands where I can see them…"

He climbs the few more steps to the next floor.

In front of him is a long, dark corridor—blackened at its end. Overhead lights extinguished, a gun-metal sky at the windows.

"You're going to call Chicago," Belaski says. "I want a helicopter…"

"We're going on the roof?"

"We go wherever the hell I say we go."

The marshal steps out, into the corridor, into its center.

"You call the FBI, you talk to them…"

At the end, Whicher sees a figure –in the shadows—a crouched figure.

Hooper.

Sergeant Hooper—his gun arm out.

The marshal slows, swallows, eyes fixed on the kneeling man.

Hooper's eyes are wide.

Whicher thinks of the Ruger just inside his coat—no way

he can get it fast enough—no way they'll make it to the end of the corridor. "That's it," he says. He stops.

"Keep moving…"

Whicher senses the man right behind him, hears the effort in Lauren's breathing.

"I'll shoot you in the back of the head, you son of a bitch."

"You ain't making it out of here." Whicher feels his heart in his ribcage. "You want to deal, the time is now. I'm turning around…"

He forces his torso to twist, lifts a leaden foot from the floor.

Belaski's gun is point-blank in his face.

The marshal shifts, one foot to the other. Feints toward Lauren—a shot explodes—Hooper at the end of the corridor.

Belaski fires back, Lauren drives sideways, legs thrashing.

Hooper fires again—as Belaski hits the side of the wall.

Lauren buckles, both hands at the arm around her neck—Belaski fires as she tries to drag him down.

Whicher whips the Ruger free, snaps a single round into the top of the man's shoulder.

The shock drops him.

He crumples with Lauren, loses grip on the gun.

She grabs it from the floor, braces—fires two times, three into the his body.

Belaski jerks sideways, face contorted.

She pulls back—takes aim, fires into the centre of his head.

Epilogue

Space and silence and empty fields running to woods. Among the bare-stripped branches, a crow sits black-winged, eying a deserted road.

Dead stems and husks of maize are bent and ragged beneath the piled snow. The sky outside the farmhouse is flat, opaque, no wind, no movement of air.

Whicher rises from his place at the window.

He crosses the room, boots loud against the wooden boards of the floor.

Inside the house, time is suspended, a world on hold.

Lauren DeLuca sits by a fire in an open grate, her face still, her eyes half-closed.

"Is Anthony awake?" Whicher studies her.

No reply.

The marshal takes up the pot from a drop-leaf table—pours hot coffee, filling up a china mug. "I'll go on and take him some up."

He walks by Lauren, toward the hallway.

She reaches out, places a hand on the arm of his suit.

He stops.

She looks up. Her eyes hold his.

Nothing moves inside the house, the only sound is flame lapping at the firewood, a clock ticking in the hall.

"It's alright," he says.

Her eyes cut away.

The marshal raises the mug, gestures at the door.

He steps from the living room, walks along the hallway to the foot of a staircase.

Climbing slow, he reaches the next floor, sets the mug down on a bureau top.

He knocks at the door to a bedroom. A muffled voice comes back.

"It's Whicher…"

He listens to the sounds of movement from inside the room.

"You want coffee?"

The door opens. Anthony stands in the frame. He's dressed in jeans, a sweater, socks.

"You catch some sleep?"

"No," Anthony smiles. "Well, maybe." He flattens his messed-up blonde hair.

Whicher holds out the mug.

The young man takes it.

"You doing alright?"

"I guess."

"Tired?"

"A little."

"Keeping warm?" The marshal looks him over.

AN AMERICAN BULLET

Anthony takes a sip at the mug of coffee. "I'm keeping warm."

Whicher scans the small room—an antique bed, a closet, a view out over white fields. "There's food in the refrigerator. You want, I could fix something for y'all?"

"I'll come down," Anthony says. He grabs a pair of new-bought boots off the rug on the floor. "At the ranch, the cookhouse was one of my jobs," he says. A smile forms across his face. It quickly fades.

The marshal steps from the room, clips back down the staircase, checks the window in the hall—nothing out there.

Lauren shifts in her seat at the fireside.

"You want to eat?" Whicher says.

"Is he alright?"

The marshal nods. "He said he's going to come on down."

Lauren stands, picks a shawl from a chair back. She wraps it around her shoulders. "Will you call the hospital?"

"I already called."

"Will you call them again?"

"They're safe," the marshal says.

She looks at him.

"Kinawa's in the hospital in Rapid City. Maddie Cook and Agent Rimes are somewhere they can be protected."

Lauren doesn't respond.

"You did all you could."

Her face is suddenly tight. "I remember every second—every second from when that man got into the Jeep…"

Anthony's footsteps sound on the stairs in the hallway.

331

"They never would've found Janice Rimes," Whicher says, "without you."

She shudders.

The marshal eyes her. Beneath his breath he says; "Don't let him see you're afraid."

The young man enters the living room.

Lauren steps from the fireside, puts her arms around him.

"What?" Anthony says.

She grins. Lets go, steps back.

Anthony catches the shawl as it falls from her shoulders, his face coloring. "I'm alright," he says. "Come on, look, I want to fix us something to eat."

"I can do it…"

"Laur…" He steps away, shakes his head.

⋏

In the kitchen, Anthony pulls open the door of the refrigerator. "Huh," he says. He runs a hand over the food on the shelves. "How about steak? Steak and eggs. Bell peppers, onions. Everybody eat that?"

Beyond the picture window at the sink, the winter fields stretch to woods—stark, vivid, etched in white. The middle of the Illinois countryside, hundreds of miles from Rapid City, from Redwood. A safe house, isolated—a farm two hours from Chicago.

"Laur?" Anthony looks at her.

She nods.

He turns to Whicher.

"You cook it," the marshal says, "I'll eat it."

The flight to Illinois was last-minute, the weather just holding—a prop plane arriving in Peoria before nightfall—an FBI agent to meet with them, drive them out to the farm.

Whicher watches as Anthony takes a fry-pan from a hanging row of saucepans and skillets.

Lauren searches in the cupboards, finds a stack of plates, lays out three on a marked-up, oak table. Anthony slices onion, lights the stove, puts the pan on the flame.

The marshal steps from the kitchen, walks back down the hallway.

Behind him is the sound of footsteps.

He reaches the living room—Lauren enters after him, she pushes the door closed.

"Something on your mind?" He walks to the window.

She studies the floor. "There's no time." She steps toward the fire, frowns. "The trial starts tomorrow…"

He levels his gaze on her.

"What have you told them—the FBI? About the money?"

The marshal takes a long breath.

"The money I stole," she says, her voice flat. "From the Coletti's."

He turns, stares out of the window—out across the frozen field of maize.

"Are you going to tell them?"

He thinks of her, her and Anthony—a life ahead of them; a world of watching the back door, of covering traces. He studies a red-stained barn at a corner of the farmyard, its timbers twisted with age. "No," he finally says.

Lauren moves to the window, pulls the shawl about her shoulders. "You're the only person I've ever told."

Whicher steps aside, takes a piece of cordwood from a stack by the fire.

"Do you remember," she says, "back on the bus—that Greyhound bus?"

He feeds the wood into the hearth.

"That Greyhound bus," she says, "when we were headed for Denver? You told me about a man you were taking out to a prison?"

Florence ADX.

Maitland—Cutter Maitland. Caught with human remains.

"He said you and he were just the same, you remember?"

The marshal doesn't reply.

"Guard dogs. Only working for different sides."

Whicher straightens. Listens to the sound of Anthony moving in the kitchen, dull noise echoed down the hallway.

"You're not," she says. "You're all that's left."

He looks at her a long moment.

"The only thing standing in the way…"

He tilts his head.

"Of the violence," she says. "All the greed, the craziness." She moves from the window. "All I want is to protect my brother. When this is over, I won't be separated from him again. I want him with me—wherever we end up." She steps closer. "What will you do? Will you go back to Texas?"

He nods.

"But if you had a choice—another choice?" She takes another step, only inches from him. "When this is all over. The trial. Everything…"

She searches his face. Doesn't let him look away.

⚜

Whicher walks the fence line in the breathless air, winter sun low above the frozen wood. An iron-smell rises from the ground, dead stalks of maize crunch beneath his boots. His eye follows a line of telephone poles—stretching out along the only road.

Nothing is moving. Nothing out there, to the far horizon. A single, burr oak, leafless. Crows gathered among its branches as the light begins to fail.

He takes a last look at the deserted road, the empty fields, the cold, dark woods. Turns in the weak, brass light of sunset, heads for the house.

He scans its board facade, its windows, empty. Snow on the shingle roof.

And Lauren.

Lauren standing out on the porch.

Arms wrapped about her. Silent. Watching.

He makes his way up through the yard—by the red-stained barn. Sets his hat.

"Teach me how to shoot?"

He looks up at her, standing on the porch deck. Low sun at the side of her face.

Beyond the house, across the empty plain, night is coming, stealing in.

"Would you teach me?"

He reaches the foot of the stairs.

"When I close my eyes," she says, "I can see that man. So close."

The marshal pictures the corridor—upstairs in the college building—blood-quick movements, shots, a frenzy, trying to stay alive.

"I never want it to be that close to me again," she says. She holds her hands together—out in front of herself, arms extended, as if aiming a gun.

He climbs the steps. "You think that can keep it all away?"

She drops her hands to her sides. "Then what?"

The chill of a breeze moves against his skin. "Witness security will keep you safe. Once the trial is done—nobody ever got killed."

"You told me that," she says. "You told me once before."

"Long as they don't break the rules."

She looks at him, head slightly on one side.

He watches the shadows start to lengthen down the side of the barn. "McBride will be here soon. He'll take you into the city."

She dips her head.

"I'll stay here with Anthony. Until they tell me where to go."

"Don't leave him." Her voice is tight in her throat. "Promise me…"

"A lot of officers work protection…"

"They're not you."

He lets his gaze sit, unfocused, on the middle-distance.

"The doctors say he needs to rest up, eat, stay warm." He shifts toward the door of the house.

"There'll be enough," she says, "when this is all over."

He lets her words run. Doesn't answer.

"You stayed," she says.

He stops, looks into her face. Feels the pull in his gut, the shard of something.

"When Kinawa was shot," she says. "You could've taken him out. But you didn't. You stayed."

"That's it?"

She places a hand on his shirt front. Blonde hair, eyes intense, a smile at her mouth. A sad smile. "That's all there is."

⁂

A single set of headlights washes over the blackened land. Flecks of ice are blowing under the porch roof, the marshal watches the slow sweep of the beams.

The vehicle is turning, leaving the long, straight stretch of road.

Anthony steps forward from the shadows on the porch deck. "Do they really have to take her tonight?"

"Trial starts in the morning." Whicher checks his jacket is open, loose—he feels for the Glock at his hip. "McBride called. He was off of eighty, south of the interstate corridor. He said to be ready."

The sound of the motor carries, now, above the soft moan of the wind.

"What about us?" Anthony says.

"We stay here tonight."

"We stay, Lauren goes?"

Whicher looks at him.

The vehicle makes another turn, coming closer now, approaching the farm.

Anthony shoves his hands into the pockets of his jeans.

"This all was set in train a long time ago," the marshal says.

The young man watches the headlights a moment longer. "I better go tell her." He steps back from the rail, crosses to the door. Disappears into the house.

The vehicle slows, pulls in from the road. It steers up over frozen gravel in the yard—a Ram pickup, black and chrome.

Rolling to a stop in front of the old barn, the driver shuts off the motor—Whicher sees McBride in the yellow glow of the dome light.

He eases forward on the porch.

McBride steps out of the truck. He breathes the cold air, eyes the dark expanse of land. Grabs his coat from the passenger seat, slips it on.

"You see anything out there?" Whicher says.

"About two vehicles since I left the interstate." The inspector crosses the yard to the raised porch. He climbs the ice-covered steps.

"Where y'all fixing for her to stay tonight?"

McBride shrugs. "Wherever the DA's office tell me. Cells maybe, at the courthouse."

"Come on inside," Whicher says. He leads the man into

the farmhouse, down the hallway, footsteps sounding from a room upstairs. "I get you something?"

McBride shakes his head. "I need to get her into the city, they're getting nervous in Chicago." His eyes cut to the ceiling.

Whicher turns from the hallway, shows McBride through into the kitchen.

The lights are out. It's warm, still, suffused with the smell of home-cooked food.

Beyond the kitchen window, the dark is unbroken.

The marshal pours himself coffee from a pot on the stove.

McBride studies the night beyond the window. "Lonely place," he says.

Whicher nods.

"But safe." The inspector crosses his arms on his chest. "WITSEC—in its essence."

The marshal leans against the countertop. "She wants to relocate," he says. "Her and Anthony."

"Together? She told you that?"

"Could she?"

"She could." McBride exhales. He turns back to staring out of the blackened window.

"It's all she wants."

"What they want," the inspector says, "what they all want, is their old lives back."

Whicher takes a sip from the cup of coffee.

"Family," McBride says. "Friends. Their roots. An end to all the lies."

The marshal glances across the room at the older man. "They ever get it?"

"Some of that," the inspector nods. "Some of that WITSEC will allow." He unfolds his arms. "Family contact's something we have to manage, but it happens. Matter of fact, we think she called her grandmother—in San Francisco…"

The marshal looks at him.

"Before she set out for the trial. We think that's how Coletti's people knew…about Lauren, about how we'd be moving her."

"Y'all think that's how they knew about the train?"

McBride studies the backs of his hands.

Whicher thinks of Lauren—in McCook, in the waiting room, at the deserted station—she'd been calling her then.

"We knew about her," the inspector says. "Her mother's mother. She lives out in San Francisco, North Beach, the Italian-American community. She probably let slip something, some small thing—to somebody she thought she could trust. We're checking phone records from Lauren's apartment."

Footsteps are on the stairs in the hallway now, two people descending.

"FBI say the Coletti's have folk out there," McBride says. "They knew Lauren had to be in Chicago; the trial's about to start. All they needed was the departure point."

Whicher pushes up off the countertop.

The inspector looks at him. "You did good."

Lauren reaches the foot of the staircase, Anthony behind her.

"You kept them both alive," McBride says.

Lauren stops. Turns around. Still the question in her face.

The marshal squares his hat, rubs a hand across his jaw. He sweeps open the jacket of his suit, leads the way outside.

Anthony stands on the porch in the light from the house.

McBride descends the steps, crosses the yard—he opens up the Ram, puts the truck keys into the ignition. He starts the motor, takes a pace away, checks his watch. "Two hours to Chicago," he says, "we better get moving."

Whicher takes a long breath, holds it.

Lauren brushes by him, walks over to the passenger side of the pickup, still wearing the ranch coat—his coat.

She puts a hand to the collar.

He shakes his head. "Keep it."

Her eyes hold his.

She breaks off. Opens up the door, steps into the cab.

McBride crosses the yard to stand at the foot of the stairs. "Once the trial is done," he says, "WITSEC will make her disappear."

For the longest time Whicher doesn't reply.

McBride studies him. Finally he nods. "Only way to protect her is to let her go."

Whicher stands silent in the raw air.

The inspector walks to the pickup, swings open the driver's door, climbs up behind the wheel.

He backs the Ram out, brakes, straightens onto the road.

The motor rumbles beneath the hood.

He hits the gas, steers the truck forward, headlights bright at the edge of the snow-bound fields.

The marshal watches.

Minute after minute. Till the light is finally gone.
Wind and the cold returning, seeping in.
To silence.
At the edge of a darkened world.

Printed in Great Britain
by Amazon